ORIGINAL EARTH CHRONICLES

The Golden Pyramid

CHRIS KENNY

Copyright © 2021 by Chris Kenny

All rights reserved.

No part of this book may be reproduced in any form or by any electronic or mechanical means, including information storage and retrieval systems, without written permission from the author, except for the use of brief quotations in a book review.

This is a work of fiction. Names, characters, business, events and incidents are the products of the author's imagination. Any resemblance to actual persons, living or dead, or actual events is purely coincidental.

For my Dad.
Gone too soon.

PROLOGUE

"You'll never... never... get away.. wit... " The dying man couldn't finish his sentence as the inferno raged around him and his fallen comrades. His assailant acknowledged the man's last breaths with little emotion, his cold blue eyes fixed with determination as he studied his prey. The killer, for that was what he was, rose to his feet, wiping the serrated knife clean on his long trench coat. At full height, he stood over six feet tall, with a muscular build that was rather well hidden beneath not only the aforementioned coat, but a kevlar vest and black overalls, designed for stealth and combat.

"Stop!" a cry erupted from the end of the dark corridor where the assassin was headed. He glanced towards the noise and fired his shotgun, the pellets exploding upon contact with flesh, concrete and anything else within their radius. A yelp of pain filled the narrow hallway, as the newcomer fell back clutching his multiple fresh gunshot wounds. His trembling hand was coated in slick blood as he felt his chest and stomach while struggling for air. Footsteps marched towards him lazily, as if the owner of those feet had become so used to the killing, the violence, that there was no need to hurry. The task would be complete either way. Private Jensen came face to face with his attacker the very next moment.

"You... you're... "

"Ulrich Kaufmeiner," the imposing figure finished, calmly slotting another shell into his menacing weapon. His voice was smooth and commanding, his accent British. Jensen was surprised to hear this legendary figure speak with such a tone, he was allegedly raised in Siberia and conscripted to the Russian army. A fanfare of rumours preceded the man. Each one was more illogical than the last, so much so that it was hard to separate fact from fiction. Ulrich pushed a stray lock of platinum blonde hair away from his eyes as he looked at the fallen soldier, regarding him just as he had done to countless others who had been in the way; utter contempt. Private Jensen saw the glint of the blade for the briefest of moments before it was plunged into his chest. Ulrich Kaufmeiner continued walking with his methodical pace as the sirens blared. The walls illuminated a deep red with every wail of the alarms.

CHAPTER ONE

"I can't stand this any longer," she announced, hurling her shovel away into the cracked and dry earth, creating a cloud of dust to appear in reply.

"Oh, take it easy!" Joseph Cullins cried out, waving away the soil that had enveloped him.

"It's so ridiculously hot here!" Luisa exclaimed, flicking her dark brown hair aside as she stood up, placing her hands on her hips, as though accusing Joe of being the one responsible. Her hazel eyes glinted in the sunlight, their spectacular twinkling quality catching Joe off guard for a second, and he had nothing to say. Finally, he rose as well, wiping the sweat from his brow.

"Have a sip of that," Joe offered, motioning to the tanker of water with the brush held in his other hand.

"Absolutely no way, Joseph!" Luisa retorted, a look of disgust scrunching her otherwise striking features, "It's filthy!"

Joe studied the container and discovered she was correct, much to his embarrassment. Their tanker, which was supposed to be transparent and holding nothing but drinking water, was instead polluted with mud, clay, bugs and debris that Joe did not wish to look too closely at.

"Yeah, you're right. I'll go get this cleaned out right away." He hastily shuffled over and unscrewed the lid, allowing the water to cascade out.

"Joe! Be careful, the site!" Luisa said, holding her hands out in alarm.

"Oh my god!" Joe re-tightened the seal, stopping the flow of water from potentially washing away their findings of the day, which were actually rather insignificant. Luisa laughed as she noticed how flustered Joe was. To Joe, the sound was like the birds singing in the morning and he relaxed and allowed himself to chuckle as well.

The two of them had been spending practically every minute together for the last ten days in Dahshur, Egypt. The temperature in July's scorching heat was becoming unbearable, so tempers would often be frayed. Yet they would always regain their composure swiftly enough, and laughter was usually the remedy for any stressful moments.

Luisa came across to Joe and sat herself down, puffing a stray lock of hair away from her face as she did.

"This sucks, it really does," she said with defeat.

"Did you expect to unearth a pharaoh every other day then?" Joe offered, smiling as he did, his green eyes lighting up mischievously.

"No, silly," she answered playfully, giving him a slight shove as Joe took a seat as well. "I just, didn't predict this, you know?" She extended her arms wide and looked about the barren space they occupied. Sand as far as the eye could see, with a few scattered tents and other archaeological sites in view. Their team had set out from the United States of America two weeks ago, arriving first in Cairo for a few days of orientation, briefed only that there had been a recent push to uncover as much of Dahshur as possible. The project had taken off thanks to a remarkable discovery earlier in the month; a single stone coated entirely in gold had been found in the region and its origins dated back to before the first dynasty of pharaohs, throwing into doubt years of historical facts. This is how Luisa and Joe found themselves here. Having just left university and with no experience in the field, it was all hands on deck and as many archaeologists that could be summoned were dispatched. Of course, the two students hadn't exactly been sent to the hub of activity within the expedition. They were instead posted to the outskirts of the site, the very edge of where the commission ended. So, it was quieter, and for now, devoid of any remarkable discoveries.

"Well, we're definitely lucky to be here," Joe remarked, remembering how proud his mom had been when he had told her. She was a single parent, raising Joe and his brother alone all their lives. Joe's brother, Brad, was two years older than him and unlike Joe, wasn't fond of studying. Brad left school at aged fourteen and taken any job he could find. His mother, a criminal lawyer and fiercely intelligent woman who valued academia highly, was devastated. But, deep down she knew Brad had inherited more from his father's side than hers; he was far from focussed on his school work and there ended the boys' knowledge of their father. However, Brad had worked hard and ultimately became a supremely talented sandwich maker. So much so, that he could open up his own shop, an enormous gamble taken at the time which was funded by their mom plus some loans from the bank. Joe was immensely proud of his brother. They had been close their entire lives, and the day Brad opened his store was one of the best days of Joe's life. He realised in that moment how much he missed his small family and he felt alone.

"Hey, you okay?" Luisa asked to his left, jerking Joe back to the present.

Her eyes disarmed him for a time, before he confirmed he was fine. "Just miss 'em, you know?" he confessed.

"I do," she said kindly, squeezing his hand. She allowed her hand to linger for a time before taking it away, resting her chin on it thoughtfully.

"What do you think will happen with us, Joe?" she asked.

Joe was taken aback, excitement coursing through his body. *Is this it? Does she like me more than a friend now?* he asked himself.

As if she had read his mind, Luisa continued, "I mean, do you think we'll become big time archaeologists, you providing for your wife and kids and telling them stories about how you and I discovered the meaning of life in this dust bowl?"

Joe's initial burst of anticipation was quelled almost instantly, and his spark of hope doused. He had been hopelessly in love with Luisa Duarte almost from the moment they had met and of course, had never told her. When Luisa arrived from Portugal to the United States almost ten years ago, she had absolutely nobody but her aunt, who lived in Upstate New York. Joe and Luisa had met in high school in Manhattan, Joe remembered it like it was yesterday; History class with Mrs. Turnstible. As usual, nobody except Joe was paying attention. Ten minutes into the lesson, the door opened Luisa walked in. Her dark hair tied back in a ponytail, he remembered the way her pink dress flowed delicately around her, she was as breathtaking then as she is now. Joe was speechless as he watched her walk towards him and sit herself down quietly at the desk next to his. She looked over nervously and flashed a welcoming smile, which did nothing to settle his nerves, only heighten them.

"Class," Mrs Turnstible began, "This is Luisa Duarte, she's transferred here all the way from Portugal."

"Oooh," some of the class responded in mock importance, causing Luisa to flush red briefly.

"Joe, you look after her, okay? You share most of the same

classes." Joe glanced at Luisa and smiled politely, which she returned, and they spent the next forty minutes of class in silence, paying attention to the lesson and not at the stirring emotions they had both felt.

"Do you want to have lunch together?" Joe had suggested at the end of the lesson. Luisa nodded silently in reply, and they headed to the cafeteria together.

"These are hamburgers," Joe pointed out, thinking he was being helpful.

"I know what a hamburger is, Joe, I'm from Portugal, not Mars," she said, laughing, and that was the first time they had shared a joke together. They talked incessantly through lunch, about their families (Luisa had a brother and sister back home with her parents in Lisbon, where she was from) and their interests (Luisa enjoyed football, which Joe called soccer and they laughed again) and Joe confessed his love for history, which Luisa also shared.

"It's gonna sound lame, but I want to be an archaeologist when I leave school," Joe had stated.

"No way, so do I! That's why I asked to come here and live with my aunt, because there are more opportunities for study! Joe, that's so cool!" Their bond was booming, and it wasn't long before they started to hang out together outside of school. Joe introduced Luisa to his group of friends, and that was where it went wrong. Luisa was pretty, charming, funny and quick-witted, so it was no surprise when boys took an interest in her. One such boy just happened to be one of Joe's best friends growing up, Devante Walker. All American athlete, popular and the nicest guy in school. He did what Joe never could; asked Luisa out on a date. Luisa, despite liking Joe herself, accepted, as she had no invitation from the former and from then on, Joe and Luisa shared a platonic relationship. Joe simply suffered in silence as he saw Luisa spend approximately two years with Devante before they broke up.

"What happened?" Joe had asked, both to Devante and Luisa in separate conversations.

"There just wasn't a spark, you know?" Luisa responded.

"Nothing there any more, man," Devante concluded.

Joe and Luisa continued to be the best of friends. They both graduated and attended the same college, where they had their own relationships and flings, guiding each other through heartbreak and triumph alike and constantly returning to the same spot when their relationships eventually broke down; together, just the two of them.

Joe realised he hadn't answered Luisa yet. "Sorry, daydreaming."

"That's okay Joe, I know you like to go for a wander in dreamland now and then," she teased.

"Well, to answer your question, Miss Duarte," he replied in mock formality, "I think we'll uncover something pretty soon and show these other guys up."

"Oh yeah? What makes you say that?"

"Well, I just have a good feeling. It's us, we always make it work."

"Yeah, we do, don't we?" Luisa concluded, smiling sincerely.

"Come on, we should finish up here and move to the next empty patch of dirt," Joe announced, standing up and dusting down his khaki shorts.

"Yes, sir," Luisa said, saluting as she did with a big grin.

△

A few hours of no interest passed by. The midday sun was now behind them as time trickled closer towards five, at which point they could officially clock off and head back to their hotel. Luisa stood up. "Joe!" she exclaimed loudly, "Get over here!"

Joe scrambled up to his feet and jogged the short distance

between them. "What's up? Woah! What is that?" Joe reacted as he saw what Luisa was talking about. Peeking out from the earth was the corner of what appeared to be a frame, perhaps for a doorway. "Come on, let's see what else there is!" They excavated the surrounding area, chipping away carefully, trying to reveal more of this discovery without damaging it. Joe wiped away some dirt and clay from the exposed corner, blowing gently on it as he did. "Hey what's that–" Joe's commentary was interrupted with an almighty *whoosh* as the surrounding ground opened up, swallowing him in an instant.

"JOE!" Luisa screamed, scrambling across to where her best friend had been crouched over just moments before, seeing the void which had now opened up as dust billowed up from the sudden gaping wound in the ground. "Joe!" she cried again into the emptiness, her voice reaching nothing and sounding so insignificantly small in the vast openness of the Dahshur plains.

CHAPTER TWO

Lieutenant Frank Williams marched with authority through the ruined corridors of Military Base Alexandria, situated off the coast of West Africa. He grimaced as he saw two medical staff carrying a stretcher with yet another casualty. Frank continued on, past gore spattered walls, blown out windows and the occasional small fire that still burned. The surrounding scene was pure destruction. The clean-up crew had been removing debris and, to his great sadness, bodies, for hours and yet the base was still in complete chaos. He moved into the mess hall, which had its tables upturned, vending machines exploded, and chairs scattered everywhere. Blood appeared on almost every surface. Frank shuddered as he made his way through the disaster towards the Armoury, which was largely unscathed.

"Atten-shun!" barked a sergeant as Frank entered the room. The five military personnel all rose from the wrecked table and saluted.

"At ease, gentlemen," Frank said, removing his cap as he did, exposing his shaven head. His eyes peered into everyone seated at the table. Some still had charrs and burns on their skin, their uniforms a patchwork of destruction, with blood, holes and other marks adorning most of them. Frank sighed, "Out of all the men here, this is all we have left?" he said, addressing the sergeant.

"Yes, sir," answered the man, who could not have been over forty years old. Frank didn't respond at once, instead again surveying the surviving members of Base Alexandria. They all displayed the same look, the "thousand-yard stare" as civilians liked to say. Frank understood what they had been through. He suspected that many, if not all who were posted here had never seen actual combat before, and had been thrust into what was a very one sided fight. Alexandria was nowhere near any active war zones, it was seen as an effortless task for most who got deployed there. *Probably not so much now*, Frank thought darkly.

"Men," he began, his voice full of authority, yet calm and somehow comforting. "What you have been exposed to today has been something I doubt many of you would ever have believed you would experience. Your bravery and courage speak volumes, and I am proud of each and every one of you." He let the words hang in the air for a minute before continuing. "Now-"

"Sir, can I, uh, say speak freely, please?" One private interjected, cutting Frank off. The sergeant was about to reprimand the inexperienced man, but Frank waved a hand to dismiss the action.

"Go on, son," Frank allowed.

"Well, it's just, uh. I don't feel all that brave, to be honest with you," the young man said, an Alabama twang in his voice.

"Why's that, private?" Frank asked, somewhat intrigued.

"Well, see, I was just dumb lucky is all. I was somewhere that he hadn't got to yet, before he just vanished."

Frank furrowed his brow, "What do you mean, private?"

"Well one minute, he's there taking down this entire base, then the next he's gone."

Frank was again caught momentarily off guard.

"You say *he* like it was one individual who did all this," Frank asked, opening his arms to gesture, inviting everyone to survey the destruction behind him in the mess hall and beyond.

"That's right, sir. One guy." The private shifted in his seat, the only remaining light in the armoury flickering as Frank planned the next question in his head, already knowing the answer.

"You know who it was, private?"

He nodded his head, "Ulrich Kaufmeiner." The name settled in the air, all the men taking it in and recognising the importance of it.

"Thank you private, that will be all. Gentlemen." Frank stood up and saluted, which was returned by the survivors.

"If you'll walk with me, please sergeant," Frank commanded, leading the way out of the room.

"Sir-" the sergeant began, but Frank cut him off with another wave of his hand.

"Sergeant, one of two things has happened here. Either this man is a superhero and should be in a comic book, or some guerrilla warfare faction has ambushed our troops. What do you make of it?"

"Well," the sergeant answered, looking at the ground first before turning to Frank as they both stepped over a small crater in the floor, "I think the rumours are true and this guy is responsible, solely."

Frank stopped walking abruptly, which made the young sergeant even more anxious than he already was.

"Son, my superiors are landing in a few hours and they expect a debrief to tell them just what in the hell happened here. Am I really going to inform them one guy did this all alone? And for what?"

"With respect, sir. I was here, I know what happened," the

sergeant answered, keeping his voice steady but quaking on the inside. "As for why? I think the higher ups probably realise. He was looking for something."

Frank had allowed the sergeant to continue with the rest of his day as he walked alone through more ruined blocks, halls that were filled with rubble, or battle-scarred by explosions and violence. He made his way to the Chief Officer's room, where the corpse of the commanding officer of the base had already been removed. Files were scattered on the floor and the computer was still active. *Was Ulrich searching for something?* Frank wondered, before his eyes settled on an open file marked as classified. He opened it, finding precious few notes inside, surmising that Ulrich had likely taken what he wanted from here. One sheet had a picture of a rock with "Project Unity" as its header. "What is Project Unity?" Frank said aloud to nobody in particular, his question wouldn't be answered as whatever information had once been here was now gone.

Colonel Charles Riggs and his entourage touched down just over an hour after Frank had visited the Chief Officer's room. The Colonel summoned Frank to a meeting almost as soon as his feet hit the ground. A hastily constructed centre of operations had been established next to Base Alexandria to allow for a secure site for meetings to be held, which in reality it was a tent guarded by soldiers. They were asked to leave as soon as the Colonel entered with his comrades, all outranking Frank Williams and all demanding answers.

"Come in, Williams," Colonel Riggs said without glancing up from his paperwork. "Have a seat," he gestured to the vacant chair that sat opposite him, flanked by his commanding officers.

"Sirs," Frank spoke to the room, saluting as he did, the gesture returned by the four seated men.

"At ease, Lieutenant," Riggs commanded in a gruff voice. "So, what did you find out? Guerrilla warfare?" he spoke, still not looking up from his paperwork.

Frank sat and adjusted his well-ironed uniform. "Well, sir," he began, "it appears not."

Riggs raised an eyebrow as he looked at the Lieutenant for the first time. "Pardon me, Williams?" he enquired.

"The surviving men all agree that this was the work of one man, Sir," Frank pressed on. Riggs didn't answer, allowing Frank to continue. "They say it was Ulrich Kaufmeiner," he finished, wondering if the Colonel had even heard this name before. Riggs was still for a minute, then exchanged glances with his other commanding officers.

"Did they say anything else?" Riggs asked, a flicker of something in his voice, *was it panic?* Frank mused.

"No, sir, but I think if it was Ulrich, he found something in the Chief Officer's room," Frank elaborated. At this, the Colonel's eyes bulged slightly, and he turned his full attention to Frank.

"What do you mean, Williams?" he asked, leaning forward slightly.

"Sir, I found a file called Project Unity, which was completely empty except for maybe one or two sheets."

Riggs sank a little in his chair before regaining his composure and addressing the four men at the sides of the table, "Alert General Hoskins at once, tell him it's what we thought it was."

"Affirmative," a chorus of reply came and simultaneous salutes as the men swiftly left. Riggs then stood up, stuffing paperwork into his jacket and tucking his chair in.

"Sir, can I ask-"

"No, you cannot, Williams," Riggs interjected, cutting off Frank's sentence before it had even begun. "This is a matter of national security, the less you know, the better. Trust me," he shot Frank a warning glare as he walked past at breakneck speed.

"Sir, what are my orders?" Frank asked, causing Riggs to stop in his tracks.

"Get away from this continent, son. Get to your family, before it's too late," Riggs said without turning around before finally vacating the tent, leaving Frank alone with no genuine answers and an entire array of questions.

CHAPTER THREE

THE SMOKE HAD FINALLY BEGAN to clear and Luisa was at last able to see what had happened to Joe. The crater which had swallowed him up swam into view as the smoke dissipated. "Joe!" She screamed again, panic gripping her. "Oh god, Joe... Joe," Luisa muttered to herself, searching around for any signs of help. Nobody was even remotely close to where Joe and Luisa had been digging. They were very much left to their own devices and told to keep out of the way. At first, this was something of a blessing. The two of them were thrilled to be working together without being watched over or micromanaged, plus she always enjoyed being alone with Joe. Now, it didn't seem so great that they were isolated without the ability to contact anyone; mobile phones didn't work in this part of the site. Luisa's dark eyebrows shot up as she remembered the walkie-talkie. She raced over to their belongings; two rucksacks dumped unceremoniously on top of one another. Luisa dropped to her knees, frantically opened her bag and found what she was seeking. "Yes!" she exclaimed as she pressed the button to turn the device on. A wave of static greeted her.

"This is Luisa Duarte calling to base, I have an emergency,

please respond! Over!" She gripped tightly on the walkie-talkie, staring at the speaker expectantly. Nobody answered. Distorted radio interference was the only reply. Panicking more she opened the voice channel and again repeated, "This is Luisa Duarte calling to base, I have an emergency, please respond! Over!" Her hands trembled ever so slightly as the seconds ticked agonisingly away. Luisa looked around, her dark hair whipping about her face as she again searched for answers that simply weren't there. "Okay, the transport won't be here for... three more hours," she said to herself, checking her watch as she did. Luisa bit her lip. If she walked to the next excavation site, that would be only roughly forty-five minutes, but that meant abandoning Joe. What if more of the ground collapsed? What could she even do if it did? Luisa's internal debate raged on, as she glanced back across to the archway that protruded from the earth. The depths of the chasm it showed were unbelievably dark.

"I can't leave him," she whispered to herself. Slowly, Luisa walked back to the opening, again shouting for Joe's name in vain, for there was no answer. She searched around and picked up a small, jagged rock. Turning it over in her hand, she threw it as gently as possible into the void, hoping to hear it ricochet off solid ground. Luisa leaned in cautiously, straining her ears to hear. She dared to lean a little further and suddenly the ground cracked and opened once more.

△

Luisa screamed as she fell, sliding on dirt and earth, her vision totally useless as darkness closed in around her. She felt herself hurtling further and further down into the depths and knew that soon she would impact with something and it wouldn't be a soft landing. After falling for what felt like an eternity, a crack of light appeared and was rapidly expanding as her momentum carried her towards it. Her screaming continued as the light grew closer and wider. Her feet broke through first as her body followed swiftly after. Luisa shut her eyes, expecting to imminently hit the floor. Her momentum stopped, but it was not with a violent jolt. On the contrary, Luisa was suspended an inch from the ground. When she dared to open her eyes, she was astounded at what she saw.

"Hey!" Joe said breathlessly. His face was covered in dust and had a few scrapes, but otherwise he looked unharmed.

"Joe!" Luisa said, as her feet dabbed the floor. She ran over to him and hugged him tightly, nuzzling her head into his neck and fighting back some tears. "Joe, I thought I'd lost you," she whispered. Joe comforted her with his embrace and the two were inseparable for a moment. At last, Luisa pulled away from Joe, she looked up at him and smiled, sobbing gently as she finally noted her surroundings. Her eyes bulged as she saw above, noticing the hole where they had both come from was ringed and surrounded by hieroglyphs.

"How are we alive?" she asked, both to Joe but also to herself

"I've got no idea," Joe admitted, scratching his head. "The same thing happened to me, I came in from up there, just as I was about to hit the floor, I stopped. I think it's something to do with the floor, look!" Joe pointed down and Luisa saw it, the same ring of ancient symbols was on the floor and had a faint blue tinge to them.

"Joe, what is this place?" Luisa asked, now properly absorbing her surroundings. They were in an immense cavern, which had lit torches lined on the walls. Ahead of them was a path, wide enough to fit three cars side by side. The trail extended onwards into the distance, which disappeared into darkness. The walls of the cavern seemed to extend for infinity both up and down. Luisa noted that on either side of the route there was a sheer drop into a darkness so absolute it gave her the chills.

"I don't know," Joe answered, equally in awe of their surroundings. "I didn't go ahead because I figured you'd probably be stupid enough to follow me," he said grinning.

"Well, I didn't plan on it, I have to say," Luisa admitted. "But I'm sure glad I did, this place is amazing!" she said, her excitement building, imagining the prestige such a discovery would bring them both.

"Don't you find it strange?" Joe asked earnestly. "I mean, how are these torches lit?" he inquired, gesturing to the neatly placed beacons of light above and ahead of them. "Also," he continued, "this pathway looks to be pristine, like nobody has ever walked on it before." Joe finished, crouching down to investigate the floor in greater detail. He was right, it looked untouched, a layer of dust and fine sand was present, but otherwise, it was spotless.

"More to the point, how was our momentum completely stopped?" Luisa asked, gesturing to the hole behind and above them. "Hey, they've faded," Luisa noted, spotting that the rings on the floor and ceiling had ceased radiating their faint blue colour. She strolled around the circular marking and wandered to the wall that trapped them. Luisa touched it, not sure what she was expecting.

"Anything?" Joe asked from behind her.

"Nothing," she responded, turning and walking back to him. Luisa looked up again at what she had decided in her head was the entrance. "I'm going to stand in this circle and see if it takes me back," she informed Joe, still looking up.

"Worth a shot, I guess," Joe shrugged in agreement. "Wait, let me come over, in case it's like a one time use kind of deal," he said, jogging the short distance.

"Good idea. Okay, ready?" Luisa said, extending her hand

for Joe to hold. He took it and for a moment, they locked eyes. They quickly turned away, both slightly embarrassed.

Luisa cleared her throat, not looking at Joe. "Okay, here we go," she said stepping into the circle with Joe, bracing herself for whatever would happen next and closing her eyes.

△

Joe and Luisa stood in silence for a few moments, Luisa opened her eyes to find Joe looking at her, with a small smirk on his face.

"Oh, it was worth a try!" she declared, yanking her hand free of his.

"It was, absolutely! But I think we both know what we have to do," Joe answered with a laugh.

"What, go forward?" Luisa answered.

"Yes! Why not? We could be on the verge of the biggest discovery of our time," Joe replied with adventure swimming in his eyes.

Luisa bit her lip again, pondering the options. "Shouldn't we wait? The transport will be along and I think it'll be obvious where we are, so maybe we should stay here?"

"That transport is hours away still," Joe countered. "Come on, when are we ever going to get an opportunity like this again in our lives? Untouched and unexplored for centuries? This is going to be huge!" he exclaimed, excitement finally bubbling over.

Luisa smiled, "Okay, let's do it," she said.

"We need to be careful though," Joe stated, somewhat obviously.

"You don't say?" Luisa mocked.

"Yeah, yeah. You know what I mean. We did just fall down a massive hole and somehow emerge in this perfectly preserved chamber, maybe something isn't quite right, you know?" Joe answered.

"You're right, let's just be careful and stay close," Luisa suggested. Joe's heart fluttered slightly at the phrasing *stay close* but he remained neutral in his expression.

"I'll lead the way, come on, let's see where this path takes us," Joe said, taking the first step onto the pathway, with Luisa following behind him.

A few hundred miles away, Ulrich Kaufmeiner tightens the silencer on his pistol. He sheathes the serrated blade into his belt and ensures he is carrying at least four grenades; two high explosive, one smoke and one flashbang. He saunters to the mirror in his dingy motel room bathroom and switches on the light. It flickers once, twice, and then at last stays. Ulrich stares at his own reflection for several moments, before whispering just three words, "It has begun." Swiftly, he turns around and leaves the area, descending the wooden staircase, past the lobby and out into the late Egyptian afternoon. He unlocks the rented Suzuki Jimney and climbs in, turning the ignition and heading for his destination; Dahshur.

CHAPTER FOUR

GENERAL HOSKINS STOOD in silence in his vast office, looking out onto the peaceful and idyllic lake. The serene setting was a stark contrast to the cold, grey walls of the US military base where he was stationed. The structure sharp and angular compared to the natural beauty of the outside world which ebbed and flowed, not deliberate and calculated. Hoskins had called this place home for over a decade now since his promotion. Dan Hoskins was following in his father's footsteps and his father's footsteps before him; all service men, all descended from a long line of proud warriors which stretched back seemingly until the very origins of time itself. Hoskins was picked for this role, put in place by those who knew the only truth; that this world needed to be born anew, fresh from the many, many imperfections that plagued it currently.

He inhaled before taking a deep swig of his morning coffee; the smell filling his nostrils and affording him precious few seconds of complete satisfaction as he closed his eyes, allowing the moment to last.

"General Hoskins," the tone of his secretary blared through his phone. He sighed, opening his eyes and giving in to reality. He walked across to his desk and pressed the intercom: "Yes, Dorris, what is it?" his deep voice answered in an even, yet irritated tone.

"Riggs on line one, shall I patch him in?"

"Go ahead," Hoskins replied, lifting the receiver. "Riggs, tell me what's happening?"

"Sir, he knows," Riggs replied, his speech revealing his panic.

"Who knows what, Riggs?" Hoskins replied, already knowing the answer.

"Kaufmeiner, he knows about *Project Unity*."

Hoskins took another sip of his coffee before replying, setting it neatly onto a coaster on his desk. "Was there anything in the file of value?"

"It had the suspected location of the artefact, sir," Riggs answered, swallowing hard.

Hoskins chuckled, "Nobody truly knows where it is, and if it indeed exists. What he's taken is nothing but an educated guess, at best."

"He's been hunting this information down for months. How did he even know about it?" Riggs asked, panic again creeping into his cadence.

"How indeed," pondered Hoskins.

"What are my orders, sir?" Riggs asked.

"Secure the site at Dahshur. This is where we pinpointed the probable location, is it not?"

"Yes, sir. Indeed. This was in the file."

"Good, this stops us chasing our tail. We know where Kaufmeiner will head to next and we can be prepared. Assemble your best forces, Colonel and good luck. We'll catch this evil man and avenge our brothers who died by his hand," Hoskins said firmly.

"Aye, sir. Will keep you appraised of any developments," Riggs finished, ending the conversation. Hoskins put down the receiver, lifted his coffee and walked slowly around his office, stopping next to the ornate chess-board that sat proudly on a glass table. Deliberately, Hoskins moved a white pawn forward. "It has begun," he whispered.

△

Frank Williams was just about to leave the base when his phone rang loudly from his jacket pocket.

"Frank Williams," he said.

"Lieutenant, this is Colonel Riggs. Sorry son, but I have a new mission for you and I need my best."

"Well thank you sir, how can I be of service?" Frank answered, rubbing his shaven head absently with his free hand.

"I need forces deployed to Dahshur, yesterday. Remember that whole national security bit I said earlier?"

"Yes, sir?"

"Well, you're in luck, you're now involved. Grab your things, meet me ten kilometres south of here ASAP."

"Roger that!" Frank clicked the phone off and hurriedly looked for a vehicle to commandeer. He settled on a black Range Rover and politely requested the privates to vacate, no questions asked. As he climbed in, his phone buzzed again, this time a message detailing the rendezvous location sent by the aforementioned Colonel. He put his foot down and drove there as fast as he could.

△

Frank pulled up outside the loading bay of a large warehouse, which had troops running left and right, vehicles being loaded with munitions and people alike. It was organised chaos, and the Lieutenant was settling; this is where he was at his best, in amongst the unpredictable whirlwind of battle.

"Williams," called out Colonel Riggs, who was approaching from the western side of the vast storage facility, flanked by his four officers as before.

"Sir," Frank responded with a salute.

"At ease, son," Riggs replied. There wasn't much of an age difference between the pair, but Frank respected Riggs immensely. His victories in skirmishes were well known throughout the corps, his reputation for dealing with enemies of the free world preceded him and Frank was admittedly excited to be working alongside him on this mission.

"We've got a rapidly developing situation out in Dahshur," Riggs began, locking eyes with Frank, a fresh sense of urgency in his voice and tone. "We believe Kaufmeiner will be en route as we speak, and we intend to stop him in his tracks," the Colonel continued. "Remember that file you mentioned?"

"I do," Frank answered.

"Well, that file contained evidence suggesting a powerful artefact is located in Dahshur," Riggs explained. "At this point, it's prudent to remind you that this is, of course, top secret information and not to be shared with anyone," he followed up.

"Of course, sir," Frank repeated, his heart rate pulsing. He had always been very satisfied with his job as it had provided well for his family, allowed him to buy a house, clothes for his daughter and take his wife out for meals. But it had never quite scratched his itch for adventure; Frank yearned to be spoken about in the same way Riggs was. Revered by peers and feared by enemies and he sensed that this was his chance to prove himself.

"Ulrich is seeking this artefact, that we know. Whether it's for him or a terrorist group, we're not sure, as we've only seen him act alone and as of yet have been unable to capture and interrogate him," Riggs elaborated before continuing, "To that end, our orders are to subdue and if we can, bring him in for questioning. Of course, neutralise the target if necessary, but it is the view of my colleagues and I that it would be beneficial to bring him in alive," he finished.

"Understood, sir. May I ask a question?"

"Of course, Lieutenant," Riggs replied.

"Do we actually know what this artefact does?" Frank asked earnestly. The four officers looked at one other uncomfortably. Riggs however simply smiled.

"Truth be told, Lieutenant, no, we do not. We understand it is potentially something that can alter the very reality we live in, but to what end, we're uncertain. But it seems this Kaufmeiner character is determined to find out," Riggs stroked the stubble on his chin as he spoke, his honesty a breath of fresh air to Frank.

"How widely known is this, if I may ask, Colonel?"

"Outside of our armed forces, not at all. General Hoskins has briefed maybe ten of us on its supposed existence, and this was only as recently as a month ago," Riggs answered.

Frank thought on this for a moment, his mind trying to think as the continued stream of action in the warehouse blew like a tornado around them.

"How did General Hoskins come to find this information out, Colonel?" This question drew yet more looks of concern from the four officers and they shifted where they stood, avoiding Riggs' eyes.

"I'm not entirely sure," Riggs said, now noticing his officers. "Gentlemen, do you happen to know? Why so bashful suddenly?"

"Sir, no sir," one replied, speaking on behalf of everyone there, standing as straight as a lamp post.

"At ease, officer," Riggs said, waving a hand, before turning his attention back to Frank. "For this detail, you'll have two squads under your command, the goal as I say is to engage with the aim of bringing the target back for interrogation. Is that clear?"

"Affirmative, sir," Frank answered.

"You'll be working in tandem with my colleagues here, each of whom will also have a squadron under their remit. We're going to create a perimeter around this location here," Riggs pointed to a red circle on a map that one of his officers held. "This was, according to our intelligence, the most likely place for the artefact to be located. There is in fact a team of archaeologists working in this area at present, so we have sent advanced communication warning them of the potential danger and have asked them to vacate the area, so by the time you arrive, there will be no civilians present. We must establish a perimeter, at least five hundred meters in radius and we simply try and catch Kaufmeiner the moment he's in range. As you can appreciate, time is of the essence, so move out at once, your troops are just over there in the hanger awaiting your arrival. I wish you luck and make sure you all come back in one piece," Riggs said, looking each man in the eye sternly. "That's an order," he finished, before snapping his feet together and saluting. He handed the map to Frank and turned on his heel. Frank and the others saluted in response before they went in their separate directions in a hurry, Frank rushing towards his new squad-mates, his heart beating fast and adrenaline beginning to course around his body.

Frank slowed his run as he approached the twenty men and women who were to be in his command. They were all ready and waiting by the transport.

"Lieutenant Williams, sir!" cried out who Frank suspected was the sergeant of the squad.

"At ease, son," Frank replied, noting how young his colleague and indeed the entire troop looked.

"Orders, sir?" the young soldier asked, his eyes lighting up in anticipation. Frank took a moment to look around at the assembly of men and women before him, their attention completely fixed upon him.

"We are to set up a perimeter at least five hundred meters in radius," Frank began, mimicking Colonel Riggs' instructions not a few minutes earlier. "Our primary goal is to ensure the threat is taken down and brought in for questioning, we need to understand his motives and who he's working for. So far he's managed to avoid being captured," Frank continued.

"Who's the target, sir?" asked one of the privates.

"Ulrich Kaufmeiner," Frank responded, the answer provoking a rippling murmur between the troops at the recognition of the name. Frank held a hand up for silence, which was immediately observed. "Now, I realise that this name may be familiar to some of you. We've been caught on the back foot before, but this time... this time we have the advantage," Frank said to the group, hoping to inspire some confidence amongst them. Behind him, armoured vehicles had begun tearing off into the desert, bearing down on their location with haste. Frank turned back to his soldiers and noticed the worried glances that met his gaze.

"I know this detail may seem daunting, you've all clearly heard the stories, hell, some of you may have had friends killed by this guy. But that doesn't mean he's anything more than a man and a threat we need to take down. By all means, if your life is in danger and you have no choice, use lethal force, but we should be able to subdue him silently and effectively. He probably expects we'll be waiting for him, true, but he doesn't know when or how we'll strike. That's what we use to our advantage. We're on the assumption he's going there right away, so he may very well be there already. My gut tells me otherwise, I'm thinking he's rested up some place first before heading out there. That's how we'll get him." Frank's rousing words caused a visible reaction in the troops, some that looked downtrodden grew in stature, others who lacked confidence were standing tall. "We do this for our country, for our fallen comrades and for our family. We do not let this man continue his crusade of destruction. Are you with me?" Frank bellowed those last words.

"Yeah!" cried a few of the soldiers.

"I need you with me! ARE YOU WITH ME?" Frank roared, and this time everyone responded with loud approval.

"Let's load up and roll out!" Frank shouted again and his soldiers obliged, hungry for action and retribution against their new enemy. Frank hoisted himself into the passenger seat of the transport and said a silent prayer that they weren't already too late, as the sun began to set in the distance.

CHAPTER FIVE

Luisa followed Joe as he cautiously stepped on to the path. His foot left a faint imprint in the layer of dust that covered the surface.

"Look at that," Joe said, pointing up and to his left. Luisa's gaze followed his gesture, and she saw the engraving just above the first beacon, the light flickering and barely illuminating the feature.

"What do you think it is?" she asked.

"I don't know," Joe replied, now drawing level with the torch and craning his neck to take in the ornate spectacle. "Woah," he said under his breath. Luisa stopped next to him and mimicked his action. Her eyes widened as she too saw the entire image in full. Etched into the dark rock was a figure which loomed some twenty feet above them. It was a humanoid creature, but with no facial features they could discern, perhaps a line for a mouth, but that was all. It had three arms, one of which was stretched directly up and holding a circle, which had inscriptions on that the pair could not read. Extending out from both sides with an impossible straightness were the remaining two arms. One was tightly gripping a rod, which narrowed at the tip to a fine point. The other held nothing, but its palm was open, so that the fingers were fully outstretched, almost as if to usher Luisa and Joe along the route. The torso was depicted as muscular and had a row of symbols in a perfectly straight line across its chest. Down at the waist, the figure had a skirt or loincloth covering the nether-regions and then four legs, with its multiple toes pointing right, as though again encouraging progress along the trail.

Joe and Luisa stood in silence for a few moments, absorbing the fascinating image before them. "It doesn't look Egyptian," Joe said.

"I was thinking the same thing," Luisa replied, biting her lip slightly. "Who could have left this here?"

"I have no idea, none of this really makes much sense, does it?" Joe admitted.

"It doesn't. Joe? I'm glad you're here with me," she added, her eyes locking onto his. Joe's heart fluttered, and he felt colour rise in his cheeks.

"Um, yeah me too. Come on, we should see where this goes," he mumbled quickly and turned on his heel, cringing slightly at his own lack of assertiveness with his response. They continued in silence towards the next torch. The direction they walked was illuminated just enough so that they could move on without incident. Joe absentmindedly looked up, seeing nothing but complete darkness as the cavern stretched on for eternity, then his foot slipped. In his carelessness, Joe had walked far too close to the edge of the trail which didn't have any guard rail to stop someone falling into the abyss.

"Joe!" Luisa screamed, lunging forward and grabbing his flailing arm with both hands, holding on as tight as she could. Joe regained his balance and his dangling foot quickly found the safety of the walkway. They both looked at each other for a second, breathing hard, and then Joe laughed.

"What is so funny? You could have fallen off the edge and died!" Luisa exclaimed.

"That really was close," he said, grinning broadly, only annoying Luisa even more.

"Be more careful!" she said, slapping his arm and adjusting her top, blowing a loose hair away from her face in annoyance.

"Sorry," Joe said, a little sheepishly. "Hey, what's that?" Joe peered down into the impossible blackness of the depths below and saw a tiny light pulsating. It blinked two, then three times before fading.

"What's *what?*" Luisa asked, now joining him near the edge and looking down at the void. "What am I looking at, Joe?" She inquired, mild irritation permeating her voice.

"It was just there, a light, I saw it!" Joe protested, doubt clouding his mind.

"It's okay, Joe," Luisa said, toning down her annoyance and softening her glare. "There's something strange here, we should just keep moving," Luisa finished.

"Yeah, you're right. We need to find a way out and then come back tomorrow with the entire team," Joe said optimistically.

"There's something up ahead," Luisa noted. "Come on, let's check it out, looks to be another engraving," she decided, this time taking the lead and walking ahead of Joe.

As they neared the next torch, some four hundred metres ahead, the image etched into the cavern wall focused and they both scrunched their faces up in puzzled concentration.

"It could be a skull?" Joe offered as they kept walking closer, the perspective shifted as they met the next torch and stopped dead centre to absorb the icon before them. Sitting a few metres above the torch was indeed a skull. However, it had intricately detailed symbols carved at the top, words Joe presumed, though he couldn't fathom what they meant, their symbols alien to him. Above the skull was a crown adorned with feathers, jewels and three distinct spokes. Joe wondered if there was a connection with the three arms they had seen on the previous image.

"This is definitely not Egyptian," Luisa mused.

"Looks almost Mayan," Joe replied, his mind trying to connect the dots but unable to fathom why and how these carvings came to be. He looked again to the path and saw that there were only three more torches left and from that point on, the way ahead was plunged into darkness. Out of nowhere there was a rumble, making the pair jump. Luisa stifled a scream and Joe gasped. The noise wasn't loud, but in the cavern's emptiness it was magnified enormously.

"What was that?" Luisa asked, panic infiltrating her usually calm voice.

"It felt like it came from below," Joe said, daring to take a peek over the side of the path. He saw it once again.

"There, look, quickly!" Joe exclaimed, ushering Luisa over. This time she arrived in time.

"Woah!" She blurted out, her eyes wide as she saw the golden light. They both stared at it in awe for a few seconds and just like before, it blinked three times and faded out.

"Unless we're both hallucinating, there's something down there, right?" Joe asked earnestly.

"Yes, I think there is," Luisa responded quietly.

"I can't wait for everyone to see this," Joe said lightly, his excitement outweighing any feelings of trepidation for the time being. "Come on, let's keep going, there may be a way out soon," Joe finished, setting off and taking the lead once more.

They pressed on and like the earlier torches, the next two illuminated carvings that were exact replicas of the others, in the same order. The path began to narrow slightly as they approached the final torch, which had the most ornate picture yet.

"This is a map," Joe said, his eyes growing wide as they came next to the torch and the carving.

"Is it Earth?" Luisa puzzled, not sure if she was looking at continents, islands or even cities.

"That might be Africa?" Joe suggested, pointing to a large land mass.

"Hey, look," Luisa said, squinting her eyes to make sure she wasn't seeing things. "It looks like a triangle," she finished, guiding Joe to where she noticed the shape.

"Oh yeah, you don't suppose that's where we are, do you?" he suggested with a grin.

"Maybe..." Luisa said faintly, looking around the corners of the map, which had scripture running along the boundaries of the frame.

"Do you think it's Sanskrit?" Joe claimed, noticing Luisa taking in the strange designs.

"It just looks... wrong," Luisa finished, the letters and symbols looking *almost* like they made sense, but also like everything was mirrored and therefore skewed.

"Hey, look there's another triangle," Joe spotted, pointing to a land mass that lay to the east of the first triangle. He scanned around the map, picking out what he assumed were mountain ranges and rivers. It certainly looked like Earth, but it didn't add up; the scale was too big for it to be a local city, yet the arrangement of geographical features matched nothing he knew to be true. Just as he was staring closely at the second triangle, the flame was extinguished with a sudden rush of wind, taking all the other light sources with it and plunging the pair into darkness.

"Luisa!" Joe shouted, temporarily blinded by the sudden loss of light.

"Joe! I'm next to you, grab my hand," Luisa answered, fumbling in the dark and attempting to locate her friend.

"Here!" Joe felt Luisa's slender fingers grip his wrist, and he sighed in relief.

"Now what do we do?" Luisa asked, her voice even, but panic simmering under the surface.

"Let's just stay still for a minute," Joe said, conscious that there was not as much room to manoeuvre as before now that the walkway was narrower.

"Okay, good idea, I think my eyes are adjusting a bit," Luisa stated.

"Mine too," Joe lied; he couldn't see anything at all.

"Joe?" Luisa hesitantly asked.

"Yeah?"

"If we don't make it out of here..." she began.

"Hey now," Joe said quickly, but with kindness. "Don't talk like that, we're gonna be fine," he concluded with confidence, despite not being entirely sure himself.

"Okay, okay, but just in case," she carried on. "I just want you to know—" Luisa was interrupted as the cavern shook again, this time much more violently than before.

"Hold on!" Joe said as he pulled Luisa into an embrace. He shut his eyes, which seemed somewhat ridiculous as he couldn't see anyway.

"Joe, look!" Luisa cried over the noise. He obeyed and opened his right eye ever so slightly, not sure whether he could take many more surprises.

"Oh my!" Joe exclaimed as he saw the dazzling beacon which had appeared just a few metres ahead of them; it was another golden light.

The cavern ceased its upheaval, and the ground was stable again. Joe and Luisa blinked rapidly as their eyes adjusted once more to the sudden intrusion of light in the unyielding darkness. The golden orb was suspended in mid-air, hanging as if by magic. They saw that the path they were on pointed to nothing, it just stopped about a hundred metres ahead and presumably led to nowhere but down. Luisa gripped Joe's arm tightly as they shuffled forwards with trepidation.

"Joe, be careful," she whispered as he inched nearer the orb. It sat there pulsating silently, inviting them to touch it. Joe cautiously held out his hand and reached forward, his fingers trembled ever so slightly as he inched closer and closer. Mere millimetres from it, Joe realised he'd been holding his breath and exhaled gently and as quietly as he could, petrified of causing a cataclysmic reaction. His fingertips brushed the object, and he pulled back rapidly.

"What's the matter, is it hot?" Luisa asked, concern etched in her features.

"No, not at all," Joe replied, confusion spread across his face. He reached back in to touch it and this time held his hand on the sphere. "It's cold, but feels soft, like you could press into it and mould it," he said, attempting to do just that. Nothing happened. "Weird," he continued, "it's almost like it reacted to my touch," he finished, taking his hand off.

"You try," Joe asked Luisa.

"Is it safe?" She looked at Joe with doubt, but found her hand was already travelling to the enticing object before them.

"Oh!" she cried, as taken aback by the strange texture as Joe had been. She mimicked his actions and pressed into the orb, but unlike Joe, she kept her fingers affixed to it. After a few seconds, the golden hue shifted to a brilliant white. Luisa's eyes widened as did Joe's, and they watched as the unearthly device continued to shine, so much so that they had to cover their eyes.

"Do you think it's going to explode?" Joe asked, suddenly aware of the potential danger.

"No, I don't think so... hey, look! It's moving!" Luisa exclaimed, watching as the still glowing device floated noiselessly forward. They looked at each other and silently agreed to follow it, careful to keep a short distance behind it though, just in case.

"Joe, it's going to the end of the path," Luisa whispered.

"I know. Also, why are you whispering?" he said, speaking just as quietly and with a grin.

"I've got no idea!" Luisa said fully voiced, finally allowing herself to smile for the first time since being trapped in the cavern. Just as she did, the orb suddenly stopped where the path finished. Luisa and Joe exchanged glances, deciding to cautiously approach their silent guide. It pulsated as it always had, but as the duo drew closer, the light faded, dimming to barely anything above a glimmer.

"What's happened?" Joe asked, not really expecting an answer, but then he saw it. Far into the distance was another path, which looked as if it was a continuation of the one they were on and beyond that, something truly spectacular.

"Luisa, do you see this?" Joe asked, straining his eyes to scan ahead.

"Joe, oh my... is that, what I think it is?"

"I think so. I think it's a pyramid," Joe answered, awe in his voice. They both stared in wonder at the enormous structure that lay ahead of them. The tip of the pyramid was level with the path they were on, some distance ahead. They could recognise the characteristic slopes of the phenomenon descend into the blackness below, and that was all they could see.

"This thing could be absolutely gigantic," Luisa surmised. Joe's features were a mixture of shock and excitement. The orb in front of them rose a little higher above them and remained there, offering a pale light so that they could just about see each other, but no further, rendering the discovery ahead just out of their vision.

"Okay, we know there's a path ahead, right?" Joe asked.

"Yeah..." Luisa responded, not following his train of thought.

"And we know things aren't really what they seem here," he continued.

"Sure, but Joe, what does that matter, we can't get across," Luisa protested.

"I think we can," Joe said with a grin, jumping into the crevasse.

CHAPTER SIX

THE EXCAVATION SITE came into view as Frank's transport dramatically tore round the dirt track. Overhead were two helicopters flying past, heading west. "Where are those birds goin'?" Frank shouted to the driver.

"Beats me, sir," the young man called back over the drone of the engine.

Frank then spotted a figure hailing them down. He was a civilian, dressed in a vest and loose fitting shorts that were covered in dirt. The vehicle screeched to a halt a few metres short of him. Now they were closer, Frank saw the panic in the man's face.

"I just told the others, you better follow, quickly!" he blurted out before Frank had even disembarked.

"Told who what, son?" Frank replied, his voice calm and carrying an air of authority. His new acquaintance wiped his clammy hands on his shorts and pointed with a trembling finger west, the same direction that the military chinooks had just flown towards. "We felt some tremors, the ground moving, and then we sent our usual coach over to check on our two colleagues," he said, words escaping him faster than he could breathe.

"Easy, son, what's gone on here?" Frank asked, dreading that Kaufmeiner had already been in the area.

"I-I don't know," the man stammered, looking again over to the direction of other military vehicles which were ahead of Frank's cohort. "We sent our coach over," he repeated, "and we saw this... this hole. And no sign of them," he finished, barely able to fumble out the words.

"What's your name, son?" Frank said, putting a hand on his shoulder. "Captain, follow those transports, meet me back here in ten," Frank ordered, his voice neutral but his insides were churning slightly. He didn't like the sound of a hole appearing out of nowhere.

"Yes, sir," the driver said, turning the key and speeding away, kicking up dust as the truck went off to join the others.

"I'm Doctor Evan Jessup," answered the archaeologist. "This is my site, my people."

"Your responsibility," Frank concluded, smiling kindly. "I get it, you feel guilty. So how many we talking over there?" he finished, gesturing over to the horizon.

"Two. Young kids, fresh out of college. Shouldn't even be here, but, as you know..."

"Yeah, all hands on deck," Frank finished for Evan. Just then, static buzzed on the lieutenant's radio.

"Sir, come in, this is Captain Mitchell, do you copy?"

"Excuse me, Doctor," Frank said, walking a few steps aside to accept the incoming call. "Lieutenant Williams, what is it, son?"

"We're a few clicks away from the site, but the perimeter is up and-"

The communication was cut dead in an instant and Frank saw and heard why; an explosion boomed in the distance.

Frank watched in a stunned silence as he looked at the small mushroom cloud form and disappear, the dark sky briefly illuminated with a flash that was over as quickly as it had started.

"What the hell was that?" cried Evan.

"Get your people out of here, right now. Go!" Frank instructed, not taking his eyes away from where the devastation had just occurred. The radio, still in his hand, screeched back to life:

"Sir! Requesting orders, what's happening?"

"Private, get that perimeter created," barked Frank. Turning to the retreating Evan, he cried out, "Doctor, I need transport, ASAP."

"You can take this, if you can ride it," Evan called back, indicating with his right arm to the lone dirt bike propped up against one of the buildings the archaeologists were using as storage. Frank cursed under his breath; he hated bikes. Turning his attention back to the radio he spoke:

"Private, I need you to stay calm, what's the situation?"

"We're heading to the rendezvous now, I can see the rest of our troops are there and securing the site. Sir, you're gonna want to look at this... "

"I'm on my way, call an evac team to your location, see if we can help those poor souls caught in the blast," Frank instructed.

"Affirmative, sir!" with that, the line was cut. Frank ran over to the two wheeled vehicle and turned the key that was dangling in the ignition. It howled into life and Frank dragged it in an arc to face it towards the right direction and hit the accelerator, praying that he didn't run into who he thought he would.

△

His jet black boots made a soft thud as the silent assailant disembarked from his small piece of high ground. He dusted off his dark trousers and tightened the belt around his waist. Plenty of ammunition to get the task done. Flames danced in an enchanting way around the carnage that he had just caused. The car carrying six troops was a mangled wreck of melting iron and steel, intertwined with the bodies of the unfortunate souls who were simply getting on with their orders. Ulrich Kaufmeiner regarded the scene with no emotion, he just examined the debris for any sign of survivors. There were none. Satisfied, the assassin melted back into the shadows cast by the great rock formations at either side of the canyon. The pathway connecting the main archaeology site was narrow and winding, flanked by jagged rocks and a wealth of places to strike an ambush; exactly what Ulrich had done. He had arrived only thirty minutes before the armed forces, but that was enough time for him to lay his trap. The rented Suzuki was parked, hidden between two larger clusters of rocks, keeping it out of sight for the helicopters that had flown overhead. Ulrich had then simply waited for the last vehicle to pass into the valley, primed one of the high explosive grenades and tossed it precisely at the speeding jeep as it thundered into range. He had allowed all others to pass as he didn't want to raise the alarm too early, for this would create even more chaos than had already occurred and Ulrich didn't need that. What he needed was to enter the chamber at exactly the right moment. To change the course of history.

△

Frank sped across the open plains and saw the jagged crater loom in the distance. Even in the darkness, he could see the thick smoke pluming up into the night sky. The sight made

Frank grit his teeth in determination. He gave the motorcycle more gas and continued to chew up the distance ahead of him, bearing towards the unknown as the jaws of darkness welcomed him in. Frank eased up on the throttle, and finally he saw with clarity just what had happened. He killed the engine and stepped off his bike cautiously, turning on his handheld device.

"This is Lieutenant Williams, what's the situation up ahead?" Silence greeted him and for a few gut-wrenching moments Frank held his breath for a response.

"This is Sergeant Mills; we were briefed together by Riggs. Over."

"Mills, what's the situation?" Frank repeated, trudging towards the smouldering, twisted wreckage in front of him.

"Perimeter established, one transport lost, what's your location?" the voice answered almost robotically.

"I'm in the valley, confirming... the damage," Frank said grimly, his eyes surveying the scene with a deep sorrow. "Those poor families," he said aloud, thinking of the extended casualties of war; those back home who would now receive the worst news possible.

"Get to the rendezvous point as soon as you can, lieutenant - we need you to see this."

The comm died and Frank was left alone in the darkness. He looked around, searching for clues, for any sign of who he knew was responsible. Crouching low, he drew his sidearm from the holster attached to his hip and inched forwards, using the decimated jeep as cover. Scanning the dark and jutting rocks, everything seemed to be bathed in complete darkness, making it virtually impossible for Frank to spot the opening where Ulrich Kaufmeiner had been perched. Almost. Frank focused his attention on this discovery and travelled swiftly across the terrain, ascending the winding natural path that had been forged. He sneaked into the space to discover... nothing. No trace of the man who had killed his comrades. No sign of the assassin who had already claimed the lives of untold men and women in his pursuit of this mythical object. Frank sighed and opened the voice communication. "This is Lieutenant Williams. Area secured, no survivors. Heading over to you now, over and out," he clicked the device off and moved to his vehicle.

Frank began his journey, taking care to not go too fast in case he missed something, but also not be so slow that he was delayed in reconvening with his troops. Mercifully, the valley widened and the rocks flanking him on the left and right suddenly branched outwards, forming an uneven circle around him with a narrow opening on the other side. It was almost as if they were locked inside a colosseum, like the gladiators of ancient times.

"Lieutenant," Mills said as Frank approached. "Perimeter created, top and bottom. We have eyes in the sky, snipers up on these rocks and of course the ground forces here."

"Very good, thank you, sergeant. What are we looking at here?" Frank said, dismounting the bike and leaving it to stand nearby.

"In layman's terms, it's a hole," the officer said in a down-to-earth tone which Frank appreciated. "But it's more than that, well, you'll see when you get to it." They walked the moderate distance to the pit that Mills was referring to. It was roughly a football field's length away from the opening to the valley Frank just emerged from. The lieutenant saluted and kept his demeanour as neutral as possible to his fellow soldiers as he continued on his walk, determined not to let anyone see any trepidation in his features. The truth of it was that he, Frank Williams, was nervous. Ulrich was here somewhere. Six heavily armed guards parted for Frank and Mills to come closer to the gap in the earth, and Frank gasped at the sight before him. Tiny golden flakes emerging from the wound in the sand floated and spiralled gently like dust motes caught in sunlight, but they were emitting their own light and moving unusually, almost as though they were stuck inside an invisible tube.

"Beautiful, isn't it?" Mills said appreciatively. "Of course, we've got no idea what we're dealing with, but we've alerted Riggs and he's told us to secure the area, maximum lockdown in effect."

"Where is he?" Frank asked, silently praying he wasn't far so more reinforcements could arrive as quickly as possible and hopefully deter Ulrich from making a move.

"Probably only an hour away, he was in Cairo last we heard," Mills said, striking up a cigarette as he did. Frank clenched his teeth inadvertently. An hour is a long while for Ulrich, he thought.

"Tell your men to stay alert, we're sitting ducks here," Frank said darkly.

"Kaufmeiner?" Mills asked.

"I'm afraid it's almost certainly him. Who else knows what's out here?" Frank answered.

"Then he's in for a shock. Now, we're ready for him," Mills said, relishing the opportunity, and flashing a rare smile.

"I hope you're right," Frank replied, nowhere near as confidently.

△

Time seemed to slow to a crawl within the confines of the Basin (as it was now called amongst those present) whilst they waited for one of two things to happen; be attacked or have Colonel Riggs arrive with the cavalry. Frank looked around again, surveying the scene before him. Two helicopters had landed at each end of the Basin and had each deposited the aforementioned snipers on the high ground. The eight elite solders had blended, as best they could, into the environment at their disposal, taking cover amongst the various rocks that scattered haphazardly across the surface. Frank again paced the perimeter and felt the watchful eyes of the snipers on him, which was both reassuring and unsettling at the same time. The six guards standing near the hole hadn't moved at all since Frank and Mills had departed, their dedication absolutely focussed on the task at hand; to preserve the discovery at all costs. Dotted around the Basin at various points were the remaining soldiers that had set out from the base. They were not afforded the luxury of protection, the Basin offered nothing like that with its vast, open terrain. On the other hand, Frank mused, it also allowed for any enemy to be spotted quickly, even in the darkness. Looking up, Frank stopped for a moment to take in the beauty of the stars above, their twinkle and shine much more pronounced out here, away from city lights. Just as this moment of serenity came, it was disturbed by the earth shattering blast as the helicopter above the entrance exploded in a shower of metal and rocks, collapsing into the valley and blocking any potential for reinforcements to arrive from the designated path.

At once there was chaos, red lines emitting from the sniper's rifles cut through the dark and homed in on the scene of the crime, orders barked out from the ground and Frank felt his adrenaline spike; he was here. Rushing to the nearest squadron, Frank asserted control.

"Men! Seek and destroy, we have a hostile in the area, do you understand!"

"Affirmative!" came the chorus of reply, the soldiers now breaking off into a low run, weapons at the ready and moving towards the flaming wreckage.

"Mills!" Frank yelled across to the sergeant, who was

sprinting across to his retinue parallel to Frank. Mills stopped in his tracks and turned.

"Get your men over to the other side! It could be a diversion!" Mills acknowledged the order silently and then barked commands out to his troops and suddenly a second explosion rocked the Basin. The other helicopter erupted, causing a similar reaction to the first. Frank realised with horror what was happening. *He's trapping us.*

△

Ulrich moved swiftly, his speed one of his greatest assets. As the red beams of the snipers span to face the direction of the new distraction, Ulrich slid down the rock surface and sprinted towards the first group of soldiers, five of them looking the other way. Ulrich unsheathed his knife and launched himself at the first unfortunate victim, plunging the dagger deep into the man's neck. In the same swift motion, Ulrich removed the blade and rolled forwards with the momentum before springing at the next man, almost cat-like. With an upward diagonal slash, another soldier was slain. Ulrich pivoted the weapon and turned the handle inwards, allowing the blade to be thrust into the side of the next person's temple, he retracted it almost as soon as it had punctured the skull and brought it down in a forward cut, meeting the fourth man. Finally, the last person managed to survive long enough to see the attack coming and in an instant, felt the cold steel of the knife in his mid-section before crumbling to the ground.

"Contact!" screamed one private near the slaughter. He opened fire and a hail of bullets flew towards Ulrich, who had vanished in plain sight. "Loss of contact!" the private yelled, fear taking hold of him. Mills dragged his soldiers over into a tight formation. "Where is he, private?" he shouted.

"He was the…" the soldier was silenced as a bullet ended his life. Mills span around, just in time to see two more men die in rapid succession, the bullets appearing out of thin air without making a sound. Then Mills saw it, the capsule landing inches from his feet and exploding loudly, emitting a terrible blinding white light. Screaming and clutching his face in agony, Mills fell to his knees, as did the other ten men that were unlucky enough to be caught in the blast. Ulrich kept moving, charging directly at the spot and the six guards who were set up in a defensive circle. Frank watched as this figure all in black threw a smoke grenade towards the pit and disappeared into the cloud.

"MOVE! Surround that smoke!" Frank bellowed at the remaining standing soldiers near him and they all sprinted towards the fog, trying to seek the culprit. The six guardians remained in their tight circle, flicking on their infra-red scanners on the headpieces they all wore. They waited with bated breath for the assailant to come, but he didn't. Ulrich had run past them all and was now traversing the large stones to the more recently exploded helicopter, where nobody was focussing any attention. He rapidly ascended the rocks, hurling a steel cabled harness to the top of the formation. It clung into the earth and twisted itself deeper, cementing firmly in place. Ulrich hastily climbed up the height as if it were no more difficult than climbing a ladder to paint a roof, advancing cautiously behind the still-burning chopper. He reloaded his handgun and saw his targets. Eight snipers, all with their sights fixed on the mist he had just deployed. Ulrich aimed his firearm at the head of one, then another, and the last two in similar fashion, without firing. In order to do this, he'd have to be quick, precise and flawless. He took a deep breath and opened fire, one bullet after the other, moving his pistol just like he practiced seconds ago, only this time with lethal consequences. Four bodies fell in a slump in rapid succession and

Ulrich moved again, gliding down the cable and reaching for another flash-bang grenade on his belt.

Confusion reigned within the smog, then Frank noticed the four scarlet lines belonging to the snipers that whipped around in wild directions. *He's just killed them,* Frank thought. Then another realisation. *He wanted us in the smoke*. "Get back, spread out!" Too late. The flash blinded everyone who had come close to the smoke. The guards with their infra-red goggles were affected the most and they were dispatched first. Ulrich sprinted into the chaos, the writhing figures before him easy targets. He plunged his knife into the first squirming man on the floor, spinning the blade up and driving it vertically into the chin of the next. Ulrich used his left hand to open fire at close range with his pistol, bringing down two more guards. Two remained and Ulrich turned to his right, calmly putting one man out of his misery with a crack of gunfire. The last guard was standing groggily to his feet and desperately adjusting his goggles as Ulrich walked almost routinely over to him, driving the knife deep into his neck and carrying on, walking to the hole which was now entirely free.

Frank pushed himself up and blinked his vision into focus. He had turned away from the flash at the last second and closed his eyes, but it still hadn't protected him fully. Though he fared much better than his comrades, who had all fallen at his feet, either dead or temporarily blinded.

"Williams! Come in, it's Colonel Riggs! What in the name of all that is good is going on there!"

"Sir, we've been compromised," Frank answered breathlessly, finally standing properly and steadying himself.

"We're about twenty minutes away, can you hold out?"

"Sir, there's nothing or nobody left. He's decimated us," Frank said wearily, noticing how quiet everything had become except for a few cries of pain here and there. The smoke was finally clearing, and Frank looked at the true devastation of what had happened. He let the voice communicator drop from his hands as he dragged himself to the scene of the crime. Bodies were littered around the crater and Frank noticed that the golden flakes were now completely still, frozen in time. He edged closer and realised what he had to do. Frank Williams jumped into the gap, not sure what would happen, but fairly certain he'd find Ulrich Kaufmeiner already down there.

CHAPTER SEVEN

Luisa watched in horror as Joe jumped into the gap between the paths... and walked on thin air. Joe whirled round, a mixture of surprise and jubilation. "Ha!" he exclaimed triumphantly. "I knew it! Luisa, it's a trick, the floor is still here, look!" Joe stamped his feet to emphasise the point, the noise echoing in the silent chamber, despite there being no visible floor underneath Joe. Luisa's emotions were a mixture of confusion and admiration; she did not know Joe could be so brave, but at the same time, so foolish.

"You could have jumped straight to your death!" she shouted, concern etched on her face, and Joe couldn't make out if it was fury in her hazel eyes or surprise.

"Look down, you see the gold lights?" he added hastily. She obliged and nodded. "Well, if this path was really not here, you'd be able to look through it to the next light, wouldn't you?" he concluded with pride. Luisa was silent for a few seconds, and then smiled coyly.

"Very clever, Joseph Cullins," she said, the smile broadening and revealing her straight white teeth. She shook her head in disbelief as she walked over to side with him, Joe's right hand twitched as he felt the urge to take her hand in his, but he held himself in check and simply waited for her to follow him.

"Over there, see that?" Luisa said, pointing to the far end of the passage that they could see in the darkness. Joe squinted and failed to understand what Luisa could. "What is it?"

"The trail curves a little to the right. You can just watch it change gradient," she explained.

"I'll take your word for it," Joe responded with a laugh. "Do you think it leads all the way down?" He asked, feeling his excitement build.

"One way to find out," she said, and they headed off into the unknown once more.

The pyramid seemed to shimmer in the distance as the duo continued on their trek, almost as though it were phasing in and out of existence as the darkness gave way to a new light emanating from the gigantic structure itself. Luisa's observation was proven to be correct. The path carved into the walls. They descended carefully, as the surface was smooth and they could easily lose their footing if they weren't careful and slide into oblivion. Fortunately, the chamber wall now served as a barrier on the right side of the track, protecting the pair from a fall to sudden death. Yet to the left was now a sheer drop. Luisa and Joe shimmied carefully along the side, taking their time and watching the pyramid loom larger the closer they got. As they were climbing down to the base level, the sheer size of it appeared overwhelming. "This might be bigger than the Great Pyramid of Giza," Joe whispered in awe.

"It's beginning to feel like it," Luisa concluded. She kept walking carefully in front of Joe, the pathway still on a relatively steep decline. Luisa looked again at the magnificence of the pyramid, her eyes unable to avoid the beauty and wonder of the structure. As she was semi-distracted, her hand slid across an uneven jagged rock. "Ah!" she cried in surprise, looking down at the damage; a slight cut that bled at once.

"Are you okay?" Joe called a few feet above her.

Luisa turned back. "Yes, I'm fi..." her sentence was cut short as she slipped on the turn, her ankle giving way. In a matter of milliseconds, Luisa was lying flat on her stomach, sliding down the path.

"No!" Joe bellowed and impulsively leapt after her, his hands stretched out to her. He barely grabbed her fingers, tightening them as they slid quicker and quicker. "Just look at me, Luisa, look at me," Joe shouted, Luisa's head turned to her right, watching the pyramid grow larger as their fall continued. She blinked tears from her eyes and closed them, turning her head towards Joe. Her mouth opened and as she was about to speak, something jarringly halted her momentum in an instant. She opened her eyes and saw Joe, one arm clutching at something. Rope? They both exhaled deeply, Joe grunted with effort and pulled himself up to a vertical base. Luisa followed and immediately threw her arms around him, hugging him tightly.

"Joe, you saved me, you saved me," she whispered, tears of joy trickling down her cheek. She pulled away from him and stared up into his clean-shaven face. His green eyes glowed as he studied at her in a way she'd never seen. Luisa reached out a free hand to touch his arm. Joe dared to let his hand gently brush her face. The two of them feeling their hearts thumping in their chest, their eyes locked on to each other, and then the beautiful silence was shattered as a bell chimed.

The drone was deep, almost like a church bell had been transformed into a gong. It was an unusual yet mesmerising sound. Joe looked at the rope he still held in his grip. "Joe your hand!" Luisa said, carefully taking it in her similarly wounded one. Joe's palm had scores of dark red marks on them. "Rope burn," he whispered. They kept their hands clasped, and the bell rang again, disturbing the moment once more. "Do you think this means anything?" Luisa whispered.

"I don't know, I just saw it and grabbed it," Joe admitted, feeling the throbbing pain begin to set. "Look, the path ends and goes right," Joe pointed out. "Let's keep moving," he decided. The pair continued down at a slower pace now, having been scared by their incident a few moments ago. As they reached the end where the path bisected into the dead end of the rocky surface and the alternative route to their left, Joe and Luisa were now looking at the Pyramid head on, almost able to see the base of the structure. Joe peered into the distance below. "I think it opens up into some sort of courtyard," he said. "We need to be careful though. There aren't any walls to hold on to by the looks of it," he realised.

The bell rang again, a deep thundering tone way above their heads, and this time the reaction was visual as well as audible. The pyramid seemed to shake with the reverberations of the tone produced and all at once there was a light, not a blinding one but a sudden reaction as down below Joe and Luisa, eighteen pillars were suddenly brightened by the beacons that were mounted on top of them. Joe was indeed correct in his assumption. The path they were on led them down into a courtyard, with nine pillars on each side that led directly into the mouth of the pyramid. Along the floor, the golden balls of light they had seen below now illuminated to their full capacity at the very edges of the chamber, stretching back behind them. For the first time, they could see that the pyramid in all of its glory; resplendent in gold and glinting as the light from the flames shone.

"Wow," was all Luisa could muster. Joe stood in silent appreciation, no words coming to him to truly justify the magnificence of what was in front of them. Finally, after a long pause, Joe spoke. "We still have a long way down, let's be careful, yeah?" he grinned, feeling comfortable enough with Luisa to mock her slip earlier.

"Too soon, Joe!" she retorted, feigning her offence. "You're right though, slow and steady." They began walking the last leg of their journey, excited, fearful and ready to make the discovery of the modern age.

Unbeknownst to them, some two hundred metres above their heads, Ulrich Kaufmeiner had just landed in the chamber.

Joe and Luisa at last left the path and made their first steps into the ancient courtyard. "Do you feel that?" Joe asked Luisa, feeling a distinct change in the atmosphere.

"It feels... thick, doesn't it?" Luisa remarked. The air was dense, still. The lit torches burned and flickered but did not falter at all, as though a constant source of fuel powered them. "Look," Joe said, squinting hard once again. "Do you see this?" He held out a hand in the air above his messy brown hair and Luisa saw it; tiny gold flecks suspended all around it. The bell rang repeatedly and was once more accompanied by a seismic shift. Luisa instinctively grabbed Joe's arm, clinging to it. Ahead of them, the pyramid rumbled and a thin sliver of blue light, perhaps a metre wide, appeared at first along the ground, before slowly rising up the face of the pyramid before them. Sprouting from this was another line coming from the top of the light and spreading across, forming a perfect right angle. Joe and Luisa glanced at each other, just as a third strip trickled down from the newly formed horizontal edge. Joe and Luisa watched as the three blue strips rose up the pyramid, extending at least ten metres high. With a last pulse, the brilliance of the blue lights faded into the pyramid. As they did, an entrance was revealed, followed by an explosion of air that rushed out of the structure like a torrent. The force of which knocked Luisa and Joe backwards a few feet, instinctively, they shielded their eyes with their arms. Mercifully, it was over almost as quickly as it had begun, and then silence descended upon them. Joe glanced at Luisa, and she looked back with fear in her eyes. Despite this, she was the first to speak. "Well, no point in staying here. Let's find out what the hell is going on," and stepped forward, the pyramid continuing to invite them both with its aura.

△

Ulrich heard the bell chime almost as soon as he landed. He quickly looked around him to ensure there was nothing at his flank and started his run forward, not for a second taking in the majesty and wonder of the chamber he was in, as if he had either been here before or expected it to be just like it was.

△

Luisa stopped just short of the entrance and looked up at Joe. "This is it," she said, a statement of intent to some degree. "Let's find out what secrets are inside this place," she finished, stepping forward and about to enter.

"Wait," Joe said. She turned to look at him, her beauty accentuated in the mystical lighting of the pyramid. "Whatever we find in there, let's stay close and keep each other safe. You scared me back there, ya know?" he finished, blushing slightly, which was unfortunately highlighted in the strange glow of the Golden Pyramid.

Luisa smiled sweetly, glancing at her dusty shoes briefly before looking up at Joe again. "Sorry to scare you, Mr. Cullins. I won't leave your side, promise. Now come on!" she said excitedly, flashing her smile and making Joe feel slightly giddy for a second. "Together," he said, this time having the courage to hold his hand out, which Luisa took without hesitation.

"Together," she repeated, gripping his hand tightly and

walking in tandem with him, both of them disappearing into the pyramid.

△

Ulrich paused momentarily, thrown slightly by the gap in the path. He unclipped his grapple hook and threw it into the hole, surprised to see it land in thin air. His lips curled into a smile of appreciation. "Clever," he said out loud and dragged his hook back in, sprinting on, seeing the monolith shining brightly ahead of him. Time was running out, but he could still make it.

CHAPTER EIGHT

Frank Williams opened his eyes and laughed out loud; he wasn't dead. Instead, he found himself underground, unharmed but unsure of where he was. He clicked the radio on his belt and was greeted by a hiss of static. "Alpha team, do you copy, this is Lieutenant Williams, over." He turned the receiver off and waited for a response. Nothing. He cursed and glanced at his surroundings, absorbing the facts as fast as possible. Lit torches, a path, something shining deep in the distance. He squinted to sharpen the image that was just out of sight, but his vision wasn't quite up to it. Frank checked behind him and was relieved to see it was a dead end. *Good, only one way to go then,* he surmised. Bending down, he noticed the imprints in the dust on the floor, footprints. Frank scrutinised them and gasped as he realised he was looking at more than just Ulrich's boot imprints here. "There are two other people here," he whispered to himself. His eyes widened as he came to the logical conclusion; they must belong to Doctor Jessup's missing personnel. Frank stood up straight and gritted his teeth. Whatever those kids had stumbled upon, there was something far worse coming for them.

△

"Where do we go now?" Joe said out loud into the dimly lit antechamber he found himself in with Luisa. They had walked a relatively short distance into the pyramid and already had a dilemma on their hands; three chambers split out from the circular room they were in.

"There are symbols up there, look," Luisa noted, pointing above the arched entrances to the strange yet beautifully ornate patterns that framed each pathway. Joe strained his eyes. The area they were in was lit by an unseen light source; it bathed the place and its new occupants in an unnatural blue hue. It seemed to originate from above, but the structure was so large it was impossible to tell. Nevertheless, it provided them with enough of a visual aid to see where they were going, as well as to spot these unusual designs marked on the walls. Luisa moved gingerly towards the path on the far left, studying the image depicted in front of her. It looked like a helmet with wings protruding out from each side, which curved upwards and joined at the tips. Here, a new carving began that depicted a semi-circular opening upon which stood three figures, with four legs and three arms, just as they had seen back on the pathway where they had entered. This time, the humanoids were all holding a huge circular object between them, which was inscribed with runes, hieroglyphs, and a mix of other symbols and scribbles that could pass for words if read by the correct person. Luisa edged closer, now underneath the archway. She felt a wave of trepidation shudder throughout her body, acutely aware that she was potentially on the verge of an enormous discovery, or in grave danger. Or both. Closing her eyes and exhaling deeply, she stepped foot into the clearing and sighed. "I think I expected something a bit more dramatic," she said out loud to Joe, forcing a laugh in an attempt to alleviate the tension.

"Yeah," Joe replied distractedly, backing away from the space on the far right. His gaze was fixed upon the image above the doorway, which was a winding, long strip of symbols that were presumably letters. They wrapped around each other, twisting and turning and forming a mind-boggling maze that could drive someone insane if they stared at it for too long. Joe finally tore himself away and turned to look at Luisa, smiling weakly, similarly, trying to diffuse the magnitude of the situation. "Guess we'll try this way first," he declared brightly, the smile a bit more genuine this time. Just as Joe was about to join Luisa, an invisible barrier, which stopped him dead in his tracks, blocked his path. "What the hell?" he stated dumbly, startled by the sudden blockage of his progress. "Joe?" Luisa asked, stepping out to help him.

"I dunno, something blocked me," he replied, realising how strange that sounded, but unable to come up with another explanation.

"Come on, let's go," she suggested, turning to the entrance with Joe at her side to find she hit the exact same barrier. "Ah!" Luisa cried, more in shock than pain.

"See?" Joe responded, vindicated, but concerned.

"I was just there though," Luisa pondered, her face scrunching up in concentration. "Joe, stay here a second, let me try something," Luisa instructed. She tentatively extended her foot forwards into the opening of the route and found no resistance. Cautiously, she allowed the rest of her body to follow and, as she suspected, had no issue. Breathing out heavily Luisa said, "Joe I think it only lets one person in."

"No way, how could it know?" Joe questioned.

"Well how could we survive that fall to even get on that path?" Luisa answered back, raising her eyebrows quizzically.

"Yeah, good point," Joe agreed. "Let me try, you step out and see if I can go in alone," he suggested. Luisa obliged, and sure enough, Joe could stand in the entrance with no challenge.

"Let's try the others," Luisa said, her nerves building now. *What if they had to split up?* she thought, not looking forward to the prospect of exploring an ancient pyramid alone. She was brave, adventurous, and outgoing, but this was on a whole different level. With Joe at her side, she had navigated this chamber. Facing it alone, however, made her anxious. Joe glanced at her and attempted a reassuring smile again, but it was clear he was feeling the same fears she was. They stopped before the arch Joe had been studying. "Okay, let's try this," he spoke evenly. He held his hand for Luisa to take, which she did, and they moved to the opening together.

△

Ulrich continued his rapid descent towards the pyramid. He was running adjacent to the same wall Joe and Luisa had carefully descended earlier, though Ulrich was covering ground at an alarmingly fast pace. His feet seemed to barely touch the surface as he continued his sprint, the gloved fingers of his outstretched hand gliding against the wall keeping him balanced. The dangling rope brushed against him, and Ulrich stopped in his tracks. Tilting his head, Ulrich followed the dangling coil as it stretched on into the heavens. He gripped it tightly, but hesitated, internally debating the reaction that could follow should he yank the tantalising object in his hands. Ulrich relaxed his grip, deciding that some things would be better left untouched for now. He glanced over his shoulder and saw the pyramid glowing and golden, almost as though it were alive. *It wouldn't be much longer,* he thought, and with that, set off again at an electric pace.

△

Frank's progress was interrupted when he saw the large, empty space in the track ahead. "Woah," he stated aloud, slowing his jog to a walk and catching his breath. He ran his hand over his shaved head, pondering his next move. Daring to look down, Frank leaned over the left side of the trail and saw, to his surprise, a thin golden line that acted as a border for the surface below. He observed its route and realised it connected further forwards, presumably to the looming structure in the distance. "Guess that rules out jumping down," he told himself. He searched around helplessly, trying to find something he could use as a bridge, or even a vault, to hurl himself over the gap. Yet there were only rocks and dust. Frank paused at that last thought. *What did the others do?* He crouched down once more and studied the floor, the footprints of his predecessors easy to spot on the otherwise pristine surface. He followed their trajectory and discovered that they had a deeper imprint just before the edge of the gap. *So they jumped across? Surely not,* Frank puzzled. And then he saw it. Floating in front of him and rather easy to miss were the outlines of shoes, dusty footprints that had been left behind for him to follow. But they were suspended in mid air. Swallowing his fear, Frank Williams puffed out his chest, closed his eyes and stepped onto nothing. He exhaled in shock and happiness when he felt his foot touch solid ground. He peered down and instantly felt vertigo. Staring into an empty abyss, his foot resting on nothing whatsoever, Frank nearly lost his balance. Regaining composure, Frank took another step, then another, and was soon across the invisible walkway. "This is some otherworldly location, that's for sure," he muttered, taking a second to absorb his environment and appreciate the brightness of the golden pyramid ahead. *I hope you're down there and I hope he doesn't find you,* Frank mused, thinking of the two missing persons Doctor Jessup had spoken of.

△

Luisa and Joe held their breath as they inched towards the opening, both silently praying that it would allow them entry. Luisa closed her eyes and tightened her grip on Joe's hand and walked into a dead end.

"No," she whispered, opening her eyes and frantically looking at Joe. He stared back in stoic silence.

"There's still one more," he muttered, already sure that this would be a futile exercise. Luisa nodded quietly, coming to the same conclusion. Releasing their hands, they walked to the middle. Joe exhaled and glanced sideways at Luisa, his mouth dry and unable to formulate a witty comment to lighten the mood for once. They strolled towards the entrance simultaneously and were met once again with the same result; no entry. "Joe, we should go back outside," Luisa said, not sure of what else to suggest.

"Yeah, maybe we should just wait. Surely the team has noticed we're missing by now, right?" Joe concluded. "Come on, let's just get out of this tomb and wait, we can't go forward, I'm not leaving you, am I?" he declared, his smile flickered for a brief moment.

"Well, I guess I won't leave you either," Luisa responded, managing a weak grin herself. As they walked towards the entrance of the pyramid, they both felt a sense of relief; they'd made an incredible discovery and had a wonderful adventure, but now it was time to invite the rest of the group to share in their findings.

They emerged back into the courtyard, their eyes adjusting to the now bright light that was emanating from the pyramid, a stark contrast to the gloomy pale blue glow present inside. "Did this thing suddenly turn on some lights?" Joe asked, looking around at his surroundings.

"Yeah, it definitely feels like it," Luisa agreed. Suddenly, she spotted a figure in the distance heading their way. "Hey, look! Someone's already coming to help!" she exclaimed excitedly. "Hello! Down here!" She yelled, waving her arms and jumping up and down on the spot. Joe watched her fondly and smiled. Her enthusiasm was contagious. He peered ahead and saw the new arrival walk a little closer, then stop. Bizarrely, the person crouched onto one knee and raised an object up to their shoulder. Joe's eyes widened in horror as he saw the glint of light reflect off of the drawn firearm.

"LUISA!" he bellowed, "GET DOWN!" As he screamed these words, he was already moving forward to where Luisa was standing. She turned around to see him charging at her, and her eyes grew large in alarm.

"Jo-!" *BOOM!* The sound split the chamber's silence in half, cracking through the serenity like a whip. Joe threw himself at Luisa and tackled her to the ground. They landed heavily and didn't move.

△

Ulrich exhaled calmly and holstered his pistol. The two bodies lay prone on the ground, unmoving since he fired the shot, which surprised him as the distance was certainly significant and thus made it difficult to hit the targets. Not that he meant to kill them, of course. After all, he needed them to move forward. The bullets were only fired to push them in the right direction. As Ulrich was trudging the same steep path that Joe and Luisa had walked not too long ago, he heard the ring of the bell suddenly chime above him. The deep, unnatural sound filled the air at once. He looked up and smiled in mild amusement; one of the army personnel had apparently followed him down here.

△

Frank stopped dead as he heard the unmistakable sound of a gunshot. It reverberated around him. Unsure of the origin, his pace quickened as much as possible on the sloped surface, his hand running along the wall to his right for support. Just then, he felt material on his fingers, which caused him to pause his descent. Frank yanked the cord and was shocked to hear the drone of a bell ringing from somewhere hidden within the chamber. He'd pulled it, thinking it was perhaps a rope revealing a ladder that the man he was following had left behind, just in case the golden pyramid shimmering in the distance wasn't the end goal after all. *Seems not,* he thought, and carried on carefully treading the path, unaware that his actions had just caused a monumental shift in the course of history.

$$\triangle$$

Joe breathed deeply, the gong of the bell a familiar and welcome noise, especially in these circumstances. He dared to incline his head upwards and learned to his relief that this mystery assailant had turned his or her back to them to discover the source of the distraction. "Now!" he said through gritted teeth, hoisting Luisa up by her arm and almost dragging her along with him. It wasn't a long way to go, but they had to get there. Luisa panted, her breath still not fully with her after Joe had tackled her to the ground. She dared to look behind her and caught that whoever shot at them still had their back turned. The pair rapidly closed the distance to the tomb, twenty metres, then ten, then five, *BOOM*! The bullet whizzed past them both, narrowly missing Joe's head by inches as it impacted the structure before them. Joe looked behind him and saw the gun being raised again. "DUCK!" he screamed to Luisa. She obliged without hesitation as another shot ricocheted off the edifice. "Inside, quick!" Joe yelled, pushing Luisa slightly ahead of him in an attempt to protect her.

△

Ulrich was patient and instead of rushing, reloaded his handgun and exhaled another deep sigh. He knew what was in there, he knew that it would trap them. What he didn't know was who had followed him. Perhaps it would be prudent to deal with that annoyance, he thought. Deciding it would be a waste of precious time that he didn't really have, Ulrich cautiously moved towards the pyramid, alternating between looking ahead and behind. It is foolish to underestimate anybody, a lesson he had learned a long while ago, so he kept pivoting his gaze between the route and the monolith, in case he was ambushed by the two inside. As he drew nearer the golden structure, he looked again to the path and saw the regulation U.S. Army boots appear at the foot of the passage. Ulrich's gloved finger hovered over the trigger of his pistol but knew a shot from here was a gambit not really worth taking. He'd need to wait for the target to be closer, so he paused, waiting for the person to reveal themselves entirely. A few seconds later, Ulrich could see the full outline and got the answer he was looking for; no sniper rifle. He turned his back and entered the shrine.

△

"Joe..." Luisa breathed heavily. "Joe, stop, please," she finished, wheezing her words. Joe obeyed, and they were still, once again, in the antechamber with the three pathways. Luisa hunched over, inhaling sharply and finally having a moment to catch her breath. Joe looked anxiously behind him. They probably only had minutes to spare before this lunatic was firing at them again. Luisa stood up straight at last, placing one hand on her hip and using the other to push her hair out of her face. "We have to split up, Joe," she said solemnly.

"No way, we can't do that, are you kidding me?" Joe protested, though with time running out, he knew it was the only choice.

"I'll take the left, you take the right, hopefully whoever that is goes down the middle and we can listen out, come back here and make a break for it," Luisa instructed, her loose plan sounding even more ridiculous out loud than it did in her head.

"But we don't know what's in *there*," Joe answered, prodding a finger towards the ominous archway.

"No, but we do know what's out here. Someone trying to hurt us. I can't let that happen to you, to us. I can't lose you," she finished, letting her head hang as she felt the familiar sting of tears in her eyes. Joe was momentarily stunned into silence, but soon snapped to his senses.

"Luisa," he whispered urgently. "Someone's coming, we have to go, now!" They crouched low, hiding from an unseen threat. Joe put his arms on Luisa's shoulders and expressed all that needed to be spoken with his eyes alone. Luisa stared back at him, her heart swelling and aching. The moment between them was stretched almost as far as it could be and with a last, longing look, the pair of them disengaged and broke into a sprint down their separate paths.

△

As Ulrich entered the chamber he stopped, listening for sound. In the distance he could hear footsteps, the direction however was a mystery to him; they were running, but where had they gone? It didn't matter. Soon they would be back. Soon they would realise they could never escape. Content, Ulrich turned his attention to the entrance he had just come from, knowing that his guest would quickly arrive and be in for a rude awakening. Ulrich's steady hand drew his sidearm, and he waited patiently for Frank Williams.

CHAPTER NINE

JOE RAN, his heart thumping in time with his heavy footsteps and his breathing becoming more laboured. The light from the foyer was waning and the darkness of this corridor rapidly enclosed Joe as he took in his surroundings in more detail. The hall was narrow, wide enough for a person to walk through, but two people side by side would struggle to fit. Joe reached out a hand tentatively to touch the wall; it was incredibly smooth, almost like silk, yet completely hard. Joe wondered if even a gunshot could penetrate it. He looked down at his feet to check the surface he was on and, like the walls; it was pleasant and unmarked by any engravings or any signs of use. He continued moving and, to his relief, felt the floor incline uphill slightly, meaning he'd be out of view momentarily.

The corridor's gradient kept climbing and Joe's pace slowed, his vision rendered useless as the last remnants of light were extinguished by the oppressive darkness he now found himself in. Using both hands, Joe fumbled along the wall, feeling for anything that might be of use. For an insane second, he thought he would feel a switch and simply flick it on to illuminate the entire corridor. Instead, he found a pressure plate, or rather, his foot did. Joe's heart sank almost as rapidly as the slab he'd trod on. His body froze and he expected to be impaled by dozens of spikes, or shot by arrows in an instant. It didn't happen. He didn't realise that he'd been holding his breath, so he exhaled slowly, barely daring to move his lips. The stone he'd walked on remained depressed. Joe thought it was most likely because he was still standing on it. Nothing had changed, so Joe took a gamble. He tiptoed off the plate and prepared for the worst.

△

Luisa ran as tears streaked down her face. She used the back of her exposed forearm to wipe them away and kept running, almost tumbling down the flight of stairs that flashed in front of her. "Ah!" she screamed, flailing her arms and finding a handrail. She let go of it essentially as soon as she touched it, as though scalded by its touch. It was perfectly cool, but she was so surprised to find it here. "This doesn't make any sense," she whispered, looking back over her shoulder nervously. She could see the staircase curved to the right and plunged down into the darkness, but the alternative was to stay there and be caught by the maniac chasing them. Taking a deep breath, she gripped the handrail tightly, noticing that the stairs themselves seemed to be made from marble. Stranger still, they were in perfect condition, as if they had been built yesterday.

She continued down the spiralling staircase until she felt it flatten, then curve to the left and up, flatten again, before plunging down and to the right, like a coiled snake. Luisa took each step with caution. The last thing she wanted to do was fall and injure herself. Sub-consciously, she placed a palm on her ribs, which were sore from where Joe had tackled her. Not that she was complaining, the alternative would have been a lot worse, she concluded. Out of nowhere, she was swiftly met with a dead end. Her hands slapped uselessly on the smooth, yet hard surface. Cursing silently, she looked around, hoping to come across a button or lever, anything to remove this obstacle. She reached out with her hands and patted the wall in front of her, desperate to discover a solution that could improve her situation. She moved along to the support rail of the staircase and dared to lean over slightly, grasping with her fingers but only finding thin air. "That's odd," she said aloud, as she hovered her hand in the air. There; a blast of cold from somewhere down below. *Maybe that's an exit,* she thought, and just as she did, the surface which obstructed her progress rumbled and shifted, beginning to move. Luisa cautiously walked back and to her relief, she noticed light peeking under the crack of the block as it lifted by an unknown mechanism. She watched in awe as the fresh path revealed itself, and then her jaw dropped when she noticed what was inside.

△

Joe heard the shifting, grinding noise as he stepped away and looked around, expecting something to happen, but there was nothing. No ambush, no trapdoor, just the peculiar tone like doors were being opened. He cautiously walked around the plate and slowly crept forward, straining his eyes in a desperate attempt to break the darkness. All thoughts of his pursuer had gone, he was focussed now on continuing and finding a way out, so he could at least see again. Joe inched ahead, squinting some more, and stopped. *Was that light?* His heart raced and fresh hope filled him. He continued to move along steadily and was delighted to see a bright spot radiating in the *dis*tance. A tiny golden dot was growing as he moved ever closer, its faint glow encouraging him to keep moving. Joe kept edging nearer and almost dropped to his doom, his foot dangling in the open as the floor wasn't where it was supposed to be in front of him.

Joe fell backwards and gasped for breath. In the distance, the shining dot throbbed, inviting him to come closer. Joe crawled forward and gripped the edge of the surface he was walking on. He dared to peer down below and, to his surprise, felt cool air blow gently back in his face. He looked ahead and spotted the familiar golden light pulsating just as it had before. *Wait a minute*, Joe thought, looking again. *It's getting faster.* A silent and dazzling eruption of colour swiftly followed. Golden rays shone outward and illuminated the corridor in all of its splendour. Joe then saw it; a thin walkway that bridged the vast gap. Joe moved quickly, deciding that the brightness might not last forever, and took the first tentative step on the thin strip of marble before him.

△

The door shuddered as it ground to a halt above Luisa, and she remained there, dumfounded at the beauty of what was before her. An enormous circular chamber was revealed, its contents filled with smaller circles that descended to one ultimate point; an electric blue stone that crackled with unearthly energy and drawing her eye at once. It sat there, unassuming, as though waiting for her to simply walk down and take it. Yet the ripples of energy that sporadically burst from it made her incredibly wary. The surrounding air became thick, just like it had done when they had left the path and stood within the pyramid courtyard. She could see the familiar golden motes suspended in mid-air, acting as silent guardians of this discovery. The ceiling stretched on far beyond her line of vision and was engulfed in darkness. But who knew how far up it went? The chamber itself was wide enough for five cars to be parked inside, and she marvelled at the considerable feats of engineering clear in the construction of this place all those years ago. *If it was years ago*, she thought cynically. Slowly, she stepped into the room and as soon as she was in, the door slammed shut behind her, making her scream. Luisa was quickly frightened. She was trapped in here alone. Frantically, she looked around for another exit, but saw there was none. She looked again to the centre of the chamber, the jewel sat there radiating with intensity, the colour the deepest and most vibrant shade of blue she had ever seen. Was it a crystal? A gem? Luisa couldn't be sure, but it was marvellous. Without realising, her left foot had taken a step forward as she was drawn magnetically towards this incredible artefact. She kept walking, the blue stone almost seemed to pull her in. She felt trapped, unable to break free of the sudden wish to reach out and touch this mystical stone. Her eyes glazed over, and her breathing became shallow. Luisa walked closer and closer, descending into the centre of the area without protest or thought.

As she drew within touching distance, she became acutely aware of her surroundings; the air was hazy, blurring the details of the chamber. The walls seemed to shimmer as though they were waves. She looked up at the ceiling and saw an opening for the first time. A small hole punctured the oval structure. Had it always been there? She didn't know, but the gold flecks that she and Joe had been seeing everywhere were tumbling down from this hole, falling like snowflakes around the blue artefact but never touching it; the curious object appeared to have a barrier around it. Luisa watched as the gold motes gracefully fell around the rock, her curiosity suddenly replaced by an urgent need. She *had* to touch it, had to feel it in her hands, so she reached out. Her fingertips felt the surface of the stone, and her world changed in an instant.

It happened in a split second. The air that had been so still and thick suddenly rushed past her like a train. The ground immediately under her feet collapsed and she fell, yet landed somehow perfectly upright as if the earth had spun one hundred and eighty degrees. Luisa breathed hard, her fingers were still clasped around the stone, its colour now faded. She slowly looked left to right, noticing that she was still in the chamber. "What?" she breathed, confused how she had fallen and yet be in the *exact* same spot. Out of the corner of her eye, she felt something approaching from the doorway where she herself had entered. A ghostly figure shuffled down towards her at an alarming rate. Luisa screamed while the... thing kept coming, and then it vanished. Behind her, Luisa felt the air grow cold. She turned and watched three people point in her direction, they disappeared just as quickly as they had appeared. Frantically, Luisa span again, hearing a humming noise fill the room. It began as a low drone and rose to a deafening crescendo. She covered her ears and gasped as she saw that impossibly, the circular amphitheatre was full of robed people, seated and rocking back and forth as they chanted in unison. She gawked at them, a mix of shock, horror and bewilderment. Their features were obscured, hoods covering their faces, but they all had an ethereal quality, not seeming to be truly part of this world. Suddenly the crystal glowed again, and Luisa almost discarded it out of surprise. She stared at it, the chanting continued and then one of the ghostly figures began walking towards her slowly, holding a fist out in front of her as if to brace herself on Luisa. She tried to go but found she was frozen in place. Panicking, Luisa dropped the gem and instead of clattering on the floor it simply hovered in the air, rotating slowly and getting brighter as the image ahead of her kept coming closer. Luisa tried to run and her legs failed her, either rooted to the spot by an unseen shackle, or her body was altogether not responding to her commands. The leader moved closer and Luisa squinted to make out who or what it was. She realised the entire chamber had taken on a grey appearance, shrouded in fog. Indeed, as the figure came closer, it appeared to be wading through mist, becoming a sharper image with each step. It suddenly raised a slender hand to its hood and pulled it back, revealing a face that was blank, with no features whatsoever. Luisa screamed in terror, then she noticed the formation of recognisable parts of the face. Eyebrows, a chin, cheekbones, a nose. Luisa watched with a mixture of confusion and horror as the face swam into vision. The figure was only a few metres away now and Luisa was staring at the impossible, the face was nearly formed, and it was almost a replica of hers, just distorted, as though from a parallel world. All the while, the gem had been spinning in mid-air, as if given momentum by the constant chanting. At once, the chants stopped. The cloaked figures rose to their feet and fled out of view, the wispy entrails of their abrupt departure lingering like smoke from car exhausts. Luisa watched as the figure in front of her span around and the connection was broken. A burst of colour from the artefact broke through the grey mist of the chamber, forcing her to cover her eyes. Instinctively, Luisa grabbed it as it continued to pulse, and within seconds, Luisa had vanished.

△

Joe cautiously kept moving along the thin walkway, his eyes fixed on his dusty shoes and not daring to look up and lose his balance. He saw the flecks of gold landing at his feet, some disappearing into the darkness below, some hovering in the air for a moment. Joe furrowed his brow in confusion. He was almost over the gap and closing in on the glowing orb of light that had illuminated the passageway. Just as he was nearing the end, the light went out in an instant, as though flicked off by a switch. Joe's balance faltered at the sudden disruption, and he almost tumbled into the depths. He composed himself and exhaled in relief, tentatively inching his right foot forward to continue onwards. Crouching low, he reached out with his arms, trying to feel if the floor was there - it was. Sighing heavily, Joe leapt forward, confident that he would land on solid ground. As he jumped, the golden light erupted before him. "Argh!" Joe screamed, shielding his eyes as he tumbled forward, the dazzling light not yielding for a second. He got up hastily to his feet and rushed forward, thinking that he could smother the object and stop the incessant abuse on his vision. So he ran, and as he did, he put his arm in front of him, allowing a tiny gap to peek through as he opened his left eye a crack to see where he was going. Joe didn't notice the surrounding air had become thick and hazy, the view ahead of him disappearing into fog as he drew closer to the sphere, which kept beaming its bright light, taunting Joe and daring him to come and stop it. His eye opened a fraction more and he realised he would be right on top of it, so Joe lowered his arm and reached for the orb, one hand shielding his eye as his fingers met with the surprisingly cool surface. As soon as they did, a gale blew from behind, deep from within the confines of the pyramid, thrusting Joe forward into the light. He yelled in surprise as he was propelled towards the orb which had now vanished and was simply a gaping hole of blinding, golden light. His arm disappeared into the void and he felt something which made his skin crawl; *a hand* tightly gripped his forearm and twisted in a violent, jerking, clockwise motion. Joe expected to hear bones crunch, but instead his world span like a corkscrew. His vision blurred, and he shut his eyes tightly, expecting at any moment to come crashing to a halt. Just as quickly as it had started it was over and Joe was standing perfectly still, unharmed and otherwise unchanged, though his pulse was racing, and beads of sweat had formed at his forehead. He blinked the white spots out of his eyes and settled his vision. He was back in the chamber, although it felt *wrong*. Joe noticed the golden ball was now emitting a dull glow and was embedded into a perfectly shaped container, obviously purpose built. Joe deliberated in his head. *Should I touch it?* He was far from certain, and yet the object had a curiously strange effect on him. Joe wanted to touch the orb, in fact, something told him he needed to. Hesitantly, he stretched out his fingers slowly, inching closer to it. He winced and prepared for the worst, but nothing could have made him ready for what was about to happen.

CHAPTER TEN

Frank hurried down the path, throwing caution to the wind as he saw the shining pyramid blur and shift at the edges, as though it were moving so fast that his eyes could not process what was happening in front of him. He reached the courtyard, and his pace slowed. "What the-" he began, stopping and looking around him. The golden flakes that surrounded the air were jerking and twitching erratically, sometimes falling over great distances, other times being incredibly still. Ahead of him, Frank could see the opening of the pyramid. A light shone through the entrance, enticing the lieutenant to venture forward. Frank paused. Ulrich was in there, he had to be. But what else was going on in this strange place? He wavered for the first time, unsure of what to do. Almost reluctantly, he unclipped the voice communicator from his belt and flicked the switch on. Static burst through again and fizzed noisily from the speaker.

"This is Lieutenant Frank Williams. Does anybody copy, over?" Nothing. He let the device dangle uselessly from his hip, without even bothering to turn it off. Waving a hand through the air, he felt a dense thickness, as if he was underwater. The golden flakes reacted to his touch like seaweed when disturbed in the ocean. He continued to tread carefully in the vast courtyard, noticing several footsteps ahead of him and an imprint that looked like two people had laid down. Frank crouched and saw the impact hole of the bullet, but no blood. *He's hunting them*, Frank surmised internally. Standing up again, he walked forward and closed the distance to the entrance. Suddenly a voice breached the silence, and it startled the lieutenant.

"Williams, this is General Hoskins,"

Even with the distortion of static, the General's deep and commanding tone was unmistakable.

"General, sir," Frank replied, still in shock that the speech had come through.

"Do not move, we're topside, evac is coming."

Frank hesitated. Disobeying a direct order was, of course, out of the question. Yet he wanted to chase Ulrich and bring the murderer to justice. Then again, where could he possibly go?

"Roger that, sir, holding ground." With that, Frank Williams cautiously stepped backwards, taking cover behind one of the colossal pillars, his gaze fixed on the entrance to the golden pyramid.

△

Ulrich sat patiently in the middle of the room, cross-legged and in a meditative state. He recognised that the irreversible chain of affairs had begun. The question was, in what order? He settled his eyes and exhaled slowly. This was the part of the mission that would always be subject to the most chaos; he couldn't control what would happen next, just simply allow things to evolve and adjust accordingly. He hated that. Ulrich had been reacting to situations all his life, never truly feeling in charge of his destiny, constantly sent down a certain path and fulfilling whatever duty needed to be done. Time after time. He sealed his eyes and reflected to when this all began. It was a secret that had almost driven him mad, but eventually, he had embraced it and he knew he was required to carry out this task, no matter what. The fate of the world was at stake. There were precious few who could influence the events that were about to unfold, and he was one of them. *It must be changed,* he thought in his head. A rumble from deep inside the pyramid snapped Ulrich back to the present moment. He gradually opened his eyes and stood tall. Straining his ears, he listened again. Silence, the usual void of sound returned, and Ulrich made a move. Striding forward, he confidently walked down the middle pathway, its dominating archway adorned with symbols that no man recognised, no historian could decipher. Yet Ulrich knew what they meant. As he entered the dark corridor, he snapped his night vision goggles down and activated them, bathing his perspective in a green hue that allowed him to easily see what Luisa and Joe could not; the tapestry of images, words, and patterns that were inscribed all over the hall. Within the madness of overlapping layers of text, Ulrich identified the key elements; he was heading to the very top of the monolith and the Chamber of Awakening. It was here that he would need to wait and hope that the other two did what was necessary. They had no idea what they were about to embark on, but they would soon understand.

He kept walking forward, the gradient of the corridor subtly inclining, boring deeper into the heart of the shrine, taking the assassin closer to the ultimate destination of his mission. Then Ulrich stopped. Crouching just in time, an intense golden laser beam shot through the gloom and almost beheaded Ulrich. He hurriedly removed the night vision goggles and blinked rapidly, adjusting his eyes as fast as he could to the dark. He kept low and looked behind him. The beam had made a neat circular hole in the walls of the tomb itself and had burst out into the courtyard from where he had arrived. Tentatively, Ulrich took his black glove off his right hand and held it to the light, allowing the index finger to touch the beam. It sizzled and hissed, disintegrating instantly. "Great," Ulrich said aloud sarcastically, and placed the mitt in one of his pockets. He moved on, the pace slower than before and caution very much the primary focus of his journey. He continued forwards and suddenly the floor split and twisted down in front of him, the walls shifted out, revealing an impossible emptiness below. Ulrich quickly grabbed the border of the track he was walking on mere moments before, which was now turned upwards at a ninety-degree angle. Grunting with effort, he reached into his utility belt and produced his grappling hook. Quickly, he latched it on to the side of the passage he was clinging on to and allowed it to dig in, supporting his body weight. Ulrich let go, and the pin gripped him in place, which meant he could turn his body horizontally and set his feet back on the trail. He was now standing straight, but instead of up, he was planted against the wall. Taking a second to process what was happening, Ulrich looked into the distance and realised the corridor was coiling and turning, leading to nothing but darkness. *Perhaps this isn't as straightforward as I presumed,* he reflected. He glanced up and to his right and noticed the intense golden beam still menacingly burning above him, its purpose though not clear. Ulrich analysed his situation; in order to move forward, he had to walk straight, but he observed the route as it changed again.

The path dipped under itself, curving to the right before coiling back anew and settling into its normal position. He noticed the pattern repeated itself over and over with no end in sight and certainly no Chamber of Awakening to aim for. A dark thought clouded his mind. *What if it was all false? What if they had got this entire thing wrong and now we were doomed?* It was the first time Ulrich Kaufmeiner had ever doubted a mission, and it frightened him.

△

Frank gasped as an intense brightness erupted from the pyramid, impacting an invisible barrier at the edge of the courtyard, where the path from above ended. He could hear the air hiss around him, and then Frank saw what was taking place. Something magnetically drew the golden flakes towards where the light had stopped and had clumped together, forming a shield. Frank quickly realised what was going on. The pyramid was *protecting* itself and closing. He fumbled for the walkie-talkie and spoke clearly, an underlying tone of panic permeating his speech.

"This is Lieutenant Williams. General Hoskins, do you copy? The pyramid is sealing itself, over." Frank waited with bated breath as he continued to see the golden shield forming, rapidly expanding like a balloon filling with air. He looked repeatedly at the unresponsive device and cursed. "Where are you, Hoskins?"

"This is Hoskins, what's happening down there?" the terse voice came through suddenly.

"Sir, the pyramid is creating a barrier, it's sealing me inside. What are my orders?" Frank said, again unable to mask the slight panic he felt.

"Do nothing. Hold your ground, we are coming."

Frank felt like throwing the device and his plans as far as he could. He was going to be shut in, and who knew when he would be out? Frank's thoughts at once drifted to his wife, Ellie and his daughter, Grace. He was due to be home in just a week for his daughter's birthday, which he wouldn't miss for the world. He swallowed hard and continued to watch the growing shield seal him in. Steadily, he controlled his breathing and raised his head to the heavens, seeing nothing but darkness. "I'll be out of here soon, don't worry, Gracie," he whispered to his child.

△

General Hoskins disembarked from the black helicopter that had landed in The Basin of Dahshur. He looked around at the carnage that had taken place a few hours earlier; the smouldering wrecks of the two ruined helicopters still lay where they had been destroyed. The bodies of the men that Ulrich had slain had thankfully been taken away, but the blood stains and gore remained. Colonel Riggs was busy organising his men by the opening that had formed on the ground. Hoskins smiled. Everything was proceeding just as planned. He walked confidently over to Riggs and the men saluted him as he did, which he ignored. "Riggs," he responded coolly, announcing his presence.

"Sir," Riggs responded, "We've secured the perimeter, but Lieutenant Williams is still down there," he added nervously.

"I am aware," Hoskins answered, mildly irritated. "We need to ensure no eyes are on us, keep the press away, the archaeologists, the government. Nobody can know what's here."

"Acknowledged." Riggs shifted. "Permission to speak, sir?"

"Go ahead," Hoskins said, scanning the horizon, surprisingly satisfied with the perimeter Riggs had established.

"What exactly is down there, Sir?"

Hoskins looked at Riggs. His eyes blazed with purpose and for a brief moment, Riggs thought he saw laughter there too.

"The most pivotal discovery of our time, Colonel," he answered simply, before walking off and leaving Riggs with more questions than answers.

CHAPTER ELEVEN

Luisa felt the world shift and turn around her as she hurtled through space and time, travelling at breakneck speed thousands of years into the past and feeling her body ripple with electricity as she burst through a tear in the very fabric of reality. Abruptly, Luisa landed with crunch onto the hard, stone floor. She gingerly rose to her knees, using her hands as a base. She heard the gentle lapping of waves as they rose and fell against the platform she was on. Blinking slowly, Luisa saw she was in a harbour, busy with fishermen, tradesmen and an assortment of people going about their daily business. Her mouth fell open in shock as she studied the inhabitants; their clothes were from an era in history she had only read about. "Am I dreaming?" she wondered aloud.

"No, you're not," came a reply from behind her. She whirled around and stumbled back.

"W-who are you?" she asked nervously, studying the man before her.

He was tall and muscular with tanned skin, his smile was disarming and lit up his features, contrasting with his long dark hair and eyes. A medium length beard that was on the verge of being unkempt framed his mouth. The stranger was wearing a simple tunic and sandals, typical attire for Ancient Greek travellers, Luisa thought. The man extended his hand out for her to take, "please, call me Zurman," he announced, still smiling. Luisa cautiously accepted his grip, and he effortlessly helped her to her feet. She dusted herself down and noticed with relief that she was nevertheless in her own clothes.

"Yes, we'll need to get you properly dressed if you are to blend in here," the mysterious man added as though reading her thoughts. "Come, I have prepared something for you to wear," he mentioned taking a step forward and turning his back to her.

Luisa didn't move. Her mind was racing with a thousand questions and she suddenly felt incredibly anxious. Her breathing quickened, and she took an involuntary step backwards, dangerously close to the edge. Zurman turned around and his smile faded for the first time, replaced with a look of concern. "Are you okay?" he asked genuinely, taking a step towards her.

"Get back!" she exclaimed, her voice quaking. Zurman raised both his hands slowly and stopped in his tracks. "It's okay, I understand your confusion, your fear."

"No, no, you don't!" she replied hysterically. "I've just gone from digging around a perfectly boring excavation site in Egypt, to falling down a hole, discovering probably the most important ancient structure in our time and now I'm somehow here, after touching this *thing*!" she finished, brandishing the electric blue rock from her right hand. A flicker of recognition flashed through Zurman's eyes. He was fixated on the gem for a second before composing himself and once again smiling his warm grin.

"You're like me," he simply said. "I was also thrust into this world," he continued, opening his arms wide and looking about his person. "I too, was in that pyramid you speak of."

"How, it was untouched?" Luisa questioned. Something was nagging in her mind not to trust this man, her instinct screamed at her to run, but where would she go?

"Perhaps in your age," he answered carefully. "But not in mine."

"What do you mean?"

"There are many, many questions for another occasion. I will do my best to answer as much as I can, but right now we need to move, there are eyes watching us already," he finished, his gaze flicking around to the onlookers that were studying Luisa with interest as they walked past. She noticed this too and decided that she had no other choice but to follow her new guide. He again held out his hand, and Luisa cautiously took it and the warmth of his grip radiated throughout her body.

"Stay close, we'll get somewhere safe," Zurman said as he led the way into the densely packed market place.

Luisa felt as if she was in a dream, the surroundings swam past her in a dizzying blur as she was led forward by Zurman. She looked at his back as he walked, his frame was huge and he stood a lot taller than most of the men and women they shuffled past, drawing the occasional look that would then shift to Luisa, her clothing making her stand out, bringing whispers and points from passers-by. Zurman quickened his pace, and they emerged from the busy stalls, ducking into a side alley, free from onlookers. "Almost there," he said, turning around and smiling at Luisa. Loosening his grip, Luisa allowed her hand to dangle back to her side as she continued to look around in awe at her new surroundings. Zurman rounded a corner and stopped at an unremarkable wooden door which was built into the left side of the narrow alley they were in. He took out a key chain which had an assortment of keys dangling from them, some ornate and large, others small and simple. They seemed to be a collection gathered from all over these parts.

"That's a lot of keys," Luisa remarked.

"I have a lot of doors," Zurman answered as he turned the key to this particular door and it opened with a creak. "Home sweet home," he announced cheerfully, holding the door wide to allow Luisa in. She studied at him warily before stepping inside and gasped. Zurman slammed the door shut behind him, and it made Luisa jump. "Sorry," he said bashfully, locking the door as he did. "Welcome to my home, you'll be able to stay here as long as necessary," he declared brightly. Luisa was still absorbing the contents in front of her, trinkets and unique items that could have been plucked out of the British Museum. There were weapons from all eras. One shield looked to be from the Middle Ages, others were simple clubs that could have been wielded by cavemen. There were spice containers and urns that matched those from Ancient Egypt, vases from Constantinople and crockery that belonged to the Tudors. "What are you?" she breathed, trying to process this information.

"Like you, I was an explorer," he began, pulling out a chair and gesturing for Luisa to sit. "I too discovered the Rift, and it has allowed me to traverse the ages, just as you have done."

"Hold on, what's the Rift?" Luisa asked, warily taking her seat on the chair as Zurman mimicked her action and sank into a comfortable armchair that had been obtained from an unknown land. He chuckled before answering, "Perhaps it would be better if I offered you my story and explained things along the way. There is so much to tell but we don't have enough time to go through it all."

"What do you mean, enough time? What's going to happen?"

"Ah, see, I should answer that first," he stated, holding a finger in the air. "Your world is about to end, in approximately three days," he stated simply.

"Sorry, what?" Luisa replied, perplexed at the casual tone in which he had announced this revelation.

"Yes, unfortunately it's true. It's been coming for millennia, we've tried to stop it a few times, but it always ends up the same way."

"Who are *we*?" Luisa asked.

"*We* are those who are have always known that the world would end like this and have been trying to prevent it since the dawn of time." Zurman answered patiently, ready for the inevitable further questioning.

"How..." Luisa began, formulating the question in her head and starting again. "How does it happen?"

"Ah, better not to ask for now, but all you need to know is that this time, things are different."

"Why?" she asked, knowing already what the answer would be.

"*You*," Zurman said, jabbing a finger towards her. "You found the stone. You have created a fresh path that wasn't there before. You can change matters."

"But how, why am I here?"

"This is where your journey begins, where do you think we are?"

"Greece?" Luisa guessed.

"Very good, Rhodes to be exact. Have you heard of the Colossus of Rhodes?"

"Of course, one of the Ancient Wonders of the World," Luisa said matter-of-factly.

"Then I'm sure you'd like to see it in person, right?" Zurman answered, the disarming smile returning.

"It's *here?*" Luisa said, her eyes wide in anticipation.

"Yes, and it is the key to our next steps. That stone you have?" Zurman began, gesturing to Luisa's pocket. "That is how we return to the right moment in time, but we need something that exists here, in this time. Buried long ago before man even walked the Earth."

Luisa exhaled deeply, trying to process the information Zurman had just given.

"I appreciate, it's a lot to accept and understand all at once," Zurman said, again as though he had read her mind. "For now, simply rest, wash, and relax. We have time still. I need to leave for a few hours, but you'll be safe here. Please, follow me to your room," he suggested, rising to his feet and walking to the open hole in the wall that housed Luisa's makeshift bedroom. She bit her lip anxiously, unsure if this was a trap. Her emotions were a whirlwind inside of her. Fear, excitement, loneliness. Luisa missed Joe. Inside, she was racked with an enormous feeling of longing for him. Even to learn that he was safe would be enough. She felt tears forming in the corners of her eyes just as Zurman popped his head back around the opening. "Please, come, relax," he asserted, inviting her in with his charming smile. She inhaled a lungful of fresh air and stepped forward into the cosy chamber, a simple bed and table were the only furnishings there, but she didn't care. She only wanted to rest, her exhaustion was overwhelming.

"Sit down for now, then we'll talk some more. I'll be back soon," Zurman said, smiling as he left, closing the door behind him and locking it. Luisa lay down and was asleep almost as soon as her head hit the pillow.

She saw him falling down a hole which never ended, then appearing again in front of her. He was falling continually. Each cycle he became more ravaged by age and rot. Luisa tried to help him, but she couldn't touch him. A golden aura protected him and trapped him all at once, he could not be rescued and all she could do was watch this horrifying loop. "No, Joe.... come back.... don't... Joe, Joe!" Luisa awoke with a violent jerk and gasped for air, the remnants of the nightmare already fading from her mind as she blinked her vision back to reality. Panting, she put a hand on her chest and felt her rapid heartbeat begin to gradually slow down. It was still light outside, so she guessed she'd only been asleep for an hour at most. The sunlight streamed in through the slit in the stone that acted as a window. She could hear the noise of the marketplace close by and then remembered where she was; Rhodes. Luisa then remembered *when* she was; thousands of years in the past. She sat up fully now and observed her surroundings, taking stock of the long tunic that had been laid out for her to wear, as well as a pair of simply designed sandals. Deciding it would be best to try to blend in, she undressed out of her modern clothes and put on the tunic, which she recalled was known as a peplos. It was refreshingly comfortable, the warm air was pleasant on her exposed arms. She let her dark hair hang loose, her natural curls very much helping her to integrate. Luisa stepped slowly and quietly out of her bedroom and called out a meek, "hello?" No answer. Good. She had time to search around and try to piece together the events of the last twenty-four hours. Carefully, Luisa approached a bookcase that was affixed to the wall, remarkably out-of-place furniture for the era, she thought. It was full of thick books that were covered in dust and cobwebs. Some appeared to be part of the same series, their dark green colouring all similar, but the text along the spine was nonsensical; symbols and etchings that didn't look like any language she'd ever seen before. Luisa bit her lip and gradually stretched her fingers out to touch one of the books. It seemed ancient, and she tentatively slid it off the shelf to let it rest in her hands. It was heavy, and she suddenly felt a substantial burden of knowledge that seemed to emanate from the text itself. She delicately opened it and was blown backwards by a howl of noise that erupted from the pages. The book clattered to the floor and sealed itself shut, also stopping the noise just as abruptly as it had begun. Luisa's heart raced again as she sat forlornly on the floor. "What the hell was that?" she said dumbly to nobody.

"Something you probably shouldn't open," came Zurman's deep voice from the doorway. Luisa jumped and placed her hand on her chest, closing her eyes as she did.

Zurman chuckled. "Sorry, did I scare you?"

"Well no, actually a book did," Luisa answered, before dramatically slapping her hands on the floor. "Can you tell me what is happening here? Where am I, why am I here and why do you have screaming books?"

Zurman simply allowed her to vent, the words came out of her at a rapid rate and he leaned casually against the doorframe.

"Finished?"

"What do you- yes, I'm finished, tell me what's going on!" she demanded.

"Come through and we'll begin," he replied naturally, walking into the adjacent area which Luisa had yet to inspect. She straightened her tunic and stood up, watching this peculiar man stride confidently ahead.

"Please, sit," he added, gesturing to the empty chair immediately to Luisa's right as she entered.

"Woah," she responded, looking up at the ceiling. The square room was relatively sparse, much like her bedroom. Two chairs, a desk and a bronze ornament in the shape of a half moon were all that filled the space, but above, that was where the detail was. Golden scripture flowed around diagrams, images and symbols that sprawled across a dark blue background.

"What is it?" Luisa asked, still marvelling at the intricate patterns above her and yet to take a seat.

"This is my map," Zurman said simply. "I find it easier to look up at something, rather than down."

Luisa looked at him with increased curiosity. She felt a flutter *stir* within her. Distrust? Admiration? She wasn't sure. "A map for what? What language is this?"

"You should get comfortable, this isn't a short story," Zurman answered. Luisa did at last sit, still fixated on the script above her. There was a familiarity about it, yet it looked completely unlike anything she had ever seen in her life.

"Tea?" Zurman offered.

"No thanks."

"Suit yourself," he replied, pouring himself a cup from a curiously shaped kettle. It was circular and had a rectangle opening that dispensed boiling water in an almost wave like motion. Luisa watched in fascination, deciding it best to not ask yet another question and simply let this man explain himself.

"So, as you know, my name is Zurman." He sipped delicately from the cup before continuing. "You'll not be surprised to learn that I can travel through time, well more specifically, travel to certain *points* in time."

Luisa nodded slowly, trying to put logic behind his words. He took her silence as a signal to continue.

"That over there?" he pointed to the bronze object in the room's corner. "That's how I do it, but it's not a quick process and requires months of planning and calculation; hence this," he said, pointing up.

"Okay, so where does the pyramid we found in Dahshur fit into this?" Luisa probed.

"Well, I'm glad you asked," Zurman replied with a smile. "That pyramid you found is the beginning and the end. It's the centre of time and the place where we'll go back to once we have collected what we needed."

"Oh, so nothing too important then," Luisa replied sarcastically. "So hang on, has this all happened before then?"

"Ah, I'm glad you asked," Zurman repeated, waving a finger knowingly. "The answer is no, it hasn't. Which is why what we're doing is so crucial. We have a chance to change history, to stop the apocalypse and save humanity."

Luisa processed this statement, a little sceptical, but she entertained the idea for now. "So..."

"I see you don't believe me," Zurman interrupted, "and I would expect that. Therefore, I have prepared a journey for us. To the future."

Luisa's mouth hung open, and she didn't know how to respond. Zurman dragged the delicate looking object into the middle of the room and fiddled with some dials at the base.

"We're going to be taken fifty years ahead of when you discovered the pyramid, to New York City." Luisa was suddenly anxious. What if he was lying and was planning on killing her? She'd been so foolish to trust him so readily. But then, what other choice was there? She was definitely not in Dahshur, unless she'd been tricked in some truly elaborate plot. "Wait, wait," she repeated, panicking slightly. "I'm not ready. How do I know I can count on you?"

Zurman looked up from his work and smiled. "Do you have another choice?"

Luisa stared back in a mixture of shock and curiosity. "No, I suppose not," she replied quietly, realising she was very much alone here, and he was seemingly her only hope.

Zurman continued to tweak the object until there was a sudden crack of electricity that burst wildly from the tips of the mysterious creation. The bright light stabilised and hummed steadily as the light seemed to grow more intense, causing Luisa to squint her eyes slightly as it became dazzling.

"Come, take my hand," Zurman said, offering his right hand for her to hold. She looked at him with distrust before reaching out and accepting Zurman's grip. With a final adjustment, he twiddled a dial and the light suddenly pulsed in an otherworldly manner, exploding immediately and then slowing down almost as quickly, expanding at a snail's pace and slowly enveloping them both. "Get ready, it has begun," Zurman said.

Luisa didn't answer, instead keeping her eyes on the brilliant white light as it absorbed them both.

CHAPTER TWELVE

Joe crashed through branches as he tumbled out of the Rift into the air. "Aaaah!" he screamed, covering his eyes as he continued to descend, finally landing shoulder first on the earthy ground with a thud. "Urgh, Jesus Christ," Joe moaned as he rolled onto his back, staring up at the lush greenery of the forest. After Joe's spectacular landing, everything was still, quiet. A flock of birds fluttered by far above him, their wings creating the only sound for miles. Joe remained flat on his rear, pushing his brown hair to one side and finding bits of soil embedded within it. A gentle breeze rippled through the air causing Joe to shiver slightly; his clothes were still the same as what he had been wearing in Dahshur, made for the intense heat of the desert, not wherever he was now. He sat up and puffed out some air. Joe patted his ribcage and spine and, to his relief, found that there were no sensitive areas. "Ah!" he spoke sharply, after putting pressure on his left shoulder with his right hand. *Yeah, that's what broke my fall*, he determined. He stood up and felt a dull pain in his left thigh. *Figures*, he added internally. Joe had landed only on one side and now that the adrenaline was fading, he was feeling very sore.

Joe glanced around. All he could see were tall trees that stretched upwards so high that he had to crane his neck. The pleasant light blue sky was visible as the trees were thin (Joe guessed they might be pine but he was certainly no expert). At ground level, it was just like any other forest; a chaotic spread of roots, divots, holes, upturned trees, fungi and more. In short, there was no discernible path for him to follow. Equally, there was no sign of *how* Joe had even ended up here. It was clear he was no longer in Egypt, but how on earth was that possible? Joe pondered this for a moment before deciding that any further inaction would get him nowhere, literally, so he parked that concern for the time being and began his new journey. Joe managed maybe five steps before he stopped dead. His ears pricked up. *There!* A snap of a twig, far too close for comfort behind him. Joe's breathing came in rapid, short bursts. He searched frantically to his left, then right, all the while remaining absolutely still. He strained his ears once again, fear mounting as the unknown threatened to overwhelm him. Nothing. The forest was still, silent. Joe exhaled in relief, dropping his guard.

"Hello there!"

"Good God!" Joe replied, almost jumping out of his skin.

"Oh dear, I am sorry," said the visitor, who was suddenly in front of Joe. He walked over, his hands held out apologetically.

"Woah, woah! Stay right there, man," Joe warned.

"Hey, okay, easy now. I'm not going to hurt you," the newcomer replied. He was wearing a long, dark robe with broad sleeves and a circular collar, which was bone-coloured by contrast.

Joe studied him up and down before speaking. "What do you want from me? I haven't got any money man, I'm sorry." He was nervous but controlled his voice. The stranger sighed and his dark eyes stared at Joe, imploring him to understand.

"I mean you no harm, I just want to help."

"Why?" Joe asked suspiciously, shifting his feet so that he could turn and run, if required.

"Because I'm sure you're very confused right now. You're somewhere very distant from home, you have no idea where you're going and I have all the answers you seek."

Joe let the words hang for a moment, digesting each syllable.

"How do you know I'm far from home?"

"Your clothes."

"What about them?" Joe glanced down at his dusty shoes and light grey shorts, which contrasted hugely with what this stranger was wearing.

"Let's just say they're definitely not from here," the man said, smiling.

"So where is *here*?" Joe challenged.

"You're in China, close to Beijing," the stranger answered matter-of-factly.

Joe blinked a few times in quick succession before shaking his head,."Whaddya mean, *China?* I was just in Egypt for crying out loud!"

"Yes, you were. Then you were brought here. What did you touch?" Something flashed across his eyes when he asked this, Joe couldn't quite make it out. Was it malice? Or excitement?

"Yeah..." Joe began, suddenly realising that the golden orb he had touched from the pyramid lay by his right foot, dropped during his chaotic entrance.

"Is that it?" The man nodded towards the object Joe was looking at.

"Yeah, look, whatever this is, I don't want no part of it. I wanna go home and get back to work and..." His speech trailed off as he thought about Luisa. What if she was here as well? Or was she still in the pyramid, trapped and desperate? The thought of this made his stomach flip. In front of him, the stranger was now taking a few cautious steps towards Joe.

"I understand, my friend." His tone was like honey, smooth and easy. "But you must come with me, I can get you back home, back to your time."

"Wait, what do you mean, *time?*" Joe asked, this fresh information causing another wave of anxiety to swell up within him.

"Ever heard of the Ming Dynasty?" the other man responded.

"You gotta be kidding me," Joe said. "What the hell happened to me in that pyramid?"

"Calm down, everything will be okay. You just have to trust me, which I know is asking a lot. Why don't we start from the beginning; introductions. What do I call you?"

Joe hesitated before answering. The voice in his head told him to run, but to where? He really needed the help. Finally, he said, "I'm Joe. Joe Cullins. What do they call you?"

"You may call me Zurman."

"Alright Zurman, so what do you get in return for helping me?"

Zurman smiled and took a few steps closer, extending his hand now for Joe to shake. "We have much to discuss, my friend."

△

"You have started a journey that cannot be undone and must be seen to its end," Zurman said after they had walked a few paces forward. "That object you found? It's incomplete, we must combine it with another artefact that exists here, in this time, in this location."

"And you just happen to know this? What's so important about this thing, anyway?" Joe replied, brandishing the orb from his pocket.

"Mister Cullins..."

"Call me Joe,"

"Joe," Zurman corrected himself before continuing, "as I mentioned, you have taken steps on a path that must be concluded, that has always been destined. I'll show you how I know all of this and more once we return to my home."

Joe wasn't exactly thrilled at the prospect of entering this man's home. But again, what choice did he really have? "How much further then?" he asked Zurman.

"Not long, and then I can hopefully answer your questions, whatever they may be."

They walked in silence for the next leg of the journey, the trees of the forest not clearing, and Joe was noticing how hungry and tired he felt. The adrenaline that had fuelled him during the escapades in the pyramid had faded, and reality now took over. Joe's stomach rumbled loudly almost as if in response to his thoughts, he gave Zurman a sideways look and grinned sheepishly.

"Don't worry, my friend. I have food, and a bed for you to rest," he spoke to Joe, almost as though reading his mind.

"That obvious, huh?"

Zurman smiled kindly. "You have passed through a time axis. This is no small feat, especially for your first time. Your body is trying to adapt to being displaced, your mind is racing with a million questions and you're scared, it's okay. I was too."

"Wait, so this happened to you as well?" Joe asked.

"Yes, in a way. Ah! Here we are. Follow me, please," Zurman said, turning right at a natural crossroads. Joe looked up at the enormous tree that blocked the path ahead, forcing them to go left or right around it. It stretched high into the sky and seemed to be ancient, yet sturdy. As he continued to stare, he heard voices to the left abruptly pierce the silence. Joe's eyed widened, and he looked to Zurman, who pressed a finger to his lips swiftly and ushered Joe to join him.

"Quickly!" he whispered, gesturing Joe across.

Joe instinctively ducked as he scurried over, Zurman

pulling them both into some dense shrubbery that gave them cover. A few moments later, a quartet of men emerged from the left-hand side of the tree that Joe had been staring at.

"Military," Zurman breathed, their obvious red attire marking them as such. They spoke in their native tongue and walked briskly towards where Joe had first met Zurman.

"Come on," Zurman said, rushing out from the cover they were in once the troops were out of sight. He moved quickly, and Joe followed closely, occasionally looking over his shoulder.

Satisfied they were in the clear, Joe inquired, "any reason the military are here?"

Zurman looked down at Joe and smirked, "you made quite an entrance, it would have been easily spotted from the Wall."

"The wall?" Joe replied, checking behind him once more.

"The Great Wall, we're close to it," Zurman answered.

Joe smiled fondly; he had always wanted to visit The Great Wall of China. *Careful what you wish for, I guess*, he thought with sadness as they pressed on, jogging at a a moderate pace.

"So what happened when I arrived?" Joe asked.

"A brilliant flash of light, the air itself seemed to melt and suddenly you were spat out and tumbling down through the trees," Zurman said, slowing down his pace.

Joe adjusted his speed as well. "So you knew I'd be here? At this time?"

"I had an idea," Zurman answered carefully, looking into the distance instead of at Joe. "Come, we're almost there, just a bit further."

Joe didn't argue and followed Zurman's lead. The pair soon found themselves at the edge of the forest and into a clearing of lush fields, with several wooden cabins dotted sporadically throughout.

"That's us - just over there," Zurman said, pointing to the third closest shelter. "Let's move, before anyone sees us, or more to the point, you," he spoke, looking at Joe's clothing once again.

Joe nodded silently and did not try to argue. He was far too hungry and fatigued at this point and just wanted to lie down for a while.

△

After a brisk walk across the rolling green plains, the travelling duo stopped in front of Zurman's hut. It was modest, with a simple door and few windows, but Joe didn't care. It would be fine for now until he figured out what he was supposed to be doing in this place. Zurman produced a heavy set of keys and found the correct one for the lock on this door.

"That's a lot of keys," Joe remarked.

"I've heard that before," Zurman said, unlocking the door and pushing it open with a creak. "Please, come in, let's eat, rest, talk. Whatever you want to do."

Joe didn't need to be asked twice. He hurried inside and immediately felt more relaxed. He looked around and discovered the interior to be nothing like he expected. There was an array of ornaments littered throughout the cabin; some were large, highly decorated, and seemingly expensive. Others were far simpler in design and well worn. A cracked pot sat upon a dusty shelf, and Joe stretched a finger out to touch it. It surprised him by how smooth it felt, yet incredibly solid at the same time.

"Please, try not to touch things," Zurman instructed, closing the door behind him.

"Sorry," Joe answered with mild embarrassment.

"Oh, it's not that I'm fussy, just that some items are very... delicate," he answered mysteriously. "Would you like some tea? Perhaps some food?"

"I really would," Joe replied earnestly.

"Good, and then we can talk about anything you want," Zurman said, boiling the water. "Perhaps starting with that object you hold."

Joe pulled the golden orb from his pocket again and studied it For the briefest of moments it flashed a dazzling light accompanied by some ancient scripture, but just as soon as it appeared, it had faded. Joe put it down to fatigue playing tricks on his mind and tucked the orb neatly away in his pocket. Meanwhile, Zurman had seen what Joe had done and smiled. It had begun.

CHAPTER THIRTEEN

Luisa was drowned in the oppressive darkness. She blinked repeatedly, hoping that her eyes would adapt and that she would soon see objects, houses, anything. Nothing. Then she noticed the silence, so eerily quiet, like a graveyard. Zurman tugged at her arm gently, and she gasped in surprise.

"Jesus!"

"Sorry," he apologised, his voice sounded close, but she still couldn't see him. "Your eyes will adjust shortly, just keep blinking."

Luisa obeyed and remained rooted to the spot, her vision picking out silhouettes of massive constructions. They looked to be in complete ruin, from what she could tell. She inched forwards and, to her surprise, found the surface crunched in response.

"What's on the floor?" she asked, whispering, despite nobody being around to hear her apart from Zurman.

"Nuclear fallout. Dust, debris, bodies. All rolled into one."

Luisa shivered involuntarily. "This is the future?"

"I'm afraid so," Zurman answered, his voice grim. He fiddled with his own tunic and then suddenly produced a tiny, bright light which he held aloft. "That's better," he said with a grin. Indeed, it was, Luisa thought; she could at least see in front of her by a few feet.

"Who else is here?" she asked, peering into the distance, struggling to work out what was on the horizon.

"We have a small... group, I suppose you could say. The last of our kind."

"How many?"

"Too few," Zurman murmured. "We will go to them, so you can see and hear for yourself what will transpire if we should fail."

Luisa didn't answer. She kept trying to look ahead, *what was that thing in the distance? It looks like a sphere.* Finally, she spoke. "What's over there?" she said, pointing ahead.

"That is where we are headed, to the Last Table. But we must be cautious, this land is treacherous. There are more than just empty shells and buildings that linger here. Stay close to me."

Luisa felt goosebumps prickle on her arms, *what on earth did he mean by that?* She decided not to press the matter and followed closely behind her guide.

The pair walked quietly, taking their time to traverse the natural obstacle course of this ruined land. Luisa tried to acknowledge the architecture of the collapsed building they were slowly walking through. She dared to let her hand brush the stone, which was surprisingly smooth, almost like glass. *What had this once been?* she wondered.

"This was a great theatre, once," Zurman announced into the silence, again as though he had read her mind. "The entire building was made of marble and decorated in the finest metals. Gold, platinum, some sapphire, it was truly a magnificent sight. I remember coming here often with my family," he added, trailing off.

Luisa hesitated, thinking she already knew the answer, but asked anyway. "Did your family..."

"No, all gone," Zurman said flatly.

"I'm sorry."

"You needn't be, it was a very long time ago, I have existed for much longer without them than with them. But I miss them every single day," he replied. Luisa could hear the pain in his voice and decided not to ask any further questions for now. Instead, she kept her focus on following his lead and trying not to impale herself on the ruined remnants of the theatre that jutted out at various angles from the floor.

Suddenly there was a noise, a scurrying sound that made her blood freeze. Zurman heard it too and held out a fist, extinguishing the light was holding, plunging them both into darkness. Luisa breathed heavily, her eyes darting back and forth in the darkness, straining to see who or what had made that clamour. A few agonising seconds passed in silence and then they heard it again, a quick shuffle of feet rushing across the surface. *It's probably just a rat,* she resolved. *It's always a rat, nothing to worry about.* Her heart rate was increasing as she heard the noise once more, it sounded closer this time.

"Zurman," she hissed, "what do we do?"

He didn't answer. She was panicking now. *What if it's not a rat? What did he say about this land being treacherous? Oh God, I wish Joe were here.* That last thought swam into her consciousness out of nowhere and caught her off guard momentarily, but she did not have long to process it. In an instant, Zurman once again lit up the surrounding area and there it was in front of them, a wild creature with dusky fur that was spiked and chaotic, its red eyes wide open in shock at the sudden source of the brilliant glow. It bared its fangs and revealed row upon row of sharp teeth, which glinted in the light. It was no larger than an average fox, but it looked completely feral. Luisa noticed the sharp talons protruding from all four of its feet and the colour drained from her face. Zurman acted swiftly, he leapt forward and in a single motion brought his heel crashing down towards the beast. But it was quick. It jumped sideways and avoided the strike, leaning on its back legs and preparing a counter charge of its own. Zurman however was astonishingly nimble. He unsheathed a blade from inside the folds of his tunic and brandished the weapon menacingly at the thing, who now thought twice about launching an an assault. It growled in retaliation, but Zurman held his ground. He slashed the air ahead of him to ward the foul beast away.

"Get behind me!" he instructed Luisa, not taking his eyes off the animal. She did as she was told and took some sideways steps to her right, keeping her body facing the beast at all times. It snarled and peeled back its lips to once again display its razor-sharp teeth, its focus entirely on Zurman, and then it whipped its head around to look at Luisa.

"Don't. Move." Zurman said slowly and Luisa froze in place, her heart thumping against her chest. The predator walked slowly, like a wolf closing in on its prey, and Luisa stood rooted to the spot in complete fear. The red eyes of the creature narrowed and out of nowhere it jumped forward, the leap covering the few metres between it and Luisa in a flash. She closed her eyes and waited for the inevitable. She heard the impact first; the wet sound of something sharp hitting flesh, and she knew it would all soon be over. Except it wasn't. She felt no pain. Opening one eye slowly, she saw at her feet the crumpled heap of the animal in its dying throes as Zurman swiftly put it out of its misery. He had timed the attack just at the right moment and plunged his knife deep into the side of the beast to save her life.

Luisa breathed heavily, wanting to say thank you, but the words wouldn't come. Her vision was fixed on the still creature at her feet, and she felt bile burn at the back of her throat. She swallowed hard and shut her eyes, taking deep breaths through her nose.

"I told you, there are a lot of nasty things out here," Zurman said, almost jovially.

Luisa regained her composure and clumsily said, "thank you," without looking at him.

"You would have done the same for me, if you could have," he declared simply. "Are you okay?"

She nodded in response, still trying to keep herself from vomiting.

"Good, then we continue on. We need to move, that commotion would have drawn attention to us. Come on, it's not too far now." Zurman sheathed his blade into an unseen fold of his tunic and held the light once more. Luisa finally moved from her spot and took one last look at the slain creature before joining her saviour.

Their pace had noticeably slowed now. The terrain was becoming harder to navigate, either with rubble blocking their path or gigantic craters that threatened to swallow them whole.

"Come on, climb up through here," Zurman said, illuminating a gap in-between two enormous blocks of stone that had crashed together. Luisa watched as Zurman athletically leapt into the space and wriggled his way through. "Now you, quick!" he instructed Luisa. She bit her lip and her body stiffened up, she'd never been the best at physical education at school. In fact, she avoided exercise altogether, much to the annoyance of her friends who were envious of her slim yet curvy body.

"Okay, hang on," she answered, taking a deliberate step onto a protruding block. *You can do this. Just a little jump up,* she thought, trying to summon the courage to make the vertical leap up to the ledge where Zurman had disappeared to. She bent her knees and was about to push off when she heard it.

The same scurrying of claws and feet as before. She turned around slowly, her chest moving rapidly up and down and the hairs on the back of her neck standing up. In the darkness, she saw one set of red eyes. Then another. Then two more. They kept multiplying as more swam into her field of vision, deliberately slow in their approach.

"Z-Zurman!" she screamed, too paralysed by fear to do anything else. His dark features appeared overhead, a look of confusion etched on his face, which quickly transformed into horror.

"Luisa, quick, you have to come now!" He let his hand dangle below for her to reach up and grab, but the jump still had to be made. At once, the beasts charged, their bodies coming into full view now thanks to Zurman's light from the tunnel above. Luisa crouched low and jumped, her hand inches from Zurman's, but she missed and landed clumsily. She gasped in fear as she saw that the first creature leading the pack was closing in on her position. There was nothing she could do; it was time for fight or flight. Luisa kept her eyes open and just as the animal was about to leap onto her, Zurman landed with crunch directly on the thing, snapping its spine instantly. Zurman moved with such speed that Luisa could barely keep track of him. He span and slashed with his knife, avoiding fangs and slicing flesh as he did.

"Luisa!" he called back over the sound of snarls and yelps of pain. "Make the jump! GO!" This time she didn't hesitate. She crouched low and jumped, her hands gripping the edge of the shaft above with all her might. With a struggle, she hoisted herself up and was flat on her stomach, watching the skirmish below. Zurman was rapidly becoming outnumbered, but the beasts were now more cautious in their approach and formed a semi circle in front of him, blocking any path ahead. Zurman stretched out a hand behind him, feeling for the stony surface of the collapsed building. His fingers found the wall, and he paused, inhaling deeply. "Luisa," he said through gritted teeth, his eyes fixed on his enemies still. "I'm going to require a distraction. There should be some rocks in that tunnel, I need you to throw them so I can have a chance to climb up. Can you do that?"

"I'm on it!" she called down, moving quickly, her fear diminished and replaced with a sense of duty to her new friend. She soon found what Zurman meant and hurried back to the opening, peering down below as she saw the horde of beasts inching closer to the trapped Zurman. Her first throw was clumsy, landing between three of the beasts, who ignored the rock and kept creeping forward. The second throw landed on one of them, who let out a feral grunt, but didn't stop it moving. *This isn't working,* Luisa panicked, her eyes darting around for another solution. She stopped throwing the rocks and used her brain instead, a far greater weapon for her. Then she spotted it. Windows that hadn't been completely shattered in the building that was to her right. She took a deep breath and aimed precisely at the glass. The rock found its target and the window burst, showering the floor with broken shards. More importantly, the sudden noise caused some of the creatures to look around. "Yes!" she expressed aloud, already priming a second throw. It missed, but she didn't let it affect her, Luisa confidently threw again and this time, hit her target. More of the creatures turned, their noses sniffing the air, and they walked away. Now there were just a few left in front of Zurman.

"That'll do," he declared, spinning and leaping with great agility first to the step and then jumping forcefully to the ledge where Luisa was. He grunted as he landed, his chest and arms hitting the edge. Luisa hurried to help him up.

"Thank you, looks like we're even now."

"Yes, well, you were brilliant," she responded, blushing slightly.

"You get used to it out here, they're easily distracted and lose interest rather quickly. As you can see," he stated, smiling a little. They both looked down at the creatures below, who had given up the chase, deciding it wasn't worth it anymore, and instead made their way back into the darkness.

Silence again engulfed the world, and Luisa and Zurman exchanged glances before walking on into the tunnel.

After a few minutes of no conversation Luisa asked, "so how did this all happen then?"

Zurman chuckled, though the laugh was without humour. "People happened."

"What do you mean?"

"Greed, corporate agendas, wealth. Powerful people with big ideas. Countries were no longer controlled by government, those who had unlimited resources ruled them. There was a technological boom, the two corporations who spearheaded the innovation both set out to control the population of the world, claiming to unite us all with their designs." Zurman paused to check where the natural tunnel they had found was leading them as they began to emerge into a clearing. Satisfied, he continued on.

"At first, it was great. Diseases were wiped out, people lived longer, but then the gap between the rich and the poor widened. More and more jobs were becoming obsolete to technology, things that humans could do were becoming more limited as everything became automated."

"Like what?" Luisa asked.

"The simple things. Transport was one of the first things to go. They said humans are too prone to error, which they are, and thus artificial intelligence was used instead to fly planes, drive buses, boats, trains, everything."

"Did it work?"

"Oh yes, there were never any casualties again. But what did this do? It lead to an ever ageing population who were using up the planet's resources. Fast forward a few hundred years, you have a world that is creaking under the weight of how many people there are. Just before the end, or what we call *The Great Collapse*, the population was close to one hundred billion humans."

"You've got to be kidding me!" Luisa exclaimed.

"I wish I was," Zurman said grimly. "The two companies had split their wealth and power equally, each controlled half the world by rationing supplies, enforcing curfews, all sorts of measures. Of course, there were uprisings, but the people were so ill-equipped. I mean, imagine, the technology that these corporations shared with the community was just a fraction of the power they truly owned. So people realised over time that nothing could be done and accepted their life as it was. Misery."

Luisa contemplated this information as they continued to trudge through the ruin of the area. "So what about here? You said there was a theatre back there that you used to go to?"

"I was one of the very fortunate few. I won't lie to you, Intelibox, who ruled the northern hemisphere held my family in high regard. My great, great, great, great grandfather worked in the business when it was just starting out."

"This is where you grew up, raised your family then?"

"Yes, around this area," Zurman said absentmindedly. "But nuclear fire doesn't care where you live, who you are. As I'm sure you can see."

"How did it happen then?" Luisa repeated her original question.

"Nobody really knows, it was all so fast. There are so few survivors from either side that it doesn't matter who started it, just that it was all finished in the blink of an eye. One company tried to do a hostile takeover of the other. There were legions of troops, tanks, aircraft that you could only imagine seeing in movies. All unleashed on each other, civilians were slaughtered in the crossfire, nobody cared. Both heads of the companies were assassinated within days of each other. Then that's when things really fell apart. Leadership crumbled, people panicked, and the first nuclear missile was launched. The impact was terrible, as I'm sure you can imagine," he said, gesturing an arm to their surroundings. Luisa again glanced at the devastation, rubble, floating bits of debris in the open that landed occasionally on the sand-like surface of the nuclear fallout. She peered ahead once more, the spherical building much closer now, and she wondered how many survivors would actually be in there.

"So we fled, up to that building there," Zurman pointed to the circular structure Luisa was just looking at. "As we were close, they came from the sky." Zurman looked up instinctively before continuing. "They had these jetpacks that screamed through the air, when they landed it was like demons from hell had come to our home. They opened fire and caught my family before we could hide. I don't know if I'm lucky to have survived or not," he said solemnly.

"I'm so sorry. This all sounds like a nightmare. I can't believe you had to live through this."

"Well, the good news is, we can avoid it. With your help." Zurman smiled and looked down to Luisa. "What they didn't know is that we had the greatest weapon of all: time. It was only through sheer luck that I was fortunate enough to be entrusted with the secret, for there were so few of us remaining. So I gratefully accepted my mission. What kills me is that I can't just go back, grab my family and flee to some forgotten era. It doesn't quite work like that, sadly."

"We have to change everything?" Luisa insinuated.

"Yes, nothing can be the same. We have existed for an eternity, trying to piece together the puzzle, the mystery of time. With your help, we can finally do it." Zurman's eyes blazed with an intensity that she hadn't seen before, it both startled her and gave her renewed focus.

"Okay, I want to help. I really do."

"Good, then you are ready." Zurman stopped, and Luisa did too.

"We're here," Zurman announced, looking up at the gigantic structure that stood a few hundred metres before them. Luisa felt a wave of trepidation suddenly wash over her, but she ignored it and instead approached The Last Table with Zurman.

CHAPTER FOURTEEN

FRANK WILLIAMS HAD REMAINED trapped inside the pyramid's shield for too long now and there was still no sign of General Hoskins or any rescue for him, or the two missing persons. The golden light that had erupted from within the enormous building had ceased its constant blazing, causing the entire surrounding area to become deathly quiet once more. Frank idly turned on the radio attached to his utility belt and was greeted with the familiar sound of static. Nobody had answered any more of his calls, and he felt very much alone. "Screw it," he stated, getting up from his seated position on the floor and making his way towards the entrance with his pistol raised. He tried to peer in, but it was completely dark. *Great,* he thought bitterly as he inched closer to the doorway. He took one last look over his shoulder at the pulsating shield behind him and hesitated. *Should I just wait? It was a direct order...* Steeling himself, Frank pressed on. "I've waited long enough," he declared as he stepped into the pyramid.

The darkness was dissolved by an unseen light source, though it was weak. Frank cautiously stepped forward into the antechamber and saw the same three paths that those he had been following had seen. He looked around for any signs of a skirmish that had occurred, blood, bullet holes, anything. To his relief, he saw none of that, however, this now opened up an additional question. *Where are they?* Frank's eyes flicked between the three archways that loomed over him. Three different paths to take, plenty of time for Ulrich to set up an ambush for him as well. Sighing, Frank moved deliberately towards the path on his left. He crouched next to the entrance and strained his ears, hoping to detect movement. Nothing. He repeated this process for the next two archways and came to the same conclusion: no traces of anybody here. He let out a slow breath, which steadied his rising nerves. Not that he was afraid for himself, but for the two missing archaeologists. Frank stared for a moment, debating which of the pathways to take. Strange markings were laid out above each one. None of them made any sense to him and he couldn't be sure if it was anything even a seasoned historian would know. Out of nowhere, his radio suddenly blasted with a stern voice, causing Frank to almost jump out of his skin.

"Williams, what's your status? Over,"

Frank fumbled with the receiver before replying, "General Hoskins, have made my way inside the pyramid, sir. No intel to report. Over."

"Those were not your orders, Lieutenant."

Frank winced at these words. Hoskins was right, but Frank felt his actions were justified.

"With respect, sir." Frank slowly began, "I have received no communication from topside and there are two people missing with an extremely dangerous assassin on their tail. I can't in good conscience ignore that." There was a moment's silence and Frank held his breath waiting for Hoskins to reply, he was certain that the General was going to be disappointed to say the least.

"Understood, Lieutenant. See what you can find. We're still working on a solution up here. Over and out."

Frank stared at the voice communicator, hardly able to believe his luck. He was positive that Hoskins would reprimand him at best, Court Marshall at worst. Frank clipped the receiver back to his belt and decided for no reason at all that the middle path was the best route forward, and cautiously made his way to the entrance.

△

General Hoskins finished sending his message to Frank Williams and almost crushed the phone in his hands. "Meddling fool," he said out loud. He walked out of the command tent that had been set up above the Dahshur Basin and surveyed the scene before him. The hole was protected by an electromagnetic fence, which guarded the entrance. It served as a gate, barring anyone from following Frank Williams or the others to the pyramid. Hoskins watched as the blue electricity danced and crackled, its energy unmatched and yet unable to penetrate the invisible aura of crater. Teams of elite soldiers had been dispatched to reinforce the troops that were stationed here. The assumption was that Ulrich would resurface at some point and he'd need to be taken out with lethal force. Hoskins knew better. Ulrich would wait patiently down below, for all to fall into place as it always will do. The general reached into his inside pocked and withdrew an old mobile phone that had been popular some ten or fifteen years ago. Opening the contacts, he dialled the only number in there and held the device to his ear.

"Yes, this is Hoskins. Everything is proceeding as planned, however, you should know there is one more down there. No, not foreseen, however shouldn't be a problem. Take out the spare, events will unfold regardless. Yes, I understand. It has begun." Hoskins clicked the phone off and slipped it back into his uniform. Just as he did, Colonel Riggs arrived by his side.

"You wanted to meet me, sir?" Riggs inquired.

"Ah, Colonel, good to see you," Hoskins flashed a crooked smile. "You had men down here, I want them to brief me on what happened, if they can."

"Sir, of course. Any word on Williams, sir?"

"Oh yes, he's perfectly fine. He's securing the site for our arrival, when we can eventually descend into the abyss below safely. We do not know how it behaves, so sending any men down is foolish."

"I concur, sir," Riggs answered.

"I am glad. That will be all, Colonel."

Riggs turned on his heel and left, leaving the General to watch over his men, smiling with content as one might if a game were being played and their team were winning.

△

Frank Williams hesitated. He wasn't sure why, but there was a nagging feeling inside that implored him to stop, turn around, and exit the structure. But he didn't. He stepped towards the arching entrance and heard the faintest sound, a fizzling noise almost like something was disintegrating. Frank pressed forward. He was unable to detect he minute specs of gold that fell to the ground, as the ancient gateway granted him access. He felt a chill run through the air, though there was no wind. It became clear after only a few steps that visibility was going to be an issue; the light from the chamber was diminishing as he progressed deeper into the passage. Frank didn't panic. He had a small flashlight on his utility belt that he unhooked and twisted on. The narrow beam of light pierced the ever-growing darkness, and Frank waved the flashlight around, highlighting more strange scribbles on the wall. But more concerning was that the gradient of the passageway itself was changing. Further forwards, Frank saw the path itself split and the walls of the hall ended abruptly. "What the..." he muttered, cautiously moving on. He stopped at the edge of the trail and raised the torch ahead once more. Frank tracked the walkway as it curved and coiled up, then down and back over itself again. One side dropped out of sight into the gloom below, the other carried on with a slight incline leading to somewhere deep inside the pyramid. Both routes were extremely dangerous, but Frank surmised that the high road would be slightly easier to traverse, so he started moving forwards, his torch guiding him. After a few paces, the track began its twisting and turning elevation. He slowly kept on walking, which soon turned into a crouch as he held on to the right side of the trail with both hands. To his surprise, he could keep going with minor interruption in momentum, despite finding himself virtually crawling as he ascended up.

Eventually, the road levelled out again. Sweating from the effort, Frank paused and caught his breath. He was a fit man, who at age forty-six could easily outlast many younger cadets on the training assault course, but navigating this track was difficult. Especially with no food, he thought, as his stomach rumbled in complaint. Frank raised his lamp again and pointed it forward. The path steadily rose up yet, without walls or railings to guard against a fall. Though the route didn't seem to get any narrower, it was nevertheless a daunting prospect. He didn't want to think about falling, so he set off with a determined stride, keeping his gaze focused ahead.

Walking for what seemed to be hours, Frank came to a halt as he heard a noise. It was a *whoosh* of air rushing from an unknown source. Frank aimed his torch higher and angled it down, trying to get any slight vantage point. Nothing. It occurred to him he hadn't actually looked left or right, so he swept his beacon in a curved motion.

"Woah!" he exclaimed as his light settled on the ornate doors that seemed to be suspended in mid-air. Frank blinked a few times, just to make sure he wasn't seeing things. The doors remained just where he saw them, hovering in the empty space around him. "I wonder," Frank mused, thinking back to the invisible path on the way down to the pyramid. He dangled a foot over to the side and was disappointed to feel no resistance and no secret invisible pathway. He moved the torch along and found many more doors, all following the same incline of the route. Frank swept the light to his left and saw more entrances, mirroring those on his right in terms of their shape, pattern, size, and positioning. He tried his luck on the left as well, just to check, but his foot dangled lamely in the air.

Frank looked up, his hand guiding the torch along with his gaze, but there was nothing above him except for the same familiar darkness. So he continued on, his focus once more on the seemingly infinite path ahead, careful to keep his balance and footing.

At long last, Frank's torch found something other than the pathway. A platform. It spurred him on and his pace quickened. Now he could see the landing ahead was like a miniature path of its own before it opened up into an enormous space, like the courtyard back on the ground level of the pyramid. Frank stepped onto the surface and his footstep echoed throughout the cavern he was standing in. Swivelling his head, Frank guided his torch around, catching glimpses of staircases, towers, archways, doors and grand statues. It was overwhelming to think about how many routes existed from this point. Frank guessed he was right at the heart of the monolith and could only wonder what treasures (or horrors) lay within.

"Welcome, friend," a voice boomed out from the shadows, startling Frank. He quickly whipped his pistol out and held it aloft, his hands crossed over so the torch could act as his line of sight.

"Who's there?"

"There is nothing to be afraid of, you can put that down."

"Show yourself," Frank replied, sweeping the area with his raised weapon.

The next thing he knew, there was a loud clap and a sudden, dazzling light. Frank covered his eyes instinctively with his arm. Then a split second later the light had faded to a more bearable brightness. Frank took a chance with his vision and gasped in wonderment at what he looked at, now fully revealed by the light. He was standing in an open space, which then merged into layer upon layer of golden architecture, containing a litany of structures that could be doors, paths or tombs. Frank stared in wonder at the gigantic statues that stood sentinel on either side of a wide, circular opening that was at ground level. They depicted human bodies, but like the carvings he encountered on his arrival to the pyramid, each had extra arms and legs. Then he noticed the man walking slowly towards him. He was tall, with dark features and tanned skin, wearing a simple tunic that looked like it belonged in a time far older than this. Frank aimed his gun again, dropping the torch and placing both hands on the pistol. "Hold it right there," he barked. The man stopped in his tracks and raised his arms submissively, smiling curiously.

"Are you one of the archaeologists working with Evan Jessup?" Frank urged.

"No."

"Do you know where they are?"

"Perhaps."

"Don't play games with me," Frank said, cocking his gun. "Where are they?"

"In there," the stranger gestured behind him. "But you can't reach them, not yet anyway."

"Boy, you better start talking some sense."

"Do you know where you are?" the stranger inquired. Frank

didn't respond. "You have stumbled into something far more important than you could ever imagine. What brought you here?"

This time Frank answered. "I'm looking for some people, perhaps you can help me find them."

"Ah, the man in black, yes?"

Frank's chest tightened. *Ulrich*. "Yes, have you seen him?"

"He passed through here, some time ago. Extraordinary fellow, very focussed, like he was doing something important."

"Where is he now?"

"In there," the man signalled casually behind him.

Frank holstered his pistol and walked forward, when suddenly his path was stopped by an an imperceptible force.

"What the..."

"I am sorry, my friend," the man said, walking closer to Frank. "But I cannot allow you to simply wander freely in here."

"Where exactly is *here*" Frank rumbled, still trying to pass through the unseen barrier with no luck.

"This is the Axis of Time."

Frank paused and looked at the man, raising a quizzical eyebrow. "The what now?"

The man chuckled in response. "There is so much you don't understand, so much to learn. But unfortunately, you shouldn't even be here, so I can't tell you much more."

"How about a name?" Frank asked, walking along the perimeter of the wall, which he couldn't see and probing the air with his hands.

"Zurman. That is my name."

CHAPTER FIFTEEN

A PIERCING HISSING sound broke the silence and snapped Joe awake from his slumber. He looked around in a confused state.

"Sorry," Zurman said. "Kettle boiled. Tea's ready for you, though," he finished.

"Nah, I'm good," Joe answered, shifting his bodyweight up from the slumped position he'd evidently been sleeping in on one of Zurman's very comfortable armchairs.

"How long was I out?"

"About an hour," Zurman replied, bringing through a tray of tea and biscuits. "Help yourself," he added, catching Joe's eyes immediately notice the sweets on offer.

Joe hesitated, but could resist no longer and devoured the food. He licked his lips and savoured every mouthful.

"These are from the nineteen eighties," Zurman stated. "Don't worry, they're fresh. I was in that decade only last week," Zurman added, catching Joe's look of concern.

Swallowing his mouthful, Joe was prompted to ask, "So, how does that work, exactly? You can just travel through time, nobody notices, and everything is a piece of cake?"

"Ah, not quite. I have very specific destinations I can visit at very specific times. There are things that have been in motion since the dawn of time. My job is to ensure that they happen, precisely as has been ordained."

"Or what?"

"Or, the world ends, just like it did originally. I was there."

Joe looked blankly at Zurman. "So, what, the world simply stops and you're able to time travel?"

Zurman chuckled. "Not quite."

"So, what, then? And what do I and this ball have to do with it?"

"The world consumes itself. An apocalypse wipes out almost everything. There are few survivors, many deaths. Everything is gone, except there is one last hope, this machine which was protected and buried several layers under the Earth's surface," he pointed to the bronze ornament which sat in the corner of the room.

"This is your time travel machine?" Joe said, his tone somewhat sceptical.

"Actually yes, it is."

"So did you invent it?"

"Me? No. This device is ancient beyond all comprehension. It won't be discovered in your present until a few days from now. Can you guess where it is?"

Joe's eyes grew wide. "The pyramid?"

"Yes, my friend, the very same. You discover it. But nobody can interpret what it does or its purpose. So it sits, idle in a museum for decades. Until it becomes activated."

"How?"

"That is where I step in. *I* activate it."

"So you're born in the future when it's in the museum already?"

"Something like that," Zurman said, smiling.

"How do you activate it?"

"Ah, Joe," Zurman leant back into his chair as he spoke. "There are many mysteries that we do not have time to go over right now. What is important is that this time, we're altering the future. Your golden orb, if you could be so kind?" He held out his hand, waiting for Joe to deposit the small object. Joe obeyed and handed the sphere over to Zurman, a part of him excited at what might happen, another side of him wary of this apparent time traveller. Zurman let the ball roll around in his hands, his fingers manipulating it as he thought silently.

"Inside the pyramid," Zurman began, "is a sort of key. It can unlock the potential to travel freely wherever one may choose. So, for me, it is before the apocalypse to warn everybody of what is to come and tell them how to stop it." He continued to hold the orb, Joe watching as he delicately turned the ball over with his fingers, his curiosity tugging at him to probe for more answers.

"So, have you tried to get in there before?" Joe eventually asked.

"Many times, my friend. The pyramid wouldn't accept me. So I had no choice but to leave and try again, in a different time. I did, and the same thing happened, I couldn't get in."

"Who built it?"

Zurman stroked his bearded chin. "That is a hard question to answer. None of us really know, we have theories, but nothing concrete."

"The Ancient Egyptians?" Joe suggested.

Zurman chuckled politely. "No, no. They were skilled, but something like this was beyond even their infrastructure and prowess. No, this is advanced, yet unimaginably old. Alien whilst still being so familiar."

"In your future, was the pyramid discovered by me?" Joe tentatively inquired.

"No, you were never in my future. Your name isn't known, nor your achievements. I'm sorry, I've no idea who you were before today." Zurman answered, his eyes not leaving Joe's. "As for the pyramid," he continued, "this wasn't discovered in my time either. Only after we made the discovery of *time* itself. It allowed us to see things that had been... missed."

"What you're saying then," Joe started slowly, "is that we can change the course of history in a major way, for the both of us?"

"Yes, that is correct. You can come back to your own present, armed with the knowledge of time. I can return to the future, stopping the end of the earth. Everybody goes home happy!" Zurman beamed, laughing. Joe cracked a smile as well, for the first time in what felt like an eternity.

"Alright, so where is the rest of this key, then?" Joe asked.

"Have you ever heard of the Forbidden City?"

△

Emperor Xing Bao sat peacefully in his chambers. Incense burned around him and all was calm. He exhaled slowly as he allowed his mind to empty, his daily meditation one of many rituals he strictly adhered to. Xing heard voices approaching and opened one eye with irritation. The next thing he knew, his space was filled with raised voices as his elite guards tried in vain to stop the trespasser, General Hang Ling, his first cousin.

"Unhand me, unless you wish to feel the cold steel of my blade!" Han cried as he shrugged off one of Xing's guards.

"Emperor," Han answered, bowing.

Xing held a hand up, the gesture enough to command his loyal elite warriors to stand down. "Leave us," he announced quietly. They obeyed, their red robes flowing as they swiftly turned around and closed the large oak doors behind them.

Han waited until the heavy door closed with a thud before speaking again.

"We have a problem."

"Enemies at our border?" Xing asked, rising from the floor where he was sitting cross-legged and coming over to Han, placing a hand on his ornate shoulder armour.

"In a way," Han replied. He looked at his cousin, his dark eyes mirrored his own. Xing's hair was long but tied into a topknot. Flecks of grey broke up the otherwise jet-black colour, which was mirrored in his thin beard, which had been groomed into a precise goatee. By comparison, Han's hair was clipped short and his face clean shaven, yet both men were not showing signs of their true age.

"What did you find, General?" the Emperor asked.

"Out in the forest, there was an unusual sound, a flash of light, and then it was gone. Several of my squads saw it, so I dispatched a group to search the surrounding area."

"And?"

"Nothing, at first. Then we found tracks. Made by two men, though one set were extremely odd. Like something from another world entirely."

Xing tensed up at this.

"You don't think...?"

"Yes, I do, my Emperor," Han started, "I think that someone is coming for it."

Xing didn't answer, instead turning around gradually to the beautifully decorated throne where he sometimes sat. Resting beside it was a large, golden staff, held in place on a ceremonial stand that allowed it to be admired from afar, but never touched. He turned back to his relative, speaking gently. "We must garrison the capital, prepare for an invasion. Nothing must be granted access in or out. We have supplies to last us for months, we will shut the entire city down. We cannot allow anybody to get close." Xing finished and removed his palm from his cousin.

"It will be done, my Emperor." Han bowed and placed a closed fist on his chest before swiftly turning on his heel and exiting. Xing walked slowly to his throne, his hand brushing the golden staff as he did, causing it to shudder ever so slightly with an unseen power. Xing relaxed into his throne and placed his hands together, the folds of his white robes billowing as he sat. He closed his eyes and prepared for what was to come.

△

"We must wait for nightfall," Zurman instructed Joe. "The city will probably be in full lockdown soon, if not already."

"They're expecting us?"

"Oh absolutely, they would have discovered our tracks and your shoes don't belong here. They know well that what they possess is not an ordinary object."

"Oh yeah?" Joe asked, walking throughout the small hut, his gaze lingering on a large bookcase.

"The Emperor has been holding it for some time, according to my research."

"How long?" Joe enquired, looking now at the various books that Zurman kept, some of them worn beyond belief, others as though they had been printed just today.

"Approximately ninety years," Zurman said.

Joe turned around, his mouth agape. "Ninety years?! He must be ancient?"

"That's just it, he's not."

"What do you mean?"

"He appears to be a man in his fifties yet has been on the throne for over a century."

"And nobody thinks this is strange?" Joe asked.

"They don't. They see him as their divine leader. He's revered like a God."

"Whatever this thing is, it's giving him immortality?"

"Yes, I believe so," Zurman began. "But, we're not exactly sure of its potential. The Emperor may have triggered all of its power or only a fraction. Similarly, the orb you possess, it will have some quality, a power, that we must try to discover before our assault."

Joe looked at the small orb with skepticism. "Really? It looks pretty unassuming to me."

"We may have to learn its secrets as we enter the city," Zurman said casually.

"Oh great, with the entire Chinese army on us?"

"Well, I never said it would be easy," Zurman replied with a smile.

"That makes it much better, thanks."

Zurman laughed before continuing. "Come, rest for a few hours. We'll wait until the middle of the night. I need to run some errands and gather supplies, you can relax here, you'll be safe."

"Alright fine, see you soon. If I'm kidnapped in my sleep, I'll kill you."

"Hey, trust me!" Zurman smiled as he left, disappearing into the rolling fields. Joe was suddenly left alone for the first time since this entire ordeal started, and he collapsed into the nearby armchair, which looked like it belonged during the Victorian era. He sighed and put his hand on his skull. "Tell me this is a dream," he whispered into the room. Obviously, no reply came, and Joe sat in the quiet, his thoughts now turning to Luisa. *Where was she?*

Joe dreamt. Vivid images of Luisa stuck on an island. Joe was swimming, fighting against the current, never getting closer.

"Joe!" she screamed as the island dissolved from the edges, closing in on her.

Swimming harder, Joe's head was totally submerged as he tried to desperately reach her. He resurfaced and found he was no closer to the island. But Luisa had gone. Joe bobbed in the water, frantically looking around for any sign of her. Suddenly she was right there ahead of him, her hair lankly hanging in front of her face and she opened her mouth wide as if to scream, but no sound came out. Joe scrambled away, and he was now on land, his feet sinking into the sand. Luisa kept walking to him, her mouth fixed open, three arms now protruding from her figure as a golden light appeared around her head. Joe closed his eyes, and he was suddenly back in the forest, but it was nightfall. He heard troops surrounding him and talking in Chinese, ordering him to surrender (he assumed). Joe placed his hands on his head, and then he felt a sword rammed through his stomach. He fell and kept falling, over and over again, in an endless loop.

Sweat formed on his brow as Joe violently woke up, breathing hard.

"Bad dream?" Zurman asked, crouching low over a bag of supplies.

"Yeah," Joe panted, "bad dream."

"Sorry to hear that. The good news is, it's nightfall and we need to move."

"Great." Joe groggily got to his feet.

"Here," Zurman said, tossing Joe a satchel. "Your equipment for the night."

Joe opened the bag, finding robes, rope, a grappling hook and "A knife?" Joe exclaimed. "Dude, I'm no killer, what do you expect me to do with this?"

"It's just precautionary. With any luck, we'll avoid detection altogether and nobody will even know we've been there."

"I admire your optimism," Joe responded.

"We have a secret weapon, don't forget," Zurman added.

"Which we have no idea how to work," Joe pointed out.

"Ah, details, my friend. All will be well." Zurman grinned and got to his feet, strapping his own bag across his shoulder. "Ready?"

Joe re-packed his bag and slung it across his back. "Ready as I'll ever be."

Zurman led the way and opened the door, allowing Joe to exit first into the darkness.

CHAPTER SIXTEEN

ULRICH KEPT RUNNING, he had to be close now. The door was only a few metres ahead, but it was shrinking in size the closer he got. "Come on!" Ulrich snarled as he quickened his pace, his footsteps thudding on the stone surface as the door became smaller and smaller. He checked himself short just as the opening disappeared entirely and merged with the floor. Ulrich slapped the blank wall in frustration at once again being too slow. His gloved hand ran through his blonde hair and he sighed, resigned to another defeat, which wasn't something he was used to. He walked back from whence he came and emerged on a platform, high above the open space courtyard at the centre of the pyramid. He'd been here for what simultaneously felt like an eternity and seconds. Ulrich had ascended several staircases to get to where he was currently and encountered dozens of hallways with doors similar to this. Each time they had rapidly reduced in size the moment Ulrich was within closing distance. He halted to catch his breath and looked down at the ground level once more. Upon his arrival to the brightly lit arena, he had seen a wide, circular opening at the base which he had avoided for the time being. He had a sneaking suspicion that going in there could lead to many unexpected results, so had instead sought to navigate the many, many layers of stairs, doors and hidden rooms that combined like a lattice to make up the inner workings of this chamber. At a guess, Ulrich assumed he was indeed at the Chamber of Awakening, or at least close to it. It would be there that the ultimate stage of his mission would take place, that much he knew. Getting there was proving to be a different matter.

Ulrich looked to his left and decided to pursue this avenue instead, as he hadn't tackled that route yet. He lined up his jump and leapt gracefully to an outstretched platform that connected to another set of openings. There were three in total, so he worked from left to right and started with the one closest to him. His footsteps echoed as he walked cautiously inside. Visibility was limited, so he attached his night vision goggles once more. A high-pitched whine greeted him as they activated and his sight was bathed in a green hue. Ulrich saw the detail of the corridor he was in. It was lined with patterns and intricate carvings, which depicted people praying to an enormous figure that straddled two islands with its feet. Ships were shown further up, carrying many tributes and trade, presumably from the city where this gigantic being was ruler. Up ahead, Ulrich noticed a wall of smoke that filled up the entire corridor. He stopped short, watching the smoke to see if it would come closer or spread. Curiously, it stayed just where it was, swirling around in a mesmerising pattern, falling yet rising at the same time. Ulrich hesitated. He didn't have any breathing equipment on him, and who knows what the properties of this gas could be? Deciding he could always return to investigate, Ulrich retreated and emerged into the open to try the middle pathway.

As soon as Ulrich entered, he heard a rumbling noise, and the ground sloped downwards so much that he lost his footing. He slid and was descending at an alarming pace, the corridor acting like a funnel leading to something that Ulrich knew he didn't want to find. Remaining calm, Ulrich detached his grappling hook from his utility belt and wrapped it around his wrist. He tossed it backwards behind him and hoped it would catch onto the entrance where he had just been, and luck was with him. He felt an immediate snag, and it halted his momentum as the iron spikes dug into the ground just outside. Ulrich was dangling for a moment, suspended only by the steel cable of his grappling device. He panted and controlled his breathing, when abruptly the pin slipped and Ulrich was once more thrown into the abyss.

Adjusting rapidly, he reeled in his grappling hook and flicked on his night vision goggles, at last being able to see whatever doom he was heading towards. In a flash of green, Ulrich saw the trap he was on course to fall right into: an enormous pit containing nothing but sharpened spikes. His eyes bulged and his heart skipped a beat as he rapidly calculated his options. There weren't many and time was running out. He looked up and spotted an opening, a tiny gap to aim for. It would require precision, skill and some more luck. Ulrich quickly prepared his device once more as his journey brought him closer and closer to the pit. He was only a few seconds away from plummeting to a grizzly death when he threw the hook directly up and it snagged at the last moment. Ulrich managed to arrest his momentum and hang precariously above the spikes.

Ulrich almost didn't breathe. He swung gently mere feet above the devious trap and delicately pressed the button on his belt that would reel him up to the grappling hook. The mechanism whirred and brought Ulrich up to the clearing. He didn't dare increase the speed as he heard the device scrape on the stone above. As he was almost at the top, the hook slipped and Ulrich's heart was in his mouth as he was dropped a few inches. He held his breath and waited, his fate literally hanging in the balance. The hook was apparently stable so Ulrich continued his ascent and at last, he could hoist himself up into the crawl space. He lay flat on his back, exhaling hard, never more relieved in his life to be laying on cold stone. He looked around. Ahead of him was a dead end. Behind him seemed to lead back into the opening where he had started. Ulrich calculated the gap, which was narrow enough that he could reach across with his arms and pull himself up. He performed this risky manoeuvre without hesitation and found himself back out in the open. Except he wasn't where he thought he would be.

Ulrich peered over the edge of the platform and instead of seeing the ledge where he had come in, he was now looking directly at a staircase which spiralled up. He craned his neck to see where it led, but it levelled out at a ceiling, blocking his view.

"How the hell?" he said aloud, searching behind him and seeing the same narrow crawlspace he had exited from. He shook his head, knowing that everything here was questionable and thought better than to think on it too hard, for it could easily drive him insane. Instead, he dropped onto the marble surface. He walked around to the side of the staircase and saw that there were even more doorways beyond it he could venture into. It was truly sinking in how utterly lost he could become here, especially with things changing on a whim. Deciding against the doors for now, Ulrich put a hand on the bannister and began to ascend.

After a short while, he reached the top and had a decision to make. He could go straight on, up a further flight of stairs which led to a huge opening, or he could take the solitary door on his left, which he couldn't see too far into. "I've had enough surprises for the time being," he said to himself, and walked ahead to climb the broad steps. Ulrich studied the engravings which ran along the curvature of the door. It was nothing he could make out, so he just hoped he hadn't walked into yet another trap or dead end. He was wrong on both accounts. Ulrich stood with his mouth wide open as he emerged into the cavernous space. He was standing on a balcony, which overlooked a vast, empty room that had burning torches lighting it up. The floor was pristine, it even looked freshly waxed and reflected the flames beautifully. All around him were enormous stained glass windows, depicting holy beings that bore some resemblance to the statues he had seen multiple times throughout this expedition. All signs pointed to one conclusion: Ulrich was standing inside a church. But was this the Chamber of Awakening?

He made his way down to the ground level and peered up, the ceiling disappeared into darkness as did the many large pillars that supported this mammoth structure. He could see multiple levels of balconies, with more entrances that zig zagged along the walls to his left and right. Then he saw them. At first they appeared like wisps of dust floating in the air, but as Ulrich focussed his vision and went nearer, he noticed they were hooded human forms. They multiplied and Ulrich found himself in the centre of a bustling crowd. He strolled up to the closest form and reached out a hand, which went straight through it. The entity had no recognisable features, it was just a cloaked figure with a hood drawn over its head. As Ulrich looked around, they all appeared to be the same. They kept arriving from unseen entrances and soon there were at least fifty of them. As if commanded, they all moved to form a circle, which Ulrich now found himself at the very centre of. Suddenly, he heard the creaking of a door opening in the distance.

Ulrich stood still, squinting to see the origin of the sound. He could make out a thin sliver of light that was blindingly bright, and it grew wider as the gates at the far end of the church opened. Those in the surrounding circle all got on to their hands and knees and remained motionless, the doors opening gradually further and further. Ulrich tried to see who, or what, was coming. He could spot an outline, but it was difficult to tell if it was one person or more. The gates prepared to close, so whatever had entered was now making its way over to him. Ulrich readied his pistol, checking the chamber and ensuring it was fully loaded. He felt his knife by his left thigh and knew he could reach for it quickly as well, if required. Ulrich kept his gaze focussed ahead, where he knew this new arrival would come from and waited. His breathing being controlled through years of strict training, though even he admitted to himself that he was slightly afraid. He raised his weapon and then he saw that there were three, just in range. Where the others who encircled him had a white form, these three were dark like shadows, unable to be seen at all, except for their outlines. They continued getting closer and then Ulrich heard a low hum, like a chant, swell from the crowd. He whipped his head left and right, watching as the robed figures on the floor started to raise their arms up in unison, their droning chant growing louder and clearer with every moment.

Ulrich looked again at the three figures walking towards him. He could make out that they were definitely human in shape and size, of unequal height and perhaps of different genders, but that was still too difficult to discern. One of them walked to Ulrich's left, another to his right, and the third stayed still, directly in front of him. The assassin turned to each character, warily watching as they took up their respective positions inside the circle. They didn't acknowledge he was there, though they stopped precisely in line with where he was standing. Ulrich gripped his pistol tightly as the figure ahead of him held up a hand. The others copied, and continued their chanting.

Deciding to take control of the situation, Ulrich tried to move, but found to his horror that he was frozen in place. He then noticed the tiny golden motes floating near and realised with a sudden dread that they had trapped him somehow. In a desperate attempt, Ulrich went to squeeze the trigger on his pistol, but his fingers did not respond. Beginning to despair, he could no longer turn his head and instead could only look straight, directly at the dark outline which was now walking steadily towards him. Ulrich's discipline taught him to stay calm under pressure, but this was something else entirely. He tried to work his mouth into a shout, cry, anything, but that too was impossible. The figure kept coming. The chanting became stronger and again Ulrich saw the golden flakes growing brighter. The shadowy person in front of him was only metres away, and it removed the hood it had been wearing. Ulrich could tell it was a male, but couldn't make out the details, the shining light around Ulrich flaring and sparking like an electrical current. The man walked closer, allowing Ulrich to notice his hair, precisely combed back. He watched the man reach out a hand, almost able to touch Ulrich's flesh, which caused him to panic for the first time in his life. The chanting grew heavier and the light brightened. The man kept approaching and then Ulrich saw, for the briefest of seconds, a piercing set of blue eyes as the features swam into view.

Almost as if in response, the light exploded with brightness and Ulrich's vision was robbed from him. He felt a great rush of wind and blinked as his sight returned to him, a cool breeze whipping around his face. His eyes adjusted to the new location and Ulrich Kaufmeiner realised he was suddenly very far from the pyramid in Dahshur.

CHAPTER SEVENTEEN

The large circular door split in half and peeled away, revealing a dimly lit lobby that was totally empty.

"Come," Zurman said, taking the lead and walking ahead of Luisa. She felt nervous, still unsure why, but followed in silence. The doors slid shut with a satisfying click as soon as they were both in, and there was no sound except for the faint hum of the blue light that hung from the ceiling. To their left was a corridor that was completely bare; exposed metal that looked rusted and weathered its only decoration. Ahead was a larger passageway, again nothing but blank steel, but it led to a staircase that was wide enough to fit four grown adults walking side by side. On the right was another circular opening that was sealed by a thick door. "Where does that go?" Luisa asked, motioning to her right.

"That? Absolutely nowhere. It used to contain one of our defence bots."

"Oh, what happened to it?"

"Same thing that happened to everything else," Zurman replied. "Let's go. Up ahead is all that remains of my world. It's not much, but it is home."

Zurman walked towards the wide staircase, and Luisa followed along silently. She expected to hear noises, perhaps a small enclave of settlers. But there was nothing. No sound. No people. Just a deathly silence. They emerged into a circular room the size of a basketball court. The ceiling was low and covered in a mesh that looked flimsy, though Luisa surmised it was probably far stronger than it appeared. In the middle of the area was a long, smooth metal table that stretched almost the entire width of the suite. There were no seats, but as she and Zurman approached, a pale blue light illuminated the table. There was a sudden whirring of machinery from inside the table itself. Luisa watched in amazement as two ends of the table came away and glided around to the front, hovering in mid-air. Then, with a hiss, they dropped steadily to the floor and waited patiently for their guests. Luisa stared at Zurman as they both approached the slabs of metal.

"Stand on it," he instructed. Luisa did as she was told, a slight feeling of trepidation building again. Nothing happened. Then Luisa looked down at her feet and saw they were *disappearing*.

"Zurman!" Luisa screamed as she tried to move, but realised she couldn't.

"Just relax," Zurman said, extending his hand to rest on her shoulder. She glanced back at him with fear in her eyes upon witnessing Zurman's body fade away as tiny blue dots worked their way around him until he was gone. Luisa came to the realisation that she was about to vanish just like Zurman had.

△

"Luisa? Luisa?" She heard a voice which sounded distant, like it was underwater. She opened her eyes slowly and saw Zurman's face close to hers. He smiled before speaking. "Ah, she's awake, great."

Luisa blinked a few times and realised she was lying on her stomach. She hoisted herself up to a standing position, using her arms and then took in her surroundings. They were in another area, much the same as before, however, this time there was no table. Instead, there were five large ornate chairs which looked like thrones placed at various heights within a circular infrastructure that encompassed the entire room. Figures in dark robes occupied each of them, all of their faces hidden by their hoods. At the centre of the room was a small circle, which had flecks of tiny golden particles drifting lazily up into the air.

"Zurman, what is this place?" Luisa whispered, not taking her eyes off the seated figures.

"This is The Last Table," Zurman answered, far louder than she was comfortable with. Turning to address the five in their thrones, Zurman spoke again. "This is Luisa. She is from the twenty-first century and possesses one of the lost artefacts." They remained seated and Luisa was still frozen in place, completely unsure of what to say or do next. Zurman declined his head towards her and said quietly, "walk to the middle and show them the stone." Luisa looked up at Zurman with fear in her eyes. He simply smiled kindly and nodded, stepping back to make her first move that much easier. Summoning her reserves of courage, Luisa tiptoed towards the dark circle in the centre. Looking to Zurman for assurance, he held his palm out to indicate that she should stop. She did, just a few paces short of the circle and reached into her pocket with a slightly trembling hand. Something inside her told her to run, flee this setting and never return, but she pushed these fears aside and slowly produced the blue stone she had taken from the pyramid. Luisa held the artefact in her outstretched hand, and she saw all five of the hooded figures lean forward in their chairs to get a better view.

"Girl," a voice said, barely above a whisper. "How did you come across this?"

Luisa looked back at Zurman, who again nodded slowly. She peered back to the five, unsure of who asked the question and spoke.

"I... we found a pyramid underground. It was strange, it wasn't like anything we had ever seen before," she stopped. Thoughts of Joe were swelling up inside her. She wished he were here with her now.

"What did you see?" A female voice this time rang out from the thrones, powerful and clipped.

Luisa regained her train of thought. "We saw carvings. Humanoid, but not. Then we saw it, an enormous pyramid. It was as though it had never been touched, yet absolutely ancient all at once. We had to run inside; we were being chased."

"Chased? By whom?" a third male voice asked. It sounded almost regal.

"I-I don't know," Luisa stammered. "He had dark clothing, blonde hair..."

"Blonde hair?" A fourth tone, another male, interrupted. Luisa placed his accent as hailing from the Netherlands.

"Yes," Luisa answered quietly. She heard whispers ripple between the five of them as they discussed something between themselves. Luisa patiently waited for the chatter to die down.

The last voice, a female who was softly spoken and sounded as though she were in her sixties asked, "What did you find inside the pyramid?"

"There were three paths. With more strange carvings above the doors. We tried to... tried to go together, but we couldn't... some sort of barrier," Luisa's voice trailed off once again. She desperately wanted to know if Joe was alright, if he had escaped the assassin. She felt tears sting at the corners of her eyes as her mind leapt to many conclusions.

"Girl," the first voice repeated. "Your companion, it was a boy?"

"Yes."

"It is written that he will find the second artefact. I am quite sure he is alive and well." The words were meant to be comforting, but it just opened up new avenues of questioning. *What did he mean, it was written? Second artefact? How many are there? What do they even do?* Luisa found her strength, that inner confidence and fire that allowed her to thrive in New York City after leaving Portugal, that same passion that made her one of the brightest students at high school and college.

"What do you mean, *it was written*?" she asked. Luisa heard Zurman's footsteps as he joined her in the centre of the amphitheatre.

"Your excellencies, forgive her, she does not know our ways," Zurman spoke, placing his hands gently on Luisa's shoulders.

She shrugged off his touch and continued talking. "No, answer me. What is this place? What are you trying to do? What does this do?" She held the blue stone out accusingly and waited for a response. Silence answered her for a few moments. None of the five wished to divulge further information, then, just as Luisa was about to give up hope, one of them stirred. The person rose from its chair, walked to the side, and descended the stony staircase, footsteps echoing in the empty space. Now, they were level with Luisa and Zurman, and approached them. Whilst the robes shrouded the person in mystery, Luisa managed to infer that it was a man who was coming to talk to them. He stopped opposite Luisa, on the other side of the circular hole in the centre of the room. Withered hands emerged from the folds in his robes, and he slowly pulled down his hood. Luisa couldn't help but gasp as she saw his features. He looked incredibly ancient, lines and scars ran deep across his face. He had no hair to cover his misshapen skull, his eyebrows too were almost faded, yet his green eyes burned with wisdom and knowing.

"You want answers?" His voice was a whisper, and Luisa recognised it as the first person who spoke to her.

"Yes," she replied, her confidence not as high as before.

"Then you must come with me," he turned and began walking towards the thrones, but Luisa watched as the stairs shifted and rearranged into a doorway and the ancient man shuffled through. She glanced up at Zurman, who had a look of surprise on his face, which she hadn't seen before.

"Follow him, I do not know what he will say, but perhaps he will give you the answers you seek."

"Aren't you coming?"

"He addressed you and you alone, I cannot attend," Zurman said. "I'll be here when you're finished."

Luisa opened her mouth as if to speak, but she turned on her heel and stepped around the circle on the floor to follow the man. She faced the arrangement of thrones. The four remaining figures all peered down at her, observing her every step. They reminded her of the ghosts her mother would tell her about in scary bedtime stories when she was a little girl, faceless and dark, without eyes yet always watching. Shivering, Luisa looked straight ahead and entered the blackness of the room.

△

As soon as she stepped foot inside, Luisa heard the stones behind her shift and realign themselves into a staircase. For a moment she was cast completely into darkness. Then a light appeared, bathing her in a yellow glow. She saw up ahead row upon row of books, all crammed onto shelves within enormous bookcases that seemed to stretch on forever. Luisa walked forward into the space from the narrow corridor she found herself in, and was relieved and awestruck as she strode into a vast chamber. All around her were bookcases and pathways between them. She could only fathom how deep the room was, Luisa scanned the shelves and watched them disappear into darkness.

"Welcome to the Archives," the ancient man whispered from her left. Luisa looked around and saw him approaching her from one of the many thin pathways that bisected the bookcases. He ambled slowly towards her. His demeanour was friendly enough, but Luisa was a little frightened of him all the same.

"Within this chamber is our entire history, past, present and some of the future."

"Who are you?"

"My name is Elder Alech, one of the last of our world."

Luisa hesitantly held out her hand in offer of greeting. "I-I'm Luisa Duarte," she said.

"Yes, I know," replied Alech, turning away from her hand. "Forgive me, I am too frail to risk contact with another, my best years are behind me, if you understand."

"Oh, of course." Luisa hastily lowered her hand before continuing. "So you knew I would be here? It's all written here, is it?"

"In part, yes." Alech walked slowly towards yet more rows of books, looking absentmindedly at the collection of great tomes as he spoke. "We knew that someone would discover the Golden Pyramid in your time, but we did not know by whom, or when exactly. When you entered, it created this," Alech pressed a small button on the side of the bookcase and after a few seconds, a plinth rose in the middle of the room. On it was a golden parchment that was shrouded in the same dust motes Luisa had seen in the Golden Pyramid's courtyard. She walked over to it and saw that there were symbols appearing, disappearing, and then reappearing.

"What is this?" she asked.

"This is the Scripture, it is recording the future as we speak."

"What, how? What does it say?"

"Ah, I can answer some of this. It is currently writing and re-writing millions of potential futures that can exist from your actions. It cannot, however, predict too far ahead, we're dealing in days, not weeks. Every movement you make can alter the timeline. Every time you eat, wash, laugh, anything can affect it. Of course, you are not the only one who has influence over this."

Joe. Luisa felt her heart leap with excitement. "Is my... is Joe alive then? He has another artefact?"

Alech's thin lips spread into a small smile. "He is, yes. And indeed, he is in possession of another piece of this grand puzzle."

"Oh thank God, where is he?"

"He is safe, he is being guided in the same way you are."

"You mean that you have more, like Zurman?"

"Zurman *himself*, is the guide."

Luisa scrunched up her face in confusion. "But how? He's out there waiting for me?"

Alech chuckled. "He can transition between time, don't forget. So he is here with you now in your present, but also with Joe in his."

"Right," Luisa said. "So, Zurman is helping Joe, that's good."

"Yes, but there is something else." Alech's face darkened, his smile fading. "There is another, who hunts you."

Luisa felt her muscles tighten. "Yes, the assassin, he tried to kill us. Why? Who is he?"

Alech walked even closer to Luisa, his already quiet voice now barely above a whisper. "He is a dark disciple of the Chaos. His mission is to bring about the collapse of your world, which would mean our future as well. He works in the shadows, but he is not operating alone. For centuries, there have been those forces trying to ensure this apocalypse in your time happens. We are now at the critical moment in history where one wrong move from either side can cause catastrophic results. If he were to stop you or your friend, Joe, then our worlds are doomed."

Luisa let this information sink in. It made sense now why this assailant had been chasing her and Joe, how he seemingly arrived from nowhere. "Is he one of the assassins who starts this whole nuclear disaster?"

Alech nodded slowly in response. "With your completed artefacts, you can allow us to properly navigate time, we can swiftly and responsibly ensure the survival of our world. Do you understand this? The importance of what needs to be done?"

Luisa gulped, the whirlwind that had been her life since discovering the Golden Pyramid had calmed. It didn't necessarily make sense why *she* was involved, but she had been chosen either way and she had to try.

"I do, I understand. Let's go, I need to get back to Rhodes."

△

Luisa and Alech exited the Archives and headed back inside the throne area. The four remaining figures were still seated exactly as they had been when she had left, and Zurman was waiting patiently in the centre of the room. Luisa smiled when she saw him, he was at least a familiar face in all of this madness. As she walked, she couldn't help but shake a nagging feeling inside her. Should she have spent more time in the Archives? Tried to read some of the information held there? Luisa turned around and saw Alech climbing the staircase, which now sealed the entrance of the Archives, and she doubted whether she would ever get a chance to be inside there again.

"Are you alright?" Zurman asked, puncturing her thoughts.

"Yes, I am. We have to move, time is running out."

"Elder Alech told you of the assassin?"

"Yes, and that you're guiding Joe! How is he?"

Zurman looked puzzled, before a wave of realisation came over him. "Ah, perhaps I have, but not in this current timeline."

"What do you mean?"

"I'll explain later. We must acknowledge the Thrones and take our leave." Zurman looked up at the five figures seated. Alech had now covered his face with his hood once more.

"Good luck in your quest, Luisa Duarte," Alech said.

"Thank you, I will not fail, *we* will not fail," Luisa added, looking at Zurman. He kept his eyes fixed on the figures and bowed his head slightly.

"You know what to do, Zurman," Alech finished.

Zurman was again silent, staring with an intensity back at the Thrones before he turned on his heel. "Come on," he stated quietly to Luisa. She followed and cast one last look at the five shadowy characters. She joined Zurman on the steel plate that waited for them, and within a few minutes, they were back in the circular room with the large table.

"Ready?" Zurman asked, unveiling his bronze instrument and firing up the contraption.

"I think so."

"Good, let's go save the world," Zurman said with a smile as a crackle of golden light spat from the machine. Within a few seconds, they had returned to Zurman's abode in Rhodes, ready to complete their mission.

CHAPTER EIGHTEEN

Joe ran, his feet hurting in the traditional sandals that Zurman had acquired for him. They didn't fit him correctly, but they were a necessity, as his trainers were too obvious. So too were his clothes, so Joe had swapped them out for a simple tunic. Zurman was ahead of him, their pace was unrelenting, but speed was their greatest ally right now, for the warriors of the Ming Dynasty didn't know when their attackers would be coming. Zurman stopped abruptly and held out a closed fist, signalling for Joe to also come to a halt. He skidded slightly on the loose soil and panted heavily, trying to catch his breath. Zurman turned around to face Joe.

"We're almost upon the wall, listen."

Joe strained his ears, and he could hear the idle chatter of troops as they went about their patrols. "How many do you think there are?" he asked Zurman.

"Could be any number. I suspect by now they've discovered our tracks where we first met and have some inclination we're on the way," Zurman whispered, crouching low.

"Excellent," Joe muttered.

"The element of surprise is not lost just yet. Come, the wall is directly ahead of us. We need to find the trade entrance for goods and supplies," Zurman finished, standing up slightly, but not at his full height. Instead of setting off at a run again, the pair moved with caution. Their view of the Great Wall was obscured, but the guards patrolling the perimeter could quite easily spot them before Joe or Zurman had any idea they had been seen, thanks to the high ground the Chinese troops occupied.

"Here," Zurman said, ushering Joe close to his side. "Look through this gap, can you see?"

Joe peered through the parting of trees and leaves and saw for the first time a glimpse of the iconic structure. The stone wall rose high above them. It looked like it had only been recently completed. Protected by scale mail armour were scores of soldiers armed with repeating crossbows which they carried loosely as they walked. Some had sabres attached to their hilt, though Joe suspected they would all have a sword on their person. He saw guards carrying spears walking back and forth and men hunched over pushing something unseen.

"What are they moving here?" Joe asked.

"Canons," Zurman remarked.

"So they have gunpowder then?"

"Indeed, they're really bringing out the big guns for us, if you'll pardon the pun."

"Oh good, I was thinking this was going to be easy!"

"Well, we can't be making things too simple now, can we?" Zurman answered with a smile.

Joe chuckled. He was starting to like Zurman, despite the insane circumstance of their meeting. He was quite confident that they could be friends in another life.

"Come, we need to move right. I believe one of the main gates is to our left, which would suggest that our entrance would be that way," Zurman nodded to the right, at more thick foliage and tall trees.

"Lead the way," Joe said, following in Zurman's footsteps once more.

△

General Han paced quickly along the ramparts of the Great Wall, overseeing the preparations for the city-wide lockdown. He stopped in front of a lieutenant.

"Report?"

"City is prepared to shut down, we have our units and scouts in defensive position."

"Very good," Han answered. "What of the devastators?"

"We have deployed them in the forest, orders to hunt and kill whatever is out there."

"How many?"

"Three squads, General."

Han nodded in silent approval. "Very good, in the name of the Emperor, this land shall not be touched." Han saluted the lieutenant and carried on making his inspections. His retinue of five warriors closely followed behind him in silence. Han paused, watching as the teams below closed the gates. The last few trade carts were snaking in to the Forbidden City along their designated routes and Han breathed out slowly. This was the calm before the storm, he knew that much, but he did not know what to expect of his enemy. The lack of intelligence put him slightly on edge.

△

"Wait, do you hear that?" Joe hissed, coming to a stop. Zurman also did the same a few feet in front of him and listened, hearing the thud of wood and metal doors closing as the Great Wall was shut down.

"Yes, they're locking down the city, we need to move, the trade entrance will not be open for much longer."

"Okay, let's go," Joe said, hurrying over to Zurman, who hadn't moved, and abruptly grabbed Joe's robes, stopping him in his tracks.

"Hey, what the..."

Zurman held a finger to his lips, his eyes widening as he overheard something else in the forest.

"Get down," he hissed, pulling Joe to a crouching position.

Joe was about to protest but then he discovered it too: footsteps, not too far away. He looked at Zurman, fresh panic in his eyes.

"They're trying to flush us out into the open, where we can be easily picked off by the scouts on the walls. Do you have that orb still?"

"Of course," Joe answered.

"Keep it ready, its power will be needed, whatever it is."

"But ho...",

"No time, come on, we must move!" Zurman said, and dashed to his feet, breaking ahead of Joe and moving with a renewed sense of urgency. Joe followed, not quite as smoothly, but he was up and running once more. Twigs snapped beneath their heavy steps, dust kicked up as they ran, but the moment for caution was over. They had to get into the city soon. Their pace quickened, the only sound was the thudding of their feet on the ground. Then, out of nowhere, an arrow whistled past Joe's face, inches from his head. Joe stumbled and slowed his run, caught completely off guard. He breathed heavily and was stood still for a moment. Another arrow emerged from the darkness, this one heading straight for him. At the last second, Zurman jerked Joe's left arm violently and pulled him down to safety.

"Are you alright?"

Joe nodded quickly, his eyes bulging with fear.

"We have been discovered. Come, stay close, we need to press on," Zurman instructed, heaving Joe up and setting off at a dash once more. Joe's heart thumped loudly in his ears. He didn't hesitate and continued moving forward. Voices shouted somewhere behind him, he couldn't quite determine the number, but he knew they were certainly outmatched. Zurman kept going and then ducked to his left as a sharp sword cut the space where his head had been seconds before. In one swift movement, Zurman unsheathed a curved scimitar and slashed upwards, cutting off the arm of his attacker. The man screamed and fell down. Joe hopped over him and kept pace with Zurman, who barely broke his stride. Another arrow shot past Joe's shoulder. He ducked instinctively but didn't look backward and instead kept running. At that moment, two blades attacked Zurman, this time, swiping at his feet and chest. Zurman's agility allowed him to leap and clear the blade that aimed for his chest, but his landing was awkward, and he rolled forward to try to keep the momentum going, when three attackers emerged from the trees ahead.

"Hold back, Joe!" Zurman shouted, holding his sword at arm's length as his pursuers circled him. Joe's heart thumped. He could sense the footsteps behind him gaining on him any second now and he was sure that they would feel dozens of arrows pierce their skin. Joe dug into the folds of his robes and found the sphere, the cool metal surprising to touch. He grabbed it and squeezed, not really understanding why but praying something would happen. It did. The orb changed temperature, becoming hotter and hotter until Joe could stand it no more. He dropped it on the floor just as Zurman was about to be impaled on a blade.

A blinding golden light pulsated out from the sphere in a flash and then there was nothing. A complete and total silence. Joe's heavy breathing broke the serenity. He searched around and gasped. The five soldiers that were bearing down on

Zurman and inches from killing him were frozen, their expressions fixed on Zurman. Their eyes moved wildly in their head and were filled with panic. It dawned on Joe that they had no control over their bodies, but they were aware of everything that was happening. Zurman slowly opened his eyes, unaffected by the orb. He looked first at his assailants and then at Joe and gave a cry of joy.

"You did it! Joseph Cullins, you saved us!" Zurman stood up, walked over to Joe, and hugged him tightly. Still grinning, he twirled his scimitar around his hand and, in a ruthless act of surprising cruelty, beheaded all five of the men that had surrounded him a a minute ago with one brutal arc. Joe watched in horror as their heads rolled to the ground, but their bodies remained standing, frozen by the mysterious power of the golden orb. He swallowed hard as he felt bile rise in his throat. Zurman turned back to Joe, his expression full of cheer.

"Shall we?"

Joe hesitated, unable to find the words to even answer Zurman at the moment.

"Joe?" Zurman repeated, still smiling.

"Yeah, yeah. Sorry, just not used to this, I suppose," he answered flatly.

"I understand, Joe, you're no warrior, but you are brave and you just saved us both."

"Yeah, you're right," Joe mumbled.

"We have a higher purpose here, Joe," Zurman said patiently. "There will be casualties, I'm afraid. Look behind you, they would have shown no mercy either," Zurman finished, pointing beyond Joe.

Joe turned around and gasped in surprise. Suspended in mid-air were four arrows, bearing down on where he had been standing only moments before.

"You're right," Joe repeated, his resolve strengthening. "Come on, let's find the carts."

"Wait, wait," Zurman instructed, stopping Joe before he bent down to pick up the orb. "We don't know what will happen if you touch it again. It might unfreeze everyone. Stay here, I'll scout ahead. I'll be a few minutes."

"Okay, yeah, that makes sense," Joe agreed, rising up. Zurman moved swiftly into the forest and disappeared, leaving Joe alone with the dead men and many more who were panicking just a few feet away, frozen in time.

△

Han watched in bewilderment as all around him his troops suddenly stopped all at the same moment. He turned back to his personal guard, who were also suspended in place. Han then noticed his fingers; they were decrepit and thin. He gasped and discovered his voice was hoarse, his breathing raspy. Panicking, Han tried to move and found his legs were resisting him. Pain exploded from his knee and he shouted in anguish, gripping it tightly. His toes felt as though they were seizing up, and he could only hobble. With a terrible realisation, Han knew that somehow, his body was showing its true age, complete with all the ailments that had gone undetected for decades. Han limped towards the nearest soldier, who had a reflective helmet and cried out in dismay. His face was ravaged with lines, his eyes were sunken, and his hair was merely silver strands. Liver spots dotted his skin, which was now almost grey. Then, Han saw it. The eyes of the soldier he was inches from were wide and moving. Han stumbled backwards in surprise and fell, the impact instantly shattering the fragile bones in his hip. He screamed out again in misery and writhed in torment. His warriors silently watched in horror as they saw their General literally falling apart in front of them, and there was nothing they could do to stop it.

△

Joe had vomited as soon as Zurman was out of sight. He heaved and breathed heavily as the remnants of his stomach emptied and he crumpled down in a heap on the floor, holding his head in his hands. Joe thought of all the times he and his brother Brad had played video games or watched television shows where they had seen people killed or murdered. It hadn't bothered them at all back then, yet the reality of seeing limbs severed and men taking their last breaths without a chance to defend themselves had struck a chord in him.

Joe vowed he would do whatever he could do to ensure that nobody else died unnecessarily during this expedition. There were fathers, brothers and friends doing their jobs here. He had arrived in their time, out of nowhere, and was now running riot through their reality. He looked at the golden orb nestled inconspicuously against some leaves and twigs. It pulsed with a gentle hum and Joe suspected Zurman was right: if Joe touched it again, the effects would be reversed, and they would be on the run once more. But how had it even happened? What had Joe done to trigger it? These thoughts swirled around Joe's head as he clasped his knees against his chest.

Closing his eyes, Joe could only think of one thought to calm him down. Luisa. He missed her. He wished they were doing this together, at least they could rely on each other as they always had. Through high school and college they were inseparable and back in Egypt, were just on the verge of their careers beginning at the same point. What a mess he was in now. Joe felt a lump in his throat as he longed to be close to Luisa, just to hold her tightly and forget about everything for a moment.

Zurman suddenly burst through the trees and into the

small clearing. Joe jumped and hurriedly stood up, dusting down his robes as he did.

"Hey, we're near to the gate, but it's closing - well, *was* closing until you did your magic," Zurman said.

"Sure, but soon as I grab this, we're gonna be stuck?"

"Well," Zurman answered before continuing. "I have a theory. I think if I touch it, nothing will happen. Shall we try?"

"Well, do we have a choice?"

"I like your optimism," Zurman joked. Joe found it hard to return the smile this time.

"Okay, let's go."

"Wait, you should get yourself here, right at the edge. If this thing goes off, run straight and then turn right when you come to the tree with an X that I carved into it. That will lead you all the way to the plains. We can reconvene at my house and come up with something else," Zurman finished, his usual confidence wavering slightly at the prospect of failure.

Joe obeyed and walked carefully around the severed heads of the soldiers, whose bodies were still upright thanks to the power of the orb. Zurman bent down tentatively over the object.

"Ready?" he called back to Joe.

"Ready," Joe answered, ready to turn on his heel and run.

Zurman moved to pick up the sphere and yelped in pain. "Ah! It's burning!"

Joe jogged over to Zurman and saw the welts immediately forming on his fingers. "Oh man, are you okay?"

"Yeah, I'm fine, just a surprise. Okay, new plan. Wait here, I'll check the path ahead and wedge the door open, I'll be back soon."

Joe nodded and looked down at the glowing orb, its power drawing him closer. He leant in close, and he could *feel* the energy coming from it. Without meaning to, Joe instinctively reached out, and before he could stop himself, his finger touched the orb. Joe inhaled sharply as he realised what he had done. "Oh no, no, no," he muttered, hoping that he hadn't inadvertently reversed the effects of the orb. Within seconds, Joe had his answer as he heard the five bodies of the headless warriors slump down to the ground behind him.

△

Zurman sprinted towards the trade gate just as the world sprang back into life and it almost slammed shut in front of him. He threw himself against it, acting as a wedge to stop it from closing completely. *What has that kid done?* he thought internally, grunting with the effort of keeping the door open. Zurman heard voices beyond the gate and acted fast. He unsheathed his blade and kicked the wooden door hard, feeling it slam against whoever was on the other side of it. He span around the frame of the entrance and killed the soldier at once. Zurman quickly looked around him and ducked behind a large wheel of an abandoned trade cart. Troops were running towards the doorway and shouting, gesturing for medical attention and backup. Zurman crept between large boxes and eventually found an opening where he could hide for the time being. He closed his eyes as he listened to the gate slam shut and realised that the mission was now in dire straits.

CHAPTER NINETEEN

Luisa and Zurman weaved in and out of the busy marketplace, careful to avoid lingering for too long and arouse suspicion. They ducked into an empty alleyway and took a moment to catch their breath.

"So, what exactly are we looking for?"

"A temple," Zurman replied, checking his surroundings frantically. "We need to move; time is running out."

"Do you know where you're going?"

"I suppose. There's no reference to this shrine, the Temple of the Colossus, it's called, in any history books, which means it is either a well-kept secret or…"

"Or what?"

"Or the scriptures are wrong," Zurman answered. "Come, this way leads to the harbour, we'll start there."

Zurman turned and moved past Luisa, who was growing increasingly frustrated at the lack of significant information being presented to her. It was feeling like a wild goose chase at this point. Despite everything Alech had told her and all she had seen; she was losing faith. She observed her surroundings again: an unassuming Mediterranean port. There was nothing extraordinary about the place, far less that a Colossus was roaming the area waiting for her to just stumble into him. She noticed a few passers-by look closely at her and heard whispers between them. Luisa realised she had been stationary for too long and needed to move with Zurman. Walking briskly and ducking her head, she pushed through the sea of people and followed the route Zurman had just taken. Luisa walked through narrow alleyways, her pace quickening as she realised with a panic that Zurman still wasn't in her sight.

Luisa emerged after zig-zagging for what felt like hours between narrow pathways into something that took her breath away.

"Woah," she muttered.

"Welcome to Rhodes," Zurman said, suddenly appearing to her left, making Luisa jump.

"Is that?"

"Yes, that is him," Zurman answered. They were both staring at the gigantic bronze statue at the opposite end of the bustling seaport. It twinkled as the early afternoon sun glinted off its spectacularly detailed body. The two feet were stretched apart, slightly wider than shoulder width and they were raised on plinths which were elevated higher than the walls that circled the harbour. Ships passed through this gap, the towering statue watching over each one silently. But what really made Luisa take note was the rest of the sculpture. It had three arms, one of which was extended directly up and holding a small object. *A stone*, Luisa thought. *This looks familiar.* From both sides, two arms pointed out with with an impossible straightness. One was gripping a rod, which narrowed at the tip to a fine point. The other held nothing, but his hand was flattened, so that the fingers were fully elongated, *just like the carving in Dahshur,* Luisa recalled.

"Magnificent, isn't it?" Zurman exclaimed.

"Yeah, it is, yeah," Luisa answered, still distracted by the realisation that this was the same image she and Joe had seen already.

"Do you see what he's holding?"

Luisa looked again to the vertical arm of the statue before retrieving the stone from her pocket.

"This?"

"Yes, I think so. So perhaps the Colossus is missing something. Look to your right, do you see?" Zurman said, pointing to the jagged rock formations that jutted out from the earth some distance away.

Luisa squinted, not really sure what she was looking for. "The rocks?"

"No, look closer."

"Is that a temple?"

"Very good, yes. This is where I suspect we need to go."

"Why?" Luisa asked.

"Because they do not mention it anywhere in the history books."

△

Luisa and Zurman began the arduous task of ascending to the shrine to discover what, if anything, was inside. Their trek had so far taken them an hour, and they were only just now at the base of the rocky formations. The sanctuary had disappeared from view. It was tucked quite far back into the geographic features, which looked more and more like they were deliberately placed there as a means to keep people out. *Or keep something in,* Luisa thought darkly.

"You've seen me climb before, Zurman, I'm not the best," Luisa said.

"There won't be much climbing, I don't think," Zurman replied thoughtfully, walking around in circles as he studied the rocks which were in front of them.

"Oh, so you've suddenly learned how to fly?"

"Not quite, but if you study closely, we don't even need to leave the ground."

Zurman ushered Luisa over and pointed straight ahead of him, seemingly at nothing but dirt, grass and of course more rocks.

"What am I looking at here?" Luisa asked.

"It's an optical illusion, look again."

Then Luisa saw it. The rocks were overlapping each other and at first, even second glance, they appeared to be a simple random formation that blocked any access. Yet as Luisa tilted her head a fraction to the left, she saw it: a direct path that climbed out of view and presumably straight to the temple.

"Quite a coincidence, isn't it?" Luisa asked.

Zurman laughed. "Yes, if you believe in such things. We know better though, don't we?"

"Well, whoever built this thing ensured that we would have a way in and out, so I'm expecting some more *coincidences* still to come."

"Very wise. Shall we?" Zurman gestured for them to leave and took the first step. Luisa followed and stepped foot on luscious grass that had been untouched for a while. The second she did, she felt the gem in her tunic pulsate.

"Hang on," she called to Zurman, who stopped and span towards her.

Luisa carefully lifted the deep blue stone out and studied in awe as she saw a haze form around it, making anything caught in its radius appear blurred.

"What's going..."

"Wait, look!" Zurman said, interrupting her. Still holding the rock, Luisa turned and saw back in the harbour a sudden flash of blue light explode quickly but then reduce in size. It came from the same rock the Colossus statue was holding.

Luisa and Zurman both stared in silence at the

phenomenon. There was no sound except for the gentle breeze rustling the long grass at their feet. Then they heard it. A deep booming noise arriving from behind them.

"The temple?" Luisa replied, fear gripping her and her eyes widening in shock.

Zurman, for once, was utterly speechless. He looked first to the stone, still in Luisa's grip and then back to the harbour of Rhodes. The blue light that had burst from the statue was now dwindling and almost invisible, but then the rocks shook again as they heard another thundering noise coming from within.

Finally, Zurman spoke. "We have to go in, hurry!"

He grabbed Luisa's free hand and pulled her along with him. She didn't protest and simply followed his lead. They snaked in and out of the narrow pathway, paying minimal attention to their surroundings and running as quickly as possible. The pace slowed a little as the path tilted upwards, climbing higher and higher until at last they emerged into a great clearing. Luisa put her hands on her knees and caught her breath as Zurman carefully studied the immense structure that stood across from them both. It was typical in design of the ancient Greeks; marble plinths supported a roof that was flat at the bottom, with two sides meeting at the top. Carvings were etched in the gap within the roof, but they were not those of Greek gods or warriors. They were different, looking completely out of place not only in this era, but at any point in time.

"Those are the same," Luisa said, still wheezing slightly from the run.

"What are?"

"Those markings. They were in the pyramid."

"You're sure?"

"Yeah, everything is. The statue, now these markings. It's all connected."

"Then what we seek is inside. Come, we have no time to

lose," Zurman insisted, drawing his blade and running towards the entrance.

"Wait!" Luisa shouted, but it was too late. She spotted the haze around the door and then with a sudden deafening noise like a thunderclap, Zurman was lifted off his feet and sent spiralling through the air by a great gust of wind. He landed with a thud and stayed motionless.

"Zurman!" Luisa shouted. He didn't stir, but Luisa saw the golden flecks of light spilling out from the opening of the temple. The enormous yet gaping hole was suddenly filled with dozens of tiny gold specks and then she heard it again. Another loud thud. Finally, she turned and rushed to Zurman's side. Dust marked his bearded face from the impact, but he otherwise seemed unharmed.

"Zurman," she whispered, lightly tapping his cheek with her hand. His closed eyelids moved slowly, and he opened them a little.

"That's going to leave a mark," he added weakly, coughing violently as he did.

"Oh thank goodness, can you move?"

"I think so." Zurman winced as he sat upright and coughed repeatedly, this time bringing up blood as he did.

"Zurm..."

"I'm fine, I'm fine," he insisted cutting Luisa off and standing up gradually. "We have a bigger problem."

Luisa whirled around and saw what Zurman was referring to. Emerging from the darkness of the sanctuary was a golden arm, it thudded into the ground with a slow and deliberate crash. Then Luisa watched in horror as the rest of its body followed, ducking to exit the gigantic temple where it was housed. The face was entirely smooth, except for a blazing blue stone sunken deep into where normal human features would be. The stone blurred the entire face of the giant and warped the surrounding space to also lose focus. Now the rest of the body followed, and the figure stood tall in the courtyard in front of the temple. Whoever had built the statue in the harbour had completely underestimated the height of the Colossus. It was at least double the size of the monument by the water. The three arms moved slowly, flexing their fingers as if needing time to adjust to being in use again.

Luisa's mouth was fully open, and she was again frozen to the spot. Zurman simply stared with grim determination on his face.

"That's what we need, the brother to your stone. Twins of power. Combined, they make one of the artefacts. Back to the harbour, we have to move, now!"

Luisa didn't answer. She just stared as this godlike being in front of her stood before them, completely silent and still. A simple robe covered its nether regions, the rest of its body was muscular, yet looked as though it were made from various alloyed metals. It was both living but impossibly smooth and machine-like, Luisa determined that its skin (if it could be called that) would be impregnable. Unlike the statue in the harbour of Rhodes, the Colossus was empty handed. It looked down at them, both the size of ants in comparison, and it moved one of its hands as it noticed the blue stone still held by Luisa.

"He wants it," Luisa breathed.

"Let him come," Zurman answered.

"Are you mad?"

"Just trust me."

The giant took a purposeful step forward, shaking the entire earth as his foot landed. Luisa wobbled and almost fell over, Zurman steadied himself and bent his knees.

"Stay there," he told Luisa, his focus fixed on the approaching deity. Another step. This time Luisa stumbled back, but nevertheless clasped the stone. Now the titan was close enough, so it reached down with the extra arm that extended from slightly above his waist. Its fingers stretched out and Zurman sprang into action, leaping onto the thumb and gripping tightly.

"Move!" Zurman shouted down to Luisa. She didn't need a second invitation and scrambled to her feet, running to her left and away from the clutches of the Colossus. Zurman plunged his knife into the arm of the giant and watched in horror as the blade broke instantly against the tough exterior. The giant didn't even look down and followed Luisa with its eyeless face.

"Go to the temple!" Zurman called.

Luisa adjusted her course and was headed for the entrance when an enormous golden foot crashed down in front of her, blocking her path. She fell back from the impact and dropped the gem as well. It tumbled away, making clinking noises as it rolled against the gravel. The giant shifted its focus from Luisa to the crystal almost instantly, moving with a sudden haste that surprised her. Zurman was clinging on to the arm of the Colossus as it swung around to try to pick up the blue stone.

"Luisa! The stone! Get it!" Zurman yelled, adjusting his stance so that he could leap to the other arm. He landed and clung on to the index finger of the second hand and dangled uselessly for a moment while he tried to hook his feet around the huge appendage. Luisa got up swiftly, ignoring the pain shooting up her right thigh, and sped over to the stone. She scooped it up in her hand and sharply turned back towards the temple once more. High above her, the giant finally turned its attention to Zurman, who had now worked to get a purchase on one of its forearms. Luisa kept running for the temple, she was only a few metres away. The opening was in complete darkness and she had no idea what was inside, but she surmised that there might be an object in there that could help her, or at least improve her chances.

"Get inside, quick! I need to go back," Zurman shouted.

"What do you mean, back?"

"My weapons are useless. I need to get something from my time that might work! I'll keep him distracted, just stay inside."

Luisa watched as Zurman let go, just as the giant was about to swat him away. Zurman fell several feet, but landed gracefully in a roll and sprinted for the path that he and Luisa had taken. The giant pursued, reaching down to grab the invader. Zurman sharply changed direction at the last second, avoiding the enormous digits of the outstretched palm. With a last look at Luisa, Zurman jumped through the gap in the rocks and disappeared from view. Luisa didn't hesitate. She ran inside the temple and was at once plunged into darkness. Frantically, Luisa swivelled from left to right, hoping either for her eyes to adjust or for some light to appear. Neither happened and she felt her heart thump in her chest faster as her panic began to set in. Joe's voice suddenly echoed in her head. *Just breathe. Count back from ten.* He had always known what to do to keep her calm. She let out a long sigh and started counting down from ten. She shut her eyes even though she couldn't see anything and when she reached the number four a moment of inspiration hit her. Her eyes snapped open and she took the blue stone out of her tunic folds. To her delight, a dull blue light radiated from it, enough to allow her to see her hand in front of her.

This brief moment of happiness was interrupted when a violent crashing noise came from outside. Luisa span around and saw the golden arms of the Colossus on the ground. It had smashed the courtyard with such force that it had split several rocks in close vicinity and had caused the soil to crack and crater. Luisa held her breath, wondering if Zurman had been under that impact. The giant slowly raised its arms out of view and then thudded them down again as it walked towards the temple. Luisa stumbled backwards and looked around in desperation. As far as she could tell, she was in a very empty space, seemingly only serving to contain this godlike being.

Looking down, Luisa watched as the haze surrounding the stone expanded, slowly at first, but it soon washed over her entire arm. The crystal itself glowed and pulsed, its light growing brighter with every passing second. Another booming sound echoed around the insides of the temple as the Colossus was making its way back inside. Luisa frantically glanced left and right, hoping to see something to help her. As the blue light coming from the stone grew, she could see that the inside of this temple was completely barren. Nothing to hide behind or use as a weapon. There was one way in and one way out. She dropped the stone when she heard a thunderous bang as the giant took another stride. Surely he would be inside soon enough and kill her. Meanwhile, the dropped artefact kept pulsating. The mysterious haze was flourishing and forming a bubble around Luisa. The featureless head of the giant ducked under the entrance first, the shining blue gemstone embedded in its head twinkling. His three arms lazily stretched outwards as he straightened to his full height. Luisa simply watched as she started to make peace with her last moments on earth. She noticed her vision appeared to blur and assumed it was from the fresh tears filling her eyes. She closed them, hearing another crashing sound as the golden deity took another step towards her.

Then there was silence. She felt goosebumps prickle along her arms and she opened her eyes slowly. In front of her was the giant, completely immobile, one hand outstretched and reaching for her, yet suspended, entirely still.

"Luisa," a distant voice called out to her from everywhere, yet nowhere.

"Who's there?" Luisa responded into the air.

"Lu-is-a," came the distorted reply.

Luisa didn't respond this time. She looked down at the

stone and noticed it was no longer pulsating a blue light. Looking up, Luisa saw a ghostly figure emerged from the shadows only a few feet from her.

"Wha-what the!"

"Luisa, do not panic, I..." A voice answered her, but faded into silence.

Luisa watched in a mixture of horror and intrigue as small white particles formed in the open, outlining the silhouette of a human, a woman to be precise. The features were slowly being pulled together, slender arms and legs, long hair, large eyes.

"Oh my God," Luisa exclaimed, recognising at last who was standing before her. She was looking at herself.

"Lui... I don't...have... mu.... ch.....ti..time," the ghostly apparition of Luisa garbled.

"What is going on?" Luisa demanded, holding her head in her hands.

"He..is... not... you... go... run... have... to...," the other Luisa spoke in riddles, Luisa simply stared at this phantom of herself in disbelief. The other Luisa raised an arm which faded in and out of reality, it was pointing past the giant back to the outside.

"St... sta.. statue.." came the single word at last. "Get.... to.... stat.... twin.... ston... stone...," then the second Luisa pointed at the blue gem on the floor.

Luisa realised what she was being told: get out of here, get the stone out of the statue in the harbour.

"Okay, I understand! What is this?" Luisa shouted, gesturing around her at the fog.

"G... go... go!"

Luisa stepped back, her doppelgänger vanished, the haze surrounding them both disappeared and the crystal on the floor pulsed once and then grew dim. More alarmingly, Luisa heard the Colossus move. It was a clumsy sound, as though dropping a fridge suddenly on its side. Luisa acted fast, scooping up the stone and rushing straight for the behemoth. She slid under its grasping hands and stumbled slightly, but carried on at full speed. She kept running and without looking back, emerged into the sun beaming down on her. Luisa made for the gap in the rocks, not daring to slow even for a second, and sprinted as fast as she could away from the giant and the temple, her only goal now to reach the statue.

Panting, Luisa arrived on the outskirts of the harbour, where to all its inhabitants, it was business as usual. Pleasantries were exchanged between traders and fisherman as Luisa got her strength back and continued quickly towards the far edge of the harbour. She entered one of the many alleyways that criss-crossed along the harbour and came to a dead end. Luisa turned around and saw a set of bright blue eyes narrow as they fixed on her.

"Luisa Duarte," came the greeting from the British man with blonde hair, as he raised his pistol to her.

CHAPTER TWENTY

Joe stuffed the golden orb into the folds of his robes and scrambled to his feet, setting off into a sprint as fast as he could manage. Around him, he could hear the confused chatter of the re-animated soldiers as they gathered their bearings. Joe kept running, wayward thin branches from the trees snapping as he hurled himself forwards. Shouts of instruction came from all directions, and Joe knew he was surrounded. He just hoped that Zurman had secured their way into the Great Wall. If not, this adventure might be over before it even started.

The trail was a small dirt track that barely stood out against the dense foliage, but Joe was able to follow it. Voices seemed to be right next to him, and Joe's heart was in his mouth. He felt as though he were running side by side with the troops, only kept apart by bushes or trees. The track opened up into a wider clearing and Joe had to sharply change direction to take cover behind a cluster of tall, thin trees.

Ahead of him was a collection of warriors, looking around closely for any sign of their prey. It was obvious that something was drastically wrong, and they were all on high alert. Joe watched as more men arrived, moving through the gate Joe assumed to be the entrance Zurman was suggesting. Joe was reminded again how close he was to danger as he heard footsteps running from behind, walking the same route he had been on mere moments ago. Taking in a big lungful of air, Joe attempted to hold his breath and do everything in his power to stay undetected. He crouched low and shuffled backwards, further into the woodland.

His stomach dropped as his heel cracked a twig in half, causing a loud snapping noise that drew attention from the guards on the path. They checked themselves and then spoke in their native tongue. Joe could just about see that they were wading through the bushes towards his position, and he realised they would catch him. Adrenaline took over and Joe sprang from his hiding place and took off to run deeper into the wood and parallel with the Great Wall. He heard shouts behind him and knew he was going to be followed, the only hope was that he could lose his pursuers and regroup at Zurman's hut.

Joe stole a backward glance as he ran and was comforted that nobody was in immediate view. Then suddenly he felt his arm being jerked violently to the right as he was pulled against a thick tree. A hand immediately covered his mouth, and Joe was captured. The initial shock lasted a few seconds and then Joe felt a wave of relief wash over him: it was Zurman.

"What the hell happened?"

"I-I don't know," Joe stammered, his breath coming in short, sharp bursts.

Zurman rubbed his beard, an expression of dismay lining his features. "I was inside, but it got crowded. Luckily I sneaked out just at the last second, but they shut the gate."

"I saw. What do we do now?" Joe urged, feeling more foolish by the second.

"Let me see. You have the sphere, right?"

"Of course."

"Hold it again, see if we can stop time once more."

Joe obeyed and produced the golden orb, clenching it in his hand. Nothing happened.

Panicking, Joe inquired, "Do you think it was a single use kinda deal?"

"I really don't know, I'm afraid," Zurman answered. "What I do know is that we must move. Come, we will travel east and find another entrance, I'm sure. Stay close." With that, Zurman turned and jogged, Joe kept close to him and prayed that the orb would work again soon.

△

Han gasped as he got to his feet. He suddenly felt life rushing into his lungs as though he had emerged from being underwater. All around him, his troops could move and several of them were looking at him in amazement. Han warily looked down at his hands and saw to his relief that they were "normal" again. He tentatively took a step forward and had no pain in his joints, and the hip he had shattered moments ago seemed to be fine. Han turned around to look at his personal guards. They all had a steely gaze in their eyes, but there was something else there, too. Doubt? Disbelief?

"Men!" Han roared over the din of noise of the units trying to reorganise themselves. At the sound of their General's voice, however, they all froze on the spot, much like they had done a short while before.

"You all know what you saw. Your eyes did not deceive you. Nor have I tried to delude you," Han began, talking and walking slowly as he connected with each soldier on the ramparts one by one.

"You saw my body as it should be, ravaged by time and plagued with injury. Yes, it is how I *should* appear, yet look how I stand before you. I am a man in his prime. I have fought with many of your ancestors and have seen some of you grow from a newborn, to a man, to my senior. It is whispered that my cousin, your Emperor, and I are descended from the gods." Han allowed a mirthless chuckle as he continued his explanation. "Alas, we are not. We do possess something of theirs though, which has allowed us to remain as you see me now." Han spread his arms wide as he spoke, but paused, choosing his next words carefully. "I believe, as does your Emperor, that we are being assailed by forces that know of this power and want to claim it. They too possess significant weaponry, or at least knowledge that we cannot explain. So, we must be vigilant. We must protect our Emperor and ensure our city does not fall. Is that clear?" Han stopped speaking, and a chorus of affirmation greeted his remarks. His men no longer looked fearful, but inspired. Han clapped a few of them on their shoulders as he walked past. Descending one of the access ladders, he waited for his personal guard to be close to him and out of earshot of anyone else.

"Make your way to the Emperor, tell him what you have seen and lock yourselves in there with him."

"Sir? Do you have no need of us?"

"My friend," Han said, holding on to his trusted sergeant's shoulder before continuing. "I need you now more than ever, but our Emperor is the priority. See that nobody gets in or out of his chambers. I will join you if I can." His troops bowed and quickly took their leave, allowing Han to be alone with his thoughts for the first time in a long time. And he was scared.

△

Zurman darted left, then right, ignoring the thousands of tiny cuts he was receiving from sharp pines or outstretched branches. Speed was essential, they had been discovered and the city was still heading into lockdown. Joe managed to keep pace, thanks largely to his athletic background, which had seen him compete for his high school in basketball and football. Yet Zurman's stamina was seemingly endless, and Joe was feeling more and more fatigued. Ahead, Zurman stopped abruptly, causing Joe to almost slam straight into him.

"Wait," Zurman breathed, barely holding his voice above a whisper. Joe obeyed and took the time to get his breath back, bending over and sucking in as much air as possible. The pair had stopped at what looked to be a random location in the forest, but soon Joe realised why Zurman had halted their progress; voices were heard and coming closer, too.

"Stay down, low as you can," Zurman instructed, lying flat on his stomach. Joe copied him, his face instantly getting covered with dirt, but he wasn't precious about that. He smiled, thinking how Luisa would feel if she were in his position. She wasn't afraid of getting her hands dirty, but face down in soil would probably be pushing it.

A door being slammed nearby brought Joe back to reality with a jolt.

"What was that?" Joe whispered.

"It's some good fortune - I believe we have our way in. Can you see it?"

Joe craned his neck to observe what Zurman was looking at and then saw it: a bunker protruding from the ground, two wooden doors sealing the entrance and being watched by just two guards. Joe returned his position before speaking again.

"Only two guards? Can we take them?"

"I can, stay here," Zurman answered, instantly rising and snaking between the dense foliage.

Joe waited with bated breath as Zurman advanced to the edge of where the small clearing was. In a split second, Zurman had darted from his cover, a knife flying from his hand and embedding itself in the guardsman to the left. Zurman was running to the guard on the right, his scimitar drawn and with a diagonal upward slash, it was all over in a matter of seconds.

"Come on, quick," Zurman waved Joe over before retrieving his throwing knife from the lifeless man on the ground, who had been the first to fall. Joe hurried out of his hiding spot before a moment of inspiration struck.

"Wait, their clothes."

"What about them?" Zurman responded.

"Let's take them. It might get us at least a few seconds more when we need them."

"You're right. Good thinking my friend."

Hastily, Joe and Zurman stripped the protective wear from their victims. There were blood stains on the armour that Joe was procuring, which he quickly wiped with the sleeve of the dead man's robes.

"Sorry," Joe muttered, the indignity of it all becoming more apparent. Joe tried not to look at the deceased and kept reminding himself that he and Zurman were doing this for the greater good.

"Ready?" Zurman asked, fully equipped with a plate metal helmet, breastplate, shoulder pads and shin guards.

"Yeah, the boots are too small," Joe stated, adjusting the rest of his armour accordingly.

"Leave them, this is only for illusion, really."

"Okay, ready as I'll ever be, then," Joe replied, taking a deep breath as Zurman flung open the doors to the underground passageway.

△

Zurman and Joe walked with caution as they followed the winding, dimly lit passageway that had been carved out under the earth. The only light source came from the flickering flames of sporadically placed torches that did barely enough to keep the darkness at bay. The tunnel itself was supported by wooden beams and joists, simple but effective engineering that kept it all from collapsing. Joe idly wondered how long this had been in place. Had it been constructed during the Ming Dynasty, or generations before?

"Are you sure this will lead us into the Forbidden City?" Joe said.

Zurman looked behind him, having to bend down slightly to avoid crashing his head against the top of the shaft. "Not positive, but what other choice is there?"

"Great point, I suppose. But if this leads us into an army of waiting guards, I'm not bailing you out this time."

"I'll bear that in mind," Zurman grinned, turning back to peer ahead. "Ah."

"What *ah*, that doesn't sound good?"

"Well, it's not the end of the world, we just have a decision to make."

Joe looked past Zurman and noticed the dilemma: two paths forking left and right.

"Well, what does your gut say?" Joe asked Zurman.

"My gut?"

"Yeah, instinct. A feeling."

Zurman laughed heartily, "Even now, Joseph Cullins, in the middle of the greatest adventure mankind has ever known, you do not lose sense of yourself. It is to be admired."

"Well, my mom always said *trust your gut* and it's worked out okay for us, ya know? So, when you saw this split, what was your immediate thought."

"To go right," Zurman answered.

"Then that's where we go," Joe replied, striding confidently past his guide and for the first time in the expedition, taking the lead. Zurman again smiled to himself, seeing just why Joe had been chosen by destiny to save the world.

△

"Any sightings?" Han asked one of his sergeants, as he moved briskly through the barracks on the ground. The Great Wall loomed menacingly over them all, but Han felt a great comfort being in its shadow. To him it was protection, it was security. Nothing could get past the perimeter, especially not here, the most important place in all of China.

"There have been killings, my lord," his sergeant weakly responded.

Han rounded on the man. "How? Where are the culprits?"

"They escaped, fled into the forest."

"Where were they heading to before?"

"The side entrance, with the trade carts."

"Clever," Han mused, "then perhaps they know our protocols and that we are locked down. We have successfully closed all entrances and exits, correct?"

"Yes, sir," the captain hastily said, not wishing to further disappoint his general.

"Very good, then we shall simply wait. They will either decide we are too impenetrable or try their luck. Regardless, they will not enter this city. Long live the Emperor."

"Long live the Emperor," repeated the soldier and with that, Han turned on his heel and moved towards the trade entrance Zurman and Joe had attempted to infiltrate only minutes ago.

△

"Quiet," Zurman hissed, stopping Joe's movement with an outstretched hand. Joe halted and listened, at first unable to detect any noise. Then he heard it, faint at first but growing louder with every second. Footsteps fast approaching.

"Oh sh...",

"We have to move," Zurman said, cutting off Joe's sentence. They broke into a run and travelled back the way they had come, to the fork in the road, now intending to take the path to the left.

"Joe, hang on a second." Zurman's run slowed to a jog and eventually a walk.

"What is it?"

"We need a plan; we can't just run into the city and hope for the best."

"I thought you had all that under control?" Joe questioned.

"I did until we had our one route blocked, plans change I guess."

"Yeah, but this is your idea. Save the world and all that stuff. I'd be quite happy to go back to Dahshur and get on with my life, thanks," Joe replied.

"Sadly, it doesn't quite work that way. Do you think you can get that orb to activate when the time is right?" Zurman asked, glancing nervously at Joe.

"I don't know, I think so, it seems to just work as soon as I touch it, but I haven't tried since."

"Well, now may be a good time, we've got company ahead."

Joe's eyes grew wide as he saw the four guards emerge from the darkness and step into the light given off by the torch hanging on the wall.

"Now, Joe!" Zurman cried, his scimitar already drawn.

Joe watched as the four soldiers noticed the trespassers. They sprang into action, drawing their weapons and sprinting over to him and Zurman. Joe quickly dug his hands into the folds of his robes, desperately looking for the golden orb. With relief he could feel it rolling around gently and at last he got his hand over it. Clutching it tightly, Joe looked up at his attackers rushing towards him and expected them to freeze instantly.

Nothing happened.

CHAPTER TWENTY-ONE

"So unfortunately, as you can see, there's nothing that can be done, as much as I'd love to help," Zurman said with a smile, though Frank doubted there was anything friendly in that toothy grin.

"Listen, son, this goes way beyond you and I, there's something far greater at play here if you..."

Zurman held up a hand, cutting Frank off. "You need not tell me of this, my friend. I realise what is at stake here, it is no exaggeration to say that all of humanity is at risk."

"What aren't you telling me?" Frank rumbled, pacing back and forth along the invisible barrier that separated him from Zurman.

"I'm afraid, Frank Williams, that is all I can say. Now if you'll excuse me..."

"Wait, wait, hold on there, son. All I'm askin' is for some information. What is this place? Who built it?"

"You're asking a lot, Frank," Zurman said cooly, turning to face the lieutenant. "But I'll provide you one answer. The Axis of Time was developed by those that see everything, have been everywhere and have infinite knowledge. There, does that satisfy your curiosity?" Zurman turned away from Frank before he could even answer.

"Hang on, how did you know my name?" Frank called out. Zurman didn't reply and simply walked into one of the many openings that were dotted around the bemusing and magnificent structure Frank was standing in front of. Uselessly, Frank tried again to breach the barrier, but found his path was blocked. So instead, he sat and waited.

△

"You understand this will be the most dangerous detail of your life. Expect the unexpected, do not engage unless you have absolutely no other choice, do you copy?"

"Sir, yes sir," the chorus rang back at Colonel Riggs. He acknowledged the five men inside his private quarters with a curt nod and walked out of his tent into the dark night sky of Dahshur. The Basin had swelled in size with many more units trickling in over the hours. Some were special operations, here to help with the proposed rescue mission that Riggs was leading on. Then there were others, all in black, that reported directly to General Hoskins. Riggs did not know what unit they reported into and didn't think he wanted to find out either. The General had been explicit in his wish not to be disturbed unless urgent, so Riggs had respected that. He checked his watch and noted the hour was 3AM exactly. Time to move.

"Alright gentlemen," he boomed into the noisy gathering just outside of the perimeter around the hole that Frank, Joe, and Luisa had disappeared into.

"Hey, do I look like a man to you?" called out a female voice.

Riggs nodded respectfully. "Apologies. Gentlemen and *ladies.*"

"Simple mistake to make Colonel, think her biceps are bigger than mine," came a crude joke from one soldier.

"Yeah, because I've actually seen the inside of a gym, unlike your scrawny, no good, trailer park trash be-hind!"

"Ohhhh!" The men whooped and yelled at this comeback, much to the amusement of Riggs.

"Alright, alright, settle down. This energy is positive. You're gonna need it, because we don't really have a clue what in the world we are dealing with down there."

At these words, the noise died down and everyone became acutely aware of the situation at hand.

"Missing persons," Riggs continued. "One of them, our very own Lieutenant Frank Williams. You all know him. Very good man, better soldier. Got a family to get back to. The first five troops you see walking over there will be point on this mission. For you six, your role is to provide backup, dropping into the void no less than five minutes afterwards. Do you copy?"

"Affirmative sir," the familiar cry filled the night air.

"Good, now let's go save some people," Riggs finished, clapping his hands. The soldiers fanned out instantly and joined their colleagues just outside of the hole. Riggs looked up to the top of the Basin and saw General Hoskins surveying the scene, his arms folded behind his back. Riggs scrunched his eyebrows together. Something didn't feel right, but he couldn't quite put his finger on what.

△

Frank sat up and uselessly turned his voice communicator on. A fizz of static greeted him and he sighed, putting it away. For once, Frank felt utterly alone and isolated. He always had his men or, when he was home, his family by his side. It was rare that Frank was allowed time to himself to reflect. He liked it that way. He'd seen too many men left alone with their thoughts and wind up dead; fixating on the horrors of war can do strange things to a man. He shuddered involuntarily, as some of the ghosts of his past swam in his mind's eye. Frank had killed several times over. Some with his bare hands, some at point blank with a pistol, and some with a sharp thrust of a knife. He'd never taken pleasure in any of the necessary acts of violence, but a vengeful spike of anger at the thought of ending Ulrich Kaufmeiner rushed through him. A man who had tormented the best of the best for months for no reason at all and had now seized two young kids hostage. *He would get what was coming to him*, Frank thought bitterly.

Frank's thoughts shifted to focus on the present, when he noticed several doors and passages moving ahead of him. His mouth hung open in awe as Frank watched entire columns of brick and stone rotate and displace themselves, like a jigsaw puzzle shuffling its own pieces. There were fresh paths where there had been nothing but air before, doors where there had been a blank wall. Frank looked down at what he assumed was the main entrance, flanked by the massive statues that eerily acted as silent guardians. There was no change here, even though Frank could have sworn he saw some tiny golden dots floating in the open.

"Dammit!" Frank cursed, thumping his fists against the invisible barrier blocking his path. He closed his eyes but opened them quickly as he heard a a slight noise, like someone had struck a metal triangle in a music lesson at school. Frank watched as ripples expanded out from where his hands were pressed against the protective shield. They kept spreading, like a pond when disturbed by a large stone hurled into it. Suddenly, the ripples stopped. The air seemed to settle, and Frank could see nothing else.

After a few seconds of holding his breath, Frank sighed and kicked his right foot out in frustration. His foot landed and

Frank was about to turn away when he realised that his foot was on the other side of the barrier. Cautiously, Frank reached out with his fingers and inched them towards where he had previously felt resistance. This time, there was nothing. Following through, Frank extended his entire arm out and again, didn't feel any force blocking his progress. Smiling broadly, he took a deep breath in and strode forward, feeling absolutely nothing blocking his way.

"Yes!" Frank exclaimed. He moved ahead a few steps and then looked behind him. To his amazement, there was a very thin rectangular outline barely visible where he had just walked through. Frank saw it close up and gulped, realising that it could well trap him. Testing his theory, Frank stepped back a few paces to try to put his arm through the barrier and found that once again there was some unseen force blocking his motion.

"Well, guess there's no other choice but to go forward," Frank said aloud and took strides towards the giant entrance on the ground floor, flanked by the mysterious statues.

△

General Hoskins watched as the first unit launched their plunge into the hole. They were going to abseil down using a steel cable, which would be secured to their utility belts and upon successful landing, were to signal up for the rest of the strike team to follow. Hoskins observed as the first of the team went, followed swiftly by another, then another, until all five were down. He reached into his inside pocket and once again pulled out the old mobile phone, dialling the only number in the contacts list.

"They're beginning their descent. How are we doing for time?" Hoskins pursed his lips as he listened to the answer.

"Good, the pieces are moving. It will shortly be our

moment. What about the spare? Ensure it is taken care of."
The General clicked the phone off and continued to survey the
Basin, content that everything had been proceeding according
to plan. Generations of preparation would soon come to a
glorious conclusion, and at the thought of this, Hoskins
cracked a rare smile. It wouldn't be long now.

△

"Well, where do you think you're going?" Zurman announced, sitting a few levels above Frank and appearing from out of nowhere.

"Seems that I do have access," Frank replied curtly, continuing to walk forwards.

"Yes, that is rather puzzling, I must admit."

"Didn't your crystal ball tell you?" Frank muttered.

Zurman chuckled. "No, not this time. Guess it must be broken. What do you hope to achieve, may I ask?"

"I just want to find these kids, get them back to their lives and stop their families from worrying."

"Do you even know where you are? Look around, this is so far beyond any mundane rescue mission. You, my friend, are treading within the very fabric of time itself."

Frank stopped walking to finally acknowledge Zurman, who wore a satisfied smirk on his face. "Son, all of that is way beyond my pay grade. I'm down here to find one man responsible for a whole lot of damage. If you don't mind, I will be stepping through that entrance and getting a first-hand look at whatever it is you got over there."

"Be my guest, Frank Williams. I will not stand in your way." Zurman jumped down from the platform he was on and landed one level above Frank. "Be warned, though, you may not return from this journey. Those who venture inside, rarely do."

Frank looked up at Zurman, whose eyes glinted with an

unusual sparkle. Was it malice? Was it laughter? Frank didn't care. "I owe it to many to at least try. I'll see you on the other side, Zee."

Zurman's lip curled into a smile. He watched Frank Williams disappear into the darkness of his own fate, and he knew it would be the last time he ever saw him. Zurman walked towards the nearest door and retrieved something from his robes, studying it carefully as he too disappeared into the void.

△

Frank felt the air drop a few degrees in temperature the second he stepped into the vast emptiness of the chamber he now found himself in. There was a small fire flickering delicately ahead of him. It was enclosed within a circular plinth that was filled with strange stones that seemed to shine with a golden hue. Frank could scarcely make out the details of the vast room before him, but saw gigantic pillars lined up on his left and right, supporting some unseen ceiling or level above him in the darkness. He could have easily put his torch on, but something was telling him to keep walking towards the fire and ignore everything else.

Slowly, Frank approached the basin and could see that the rocks inside were indeed golden, glowing gently in the light of the fire. He dared to reach out and touch a rock. The flame itself seemed to respond, and it flared up in warning, startling the lieutenant. Frank hastily removed his finger and walked carefully around the circle, intrigued but slightly fearful of the fire. He couldn't explain it, but he had the feeling as though the flame was *watching* his every step. Out of nowhere, fire licked out and lashed Frank on the arm. He retracted it instantly, yelping out of instinct, but realised that there was no pain. It wasn't hot. Another flame reached out, landing on

Frank. This time he didn't move. The spark just sat against his skin, not burning. Without warning, the small tentacle of fire burst into a million pieces, which circulated around Frank's body. He was frozen by the suddenness of it all, yet all he could do was watch as he witnessed his limbs become totally consumed by the blaze. The fire then advanced to his face. Frank panicked and looked around, but before he knew it, the incessant fire completely blinded him. Frank screamed, though he again couldn't feel anything. The next sensation to disturb his senses was as though a strong wave had swept him up at the beach. Frank shut his eyes, unsure why he did so, given that he couldn't see, anyway.

A few moments passed, and Frank felt like his feet were on solid ground. He shifted his weight and felt like he was standing on soil or gravel. Taking a deep breath, Frank opened his eyes to find himself staring at a blonde man dressed all in black. He was pointing a gun directly at a young woman in a narrow, cobbled alleyway.

CHAPTER TWENTY-TWO

Joe stared in disbelief as the soldiers kept charging him and Zurman. He clutched the golden orb in his hand and thrust it forward, expecting something to happen, but nothing did. Panicking, Joe backed away, but Zurman leapt into action. He twirled his blade skilfully and parried two attacks meant to decapitate him. With a powerful punch he broke a man's nose, then ducked as an enemy sword clanged loudly off the wall where Zurman's head had been a second before. Snarling, Zurman thrust his own weapon deep into the side of one attacker and pirouetted away from the fight to recover a smidgen of space. There were three men still standing, and they huddled together, cautiously inching forwards towards Zurman.

"Now would be a great time to get that thing working, Joe!" Zurman exclaimed.

"Yeah, trying my best here. It didn't exactly come with an instruction manual!"

"Forget it, take this," Zurman said, tossing a small blade on to the ground behind him for Joe to pick up.

Joe stared at it blankly for a second, then hurried to pluck it up as the soldiers began their assault. Two of them rushed Zurman and there was an instant clashing of metal on metal as swords collided. One warrior broke off from the pack and ran past the skirmish towards Joe. Realising this, Joe quickly stuffed the orb back into his tunic and picked up the dagger with trembling hands. He clutched the weapon tightly as he watched his attacker close the distance between them in seconds. Joe saw the malice in the other man's eyes, the intent to harm, *to kill*. Joe was frozen. A rabbit caught in the headlights. He didn't know which way to go, or how to defend himself from the attack, or anything. He watched as his enemy pulled his sword back, ready to slash Joe in half with a diagonal strike, and all Joe could do was stare as his life was about to end.

Uselessly, Joe held his dagger up to protect himself from the incoming blow. He winced and closed his eyes completely, preparing for the inevitable. Nothing happened. Joe opened his right eye a little and saw the attacker in front of him, suspended in place. For a second, Joe wondered if Zurman had saved him, but then Joe saw him still fighting off the two other soldiers. Then he realised: *the orb*. Joe reached inside his clothing and once again retrieved the object. It was now glowing and had apparently affected only the man who was trying to kill him. Joe looked in amazement from the sphere to the guard, who was watching Joe, his eyes filled with fear and panic. Joe took one last look at the frozen soldier and ran past him, straight into the thick of the fight Zurman was embroiled in.

A sword lacerated Zurman's left arm, and he cried out in pain, dropping his guard for a second. It was just long enough for the other attacker to find the opening he needed, and he could thrust his blade into Zurman's left shoulder. Zurman fell back, his left arm rendered completely useless. He feebly held off the attacks with his one good arm, but he accepted it would only be a matter of time before he was defeated. Zurman felt a slash across his right leg, the deep wound instantly making him drop to a knee. He blocked another blow that was destined for his neck and another straight after that, but the third strike lifted his scimitar straight from his hand. Panting, Zurman looked at his attackers as they moved in for the kill. They had no mercy in their eyes, and they raised their weapons high.

Zurman closed his eyes, ready to accept his fate. He had failed. He did not know what implications this would have in the wider course of events, but he knew that this was not ordained. One warrior let out a cry of victory and Zurman prepared himself for the inevitable, but it never came. Just like Joe had done only moments before, Zurman cautiously opened his eyes and saw to his confusion that the soldiers were completely fixed in place, their eyeballs moving rapidly in a state of panic.

Joe walked past the two men, frozen in time, and grimaced when he saw his wounded companion.

"You figured it out then?" Zurman said, wincing as he tried to stand up before collapsing in a heap on the floor.

"Not really, it activated when my life was in danger, I was a dead man."

"So was I, a little help here?"

Joe hoisted Zurman up, the latter using the wall to support himself.

"Are you okay?" Joe urged, immediately regretting the phrase.

"Well, I've been better," Zurman replied flatly.

"Yeah, sorry. I mean, can you walk? Are you hurt anywhere else?"

"They have stabbed me in the shoulder and cut me badly in the same arm," Zurman announced, signalling at his left arm with his head. "I should be fine, but we need to hurry."

Joe watched as Zurman tried to put weight on his legs and winced as he saw the pain etched across Zurman's face.

"Can you make it?" Joe asked tentatively.

"I think so, but we have to move fast. Not only is time running out, but there will be more guards and we don't have the strength to keep fighting."

"You're right. Come on, we got this," Joe declared, throwing an arm around Zurman and helping him hobble forward, whilst leaving their three attackers suspended in their state of being for the rest of time.

△

Emperor Xing welcomed the royal guard inside and greeted them all by name, bowing as he did.

"Thank you for coming, you do a great service to your country and your Emperor."

"We are at your disposal our lord. What would you have us do?"

"I am certain that we will be found, sooner rather than later," Xing said, the words causing a few puzzled glances to be shared amongst the soldiers. "Whilst our defences are fearsome, this day was always destined to happen."

Xing walked slowly towards the golden staff that rested on its ornamental platform. He unfurled a small roll of parchment, which was inscribed with dark ink and had mysterious markings all around its border. However, written clearly in a language he could understand was a simple message.

"I read to you the words delivered to me, when I received this divine gift." He cleared his throat and continued. "At the hour of change, will come your end. What has always been will be undone and what has yet to be, will transform. Your time will cease, but our time will take place. Your part is over. Go with peace. Do not fear the next life, for you have served in this as a being of divinity and glory. For the One."

Silence followed the end of the transcript. Xing carefully rolled up the parchment once more and sat down on his throne.

The captain of the squadron finally spoke. "My Emperor, what does this mean?"

Xing smiled. "I honestly don't know, but only that somehow, deep down, I have always been ready for this day. We will fight a glorious last stand, my brothers. Send for Han, I need him here with me as well."

Bowing, the captain delivered instructions to two of his men and they were sent back out into the night, rushing to General Han. Emperor Xing simply sat in his chair and waited for his destiny to come, unsure of the form it would take.

△

After hobbling along together for what felt like hours, with multiple stops along the way, at last Joe and Zurman arrived at the end of the underground tunnel and were face to face with a wooden ladder underneath a trapdoor.

"So what's the plan, push the door open, rush in and hope this little ball protects us?"

"Something like that," Zurman answered with a grimace as he sat down to catch his breath. He'd torn some of his tunic and tied it into a makeshift bandage to stem the bleeding in his leg and was checking on the wound as he spoke. "I'm fairly sure this will take us into the heart of the Forbidden City, meaning the Emperor's temple and the artefact won't be too far out of reach."

"I'm guessing we won't just be allowed to walk straight in, though, right? Plenty of guards and searches I'd imagine."

"Well, perhaps. But we may be lucky in that they focused

their attention on the perimeter. We have the advantage that nobody knows we're down here and I don't believe they would have counted on us coming this way. Why would they?"

"There's only one way to find out, I guess. Ready?" Joe asked, his foot already on the bottom rung of the ladder.

"Lead the way, you'll probably need to pull me up," Zurman said, forcing a smile.

Joe nodded and climbed as quickly and quietly as he could up the short incline. He gently pushed against the wooden door above his head, but it didn't move at all.

"It's blocked," Joe hissed.

"Push harder," Zurman called back. He shuffled forwards, wobbling slightly as he stood and climbed.

Joe bit his lip and put a bit more force behind his upward thrust. A little bit of give.

"Okay, I'm going to push really hard this time. Ready?" Joe whispered. Zurman signalled back with a thumbs up, and Joe turned his focus to the door and silently counted down in his head.

Three... two... one... with a grunt of determination, Joe forced himself into the trapdoor as hard as he could with his shoulder, and it flew open dramatically, crashing down onto a stone surface loudly. Chickens clucked and flapped their wings noisily in surprise and Joe waved them away as he climbed up into a a shed. Looking around quickly, Joe surmised it was safe and ushered Zurman up. Joe dangled his hand down and helped him ascend the last few steps. Zurman clapped Joe on the shoulder with a big smile as he investigated his surroundings.

Limping towards the entrance of the barn, Zurman watched as the morning sun rose, blood red in colour. He leant on the wooden structure and called Joe over.

"See that?"

Joe followed Zurman's finger, which pointed at a large

temple in the distance. Joe thought they designed the roof like a Christmas tree, three tiers which grew smaller as they got higher.

"That's where we're headed, right?" Joe assumed.

"Correct. Well, it's my best guess. It's the Emperor's temple. It's where he eats, sleeps and breathes. He only ever leaves it once a year, ushering in a new start for the population."

"You think the artefact is with him?"

"Oh, I know it is," Zurman answered.

"So how do we get there?"

"That isn't as easy to answer. Originally we were going to arrive somewhere over there," Zurman began, waving his hand over to the right. "But now, we've arrived a lot further south than I anticipated. We need to be smart. They locked the entire city down, people will notice us skulking around."

"So, do we wait for nightfall again?" Joe offered.

"No, that's going to be too late. We need to be *back* before sundown, otherwise we'll miss our exit out of this time and hence, our chance of saving everyone and everything we know, to be blunt," Zurman answered, concern spreading across his dark features.

Joe was silent for a moment, processing the continually evolving mess he was in. After a minute, he spoke. "There must be something we can do with this. Properly I mean?" Joe asked, holding out the golden orb.

Zurman pondered the question. "May I?"

"Sure, go ahead," Joe replied, handing the curious object over to Zurman.

Joe watched as Zurman silently studied the golden ball, turning it over several times in his hands and narrowing his eyes as he tried to twist and pry it open, to no effect. Sighing, he resigned to giving up and handed it back to Joe.

"I'm sorry, Joe, it really doesn't appear to work for me. But you said it seemed to activate when you were being threatened?"

"Yeah, I mean, one minute there's a guy running at me about to stab me, the next minute he's frozen still, and this thing is glowing."

"Interesting. Perhaps it is linked to your emotions, the stronger they are, the greater the response. Obviously you were scared in the forest as well?"

Joe glanced down, hiding his embarrassment. "Well... erm, yeah, I was."

"It's okay. In fact, it may be the key to helping us. Let me try something," Zurman finished, hobbling closer to Joe.

"What are you- ow! What the hell!" Joe reacted as Zurman punched Joe's arm.

Zurman looked down at the orb. Nothing. Sniffing, Zurman adjusted his stance and back handed Joe across the face.

"Yo! Dude, not cool!" Joe exclaimed, rubbing his face. Before he could say another word, Zurman's palm slapped him hard again, this time causing Joe's lip to split. Joe touched his index finger to his bottom lip and looked at the fresh blood. His eyes then slowly worked their way to Zurman.

"Alright, you better just back up!" Joe spat whilst walking closer to Zurman. The second the words left his mouth, something suddenly catapulted Zurman into the side of the barn, the impact shaking the entire structure and provoking the many chickens to cluck and panic.

"Oh my... I'm so sorry, are you okay?"

Zurman stood up and, to Joe's surprise, was laughing.

"Your emotions Joe! You were angry! Look at the sphere!"

Joe did and saw that the small golden ball was pulsing, radiating a tiny haze of red mist around it. Breathing faster, his eyes grew wide with the realisation of the power that he held in his hands.

"It actually worked," he breathed.

"Yes!" Zurman cried, ecstatic that his experiment had paid off. "Sorry about the lip, though," he added sheepishly.

"Huh? Yeah, it's fine," Joe answered, still staring at the orb, enchanted by this newfound power.

CHAPTER TWENTY-THREE

Frank didn't hesitate. He charged into Ulrich Kaufmeiner, the man he had been hunting down for so long now. Ulrich turned at the last second and fired off a shot. The bullet ricocheted noisily off of the stone wall behind Frank as he scooped Ulrich up and slammed him down with a hard tackle.

Luisa was frozen to the spot, watching the fight unfold between these two men who seemed to have appeared out of thin air. She watched as the blonde-haired man struggled with the assailant, who was wearing a U.S. Army uniform and a realisation dawned on her: the person dressed in black was the attacker from the pyramid. He had followed her across time and was clearly intent on killing her. Finally, she ran, and she skated past the men tangled on the floor, desperately trying to get her bearings and head for the harbour and the statue of the Colossus.

Ulrich heard Luisa hurry past, and with a sharp kick to Frank's stomach, pushed the lieutenant just far enough away from him to scramble to his feet and watch Luisa disappear behind the corner. Gritting his teeth, Ulrich set off in a jog, but had his legs swept aside with a powerful kick from Frank.

Ulrich landed hard, the shock of being so easily grounded making him gasp almost as much as the impact. Frank was swift. His movements were more in line with someone half his age, and instantly he was applying a choke hold on Ulrich. The assassin felt Frank's large forearm tighten around his neck and an unusual sensation crept up on him: panic.

A sharp elbow was driven hard into Frank's stomach. He coughed and grunted, but didn't relinquish his grip on Ulrich. Not now, not after everything, all the lives he had taken. It was time for him to pay. Ulrich clawed at Frank's arm with his fingers. His face was turning purple and his eyes were bulging with fear. With a last gasp of effort, Ulrich shifted his entire bodyweight to one side and turned them both. With this sudden movement, Ulrich wriggled out of Frank's powerful grip. Ulrich was hunched over, trying to catch his breath, when Frank's fist crashed into the side of his face. Ulrich fell to one knee, fresh blood filling his mouth as Frank approached for another attack, though Ulrich reacted quicker this time. He dragged Frank to the floor using the lieutenant's own momentum against him and locked Frank's arm into place.

Instantly recognising the danger he was in, Frank swung his free elbow back as he pivoted his body to get a better angle. The force of the blow caused Ulrich to release his hold instantly, and both men were momentarily breathless on the floor, the short but intense battle taking a lot out of them both already. Ulrich, however, was the first one up within an instant had launched a barrage of throwing knives at Frank, who rolled swiftly to his right and narrowly missed being impaled by the sharp daggers. Frank sprang to his feet and drew his pistol at last, releasing the safety and firing at the oncoming Ulrich, who was bearing down on him with determination. The shot missed, the bullet embedded into the wall behind them and Ulrich punched Frank with such force that the latter was sent spiralling to the ground, blood pouring from his shattered nose.

Maintaining the advantage, Ulrich mounted Frank's back, instantly placing a thin piece of steel around Frank's neck. He pulled, choking him and cutting into his throat. This time it was Frank who felt the intense fear of air struggling to reach his lungs. He clawed desperately with his hands, fingers digging into the clay on which they fought. Frank spotted a small rock just out of the corner of his eye and frantically made for it, willing with all of his might to grab it. His fingernails scraped it and with an almighty push, Frank fumbled the rock into his palm and in one swift motion, threw his hand back, catching Ulrich on the side of the skull with the stone.

Both men again collapsed in a heap, breathing hard, blood congealing around fresh wounds. Frank coughed violently, holding his neck with his left hand. Ulrich nursed the fresh cut on his head, his blonde hair now tainted with an ever-growing crimson patch. During this brief moment of respite, they both heard voices approaching as confused onlookers had gathered, investigating the source of the noise. Ulrich watched as the residents of Rhodes studied him, bewilderment and fear in their eyes. They looked at Frank and then back to Ulrich, talking in hushed voices and backing away slowly. Frank stared at the bystanders with equal confusion. Their clothing was unlike anything he had seen before. Then he realised. He was in an entirely different time, let alone place.

Ulrich seized his chance, as more people spilled in from various side streets and alleyways, and Frank became distracted, he hurriedly took to his feet and pushed through the cluster, searching for the girl he had been so close to stopping only moments before. Frank came to his senses as he saw Ulrich disappearing through the crowd. He took to his feet a little too hastily and his vision blurred momentarily. Shaking it off, Frank set off in pursuit, the eyes and words of the natives following him as he went. Frank clumsily bounced off a building as he rounded the corner. He suddenly felt very dizzy and glancing down, found a plausible reason. Embedded in his thigh was a small throwing knife, one of the cluster that Ulrich had launched at him.

"Son of a..." Frank grimaced, noticing the trail of blood he had left behind him as he advanced. Inhaling deeply, he gripped the handle of the weapon and yanked it swiftly out of his skin. He cried out in pain and threw the knife to the side before sliding down the wall and resting on the ground. Reaching into his utility belt, Frank retrieved the bandage inside and wrapped it around the wound. He winced at the soreness, but fastened it securely and gradually stood up, applying gentle pressure on his leg. A sharp pain ran up his thigh. Frank tilted his head and closed his eyes, grunting through the discomfort. Breathing out again, he finally started. A few awkward steps at first but soon breaking into a light jog, anxious that he was losing Ulrich.

△

Luisa felt as though she were going around in circles. The marketplace where she and Zurman had travelled through was nowhere to be seen. The harbour seemed like a figment of her imagination and she was totally and utterly lost. She leant against the side of a house, catching her breath. Her mouth was dry, and she realised how thirsty she was. Instinctively, she reached to her hip where her water flask would have been had she still been on the archaeological site in Dahshur. She snorted, shaking her head as the strange reality she was living in was brought back to her. Luisa touched her forehead; beads of sweat had formed from a combination of the hot weather and the sheer amount of running she had done. It felt like she hadn't stopped for a moment since climbing that awful mountain, and fatigue was really settling in. Passers-by walked through the alley where she was standing, some of them glancing at her with quizzical looks, but most paying her no attention.

What if I stayed here? Luisa thought absurdly. She was growing tired of having to constantly be thinking about the future, saving the world, and all that came with it. *Why not hide away, start life anew here? It seems peaceful enough*, she considered. Well, that was, until she had arrived with Zurman. *Where the hell did he go, anyway?* A flash of anger punctuated her plans. She felt truly abandoned now, caught up in the middle of something much bigger than her. Luisa felt her mind wander farther and her concerns were on Joe. It had only been a few days, yet she felt like he had been away from her for a lifetime. A wave of sadness washed over her as her thoughts trailed off to the inevitable question of whether she would see him again. Equally, Luisa realised just how much Joe meant to her and if it was something she had truly considered before.

Luisa turned as she heard rapid footsteps approaching, feeling her heart leap as she saw a man appear around the corner. He studied Luisa with a look in his eyes that made it clear he meant her no harm.

"Dahshur?" he suggested, a slight southern twang in his accent.

"Yes," Luisa answered slowly.

"Oh, thank God, have you seen anyone else come through here who, er, doesn't fit in?"

"No, I've just stopped to catch my breath. The other guy, he's trying to kill me, and he has been since..."

"The pyramid? Yeah, I was there too," the man added, coming closer. "Lieutenant Frank Williams, very glad to meet your acquaintance, Miss..?"

"Luisa Duarte," she returned, extending her hand out, which Frank shook firmly.

"Ms Duarte, I hope you don't mind me saying, but we need to get all the way out of here. I don't even know where here is, come to think of it."

"We're in Rhodes, sir."

"Rhodes, huh? What about *time*? When is this all happening? 'Cos it sure as hell doesn't look like two thousand and twenty-one."

"No," Luisa agreed. "Judging by the architecture, clothing and the fact that the Colossus of Rhodes statue is still standing, sometime around two hundred BC."

"Go-lly, well, we require a minute to really digest all this but for now, if you'll come with me, we have to find somewhere safe."

"We do, but I need to get to the statue, it's kind of the end of the world if I don't," Luisa answered.

Frank looked her over and quickly surmised that she was being honest. "Okay but we gotta move. I don't know where he's got to, but he's looking for you, that's for sure."

"Alright," Luisa nodded, taking in Frank's full appearance. His shaved head was glistening with sweat. There was a light stubble on his tanned face but despite his rough and imposing figure, Luisa thought he had kind eyes. Then her gaze noticed the bloodied bandage wrapped around his leg.

"Don't mind that," Frank said gruffly as he stepped past her, the slight limp in his walk now clear.

Luisa did as he asked, and hurried to catch up to him.

"Um, Mister Williams, sir?"

"At ease, call me Frank."

"Okay, Frank, well, I think we need to get you changed, you're kind of easy to spot, no offence."

Frank stopped and smiled before speaking. "You know, you're absolutely right, come on…"

The loud crack of gunfire cut the words short as a bullet missed Luisa's skull by millimetres. There was screaming from the locals as they ducked and covered their heads. Ulrich bared his teeth, taking aim again from where he stood. He was at the other end of the crowded alley and his window of opportunity was closing rapidly.

"Get down!" Frank bellowed, hurriedly cradling Luisa's head. Alarmingly, he could feel his fingers sticky with fresh blood.

"Are you hit?"

"No, no, I'm fine. Just shards of stone, or something. I'm okay," Luisa repeated, the colour draining from her face as she felt the blood from the back of her head drip down to her ear.

"Move!" Ulrich shouted, shoving aside two onlookers who fell down in a heap. He aimed his pistol and pulled the trigger. The tiny gap between the huddle of people meant he had Luisa in his sight, giving him a window of opportunity. The bullet whizzed past her, missing her by a fraction.

Frank and Luisa ran, keeping their heads low. They were weaving in and out of bodies, all of whom were running in various directions. The confusion of the loud noise attracted some to come towards the scene and investigate the disturbance, making progress difficult not only for Frank and Luisa, but Ulrich too. People stared as Frank bustled past them, his uniform marking him out so clearly as its greens and browns clashed with the cream and beige of the town's walls and buildings. Ulrich drew just as much attention with his all-black clothing. People were equally fascinated as they were afraid, and he had no qualms in using violence to move anyone out of his way.

Another bullet cracked loudly as it hit the stone behind Frank. This time he was the target, as Luisa was being held low and out of sight.

"Son of a..." Frank cursed, daring to glance at the menacing sight of Ulrich bearing down on them. He was still far enough away that he couldn't get a clear shot, but they couldn't keep up this game of cat and mouse forever. With a jerk, Frank pulled Luisa into a narrow side street, which was thankfully free of people. Frank's eyes darted around as he continued running, finally finding what he was looking for: a wooden door. Stopping suddenly and hoping that Ulrich was still out of sight, Frank barged into the door and landed, shoulder first, on a cold stone floor, Luisa also crashing into him. Standing over them were a family of three, a woman cooking a broth in a large pot and a man and young boy playing with toys.

For a moment there was a stunned silence between them all. Then Frank acted fast and bolted wooden barricade shut, pressing his back against it. He put a finger to his lips, signalling silence, and prayed that they recognised the gesture. It seemed to work as everyone remained motionless, probably more from the shock of these sudden trespassers forcing their way into their home, Frank surmised. Then he heard it. Footsteps approaching outside, the ground crunching with Ulrich's boots as he ran. Frank slowly drew his own pistol and kept his body firmly against the exit, ready to open it if necessary and blast his enemy away. The footsteps slowed down and stopped. Frank breathed in hard, looking hastily at the others inside and again motioning for them to be quiet. He heard Ulrich take a tentative step. He was clearly looking around for a sign of where Frank and Luisa had disappeared. Frank shut his eyes for a second, praying that he hadn't splintered any wood or caused any noticeable damage to the door. Ulrich took another step. Then Frank's breathing tightened as he heard a weapon being reloaded. Frank looked down at Luisa, who was sitting with her back against the wall and his eyes said, *don't move a muscle*.

At last, Ulrich moved away and carried on in his pursuit, his pace gradually quickening from a walk to a jog. Frank finally breathed a long sigh of relief.

"Are you alright?" Frank asked Luisa, helping her to her

feet.

"I am, what about them?"

"Oh, right. How's your Ancient Greek?"

"Not the best," Luisa answered, now turning to the still shocked and silent family. "Thank you. We are sorry," Luisa mouthed the words with added exaggeration, and she was met with blank stares.

"Thank you," Frank mirrored, declining his head and holding up a hand apologetically.

"Let's just go," Luisa said quietly.

"Good idea, stay behind me and keep close." Frank opened the door slowly, wincing as the hinges groaned in protest. He looked both ways and, satisfied that the coast was clear, opened the door fully, ushering Luisa out. With a final awkward bow of apology, the pair left and were alone in the alley.

"Okay, we need to get ourselves back, I guess, to the pyramid?" Frank spoke.

"Not until I've been to the statue, that's the whole point in being here."

"Right, where exactly is that?"

"The harbour, but I'm so lost," Luisa admitted.

"Let's go back this way and see if we can find our bearings. Come on," Frank instructed, turning and head backward to where they had come from.

He walked a few paces and then paused.

"What the..."

"Frank?!"

Luisa watched in panic as she saw a haze appear around Frank's body. It slowly obscured portions of his legs and then crept up the rest of his body.

"Frank! What's happening!"

"I don't know," Frank replied, fear creeping into his voice as he struggled desperately to move his limbs.

Luisa attempted to grab Frank's arm, but her hand went straight into an invisible barrier. She looked into his eyes with fear and confusion.

"I-I..." Luisa tried to speak.

"Don't worry Miss - I'll be back for yo..." With that, Frank's frame was entirely consumed in a blurry haze and the next second he was gone. Luisa was all alone again in Rhodes.

△

"Sir, the first team has made it down, proceeding ahead as assigned."

"Very good," General Hoskins answered, a satisfied smile creeping across his face. "Send the rest," he directed over the communication array.

"Roger that, sir," Riggs said, and Hoskins watched from his position above the Basin as all the pieces on the board moved. It was almost time.

Hoskins walked back into his private tent and once more retrieved the old mobile phone from his pocket. He dialled the solitary number and waited patiently for the person to answer. There was no response. Hoskins scrunched up his face. He wasn't worried, but it was unusual. There had never been a missed call in all this time. Almost right away, his phone rang, and Hoskins immediately answered.

"Has it been done? Is the spare taken care of?"

"There's been a slight delay, but he will be out of our way soon enough," the male voice on the other end of the line spoke.

"Do not disappoint me, we are very close now. There can be no mistakes," Hoskins said curtly, and with that, clicked the phone shut as he watched the men and women below moving just as he had planned. The best of the best were ready to find the Golden Pyramid.

CHAPTER TWENTY-FOUR

The rising sun cast a mysterious light over the Forbidden City. The mixture of pinks, reds and oranges made the place feel to Joe as if it were from another planet entirely. Walking slowly next to Zurman, the pair crept forward, moving as stealthily as they could between buildings. The city, Joe realised, was more than just a military stronghold, as he had once considered. It was filled with very normal houses, farms and barns, like the one they had emerged from only a short while ago. However, despite this, the Great Wall rose ominously around them, a constant reminder that they were trapped inside. Their mission coming was at a crossroads. They needed to complete it as soon as possible or risk being captured and tortured for information. Joe shuddered at that last thought, he'd read about how vicious the Ming Dynasty could be with their enemies and he very much wanted to avoid that fate.

Zurman tapped Joe on the shoulder, stirring him from his dark thoughts.

"See that?" Zurman said, pointing up at a wooden tower in the middle of the road. The structure stretched fairly high into the sky, though it still didn't draw level with the top of the Great Wall.

"The watchtower?"

"Right. Do you think you can climb up it?"

"What, are you kidding? There's going to be someone in there, surely?"

Zurman nodded solemnly. Speaking slowly, he asserted, "Yes, there will be. But this is where we need to put into practice what can be done with that special object of yours."

Joe looked quickly down to his robes, where the golden orb was concealed.

Zurman read the anxiety on Joe's face and spoke again, his hand resting firmly but with a friendly touch on his shoulder. "You can do this. That orb listens to you. It was meant for you. Think of something that makes you mad, really concentrate as you're climbing. You need to get enough rage that the reaction causes the guard to be knocked down unconscious. Can you manage it?"

Joe hesitated before answering, really not sure if he could.

"Can you do it, Joe?" Zurman repeated.

"Yes. Yes," he finally answered.

"Good. The vantage point will give us our best chance of getting to the temple so we can retrieve the missing piece and get ourselves home. Sounds good, right?"

"It does. Okay, stay here, your leg is too unstable," Joe added, shuffling forwards with his gaze fixed upon the tower.

"Okay and Joe?"

"Yeah?" Joe answered, turning around.

"Remember you have the knife, in case things go bad."

Joe simply nodded in response. The thought of having to use a knife on someone made him feel very uneasy.

Joe scuttled along the ground, keeping his body low and his movements quick. He kept the tower directly in front of him and took a very direct approach, practically walking in the middle of the path between the households that flanked him. Joe was gambling on the residents not being awake yet or being too busy with their morning routines to notice him. His idea being to close the gap to the tower as soon as he could, in order to be in the blind spot of the lookout. In a few minutes, Joe was right where he needed to be and directly below the tower. He pulled the golden orb out from his pocket and studied it. There was a slight glow around it. Joe wondered briefly if his heart rate was causing it to pulsate the way it did. Joe stuffed the sphere into his pocket and checked his surroundings. At best, he knew he had maybe minutes before the townsfolk would start to leave their houses, so he didn't hesitate. He climbed up the ladder athletically, jumping up the first five or six rungs and quickly adjusting his grip to latch on to the steps to begin his ascent.

Blood was pounding in his ears, his adrenaline was spiking, and with each step towards the top, he tried to focus his mind on something that made him angry. *That time my brother got his shop window smashed by thugs. No not powerful enough.* Another step. *When my last girlfriend dumped me. No, she was awful anyway.* Two further rungs climbed. The platform at the top was getting excruciatingly close. *Luisa. Luisa being hurt, Luisa alone facing all of this. When Luisa broke up with Devante.* Joe's mind was racing through these thoughts, but none of them were deep enough. But something struck a chord with Luisa and Devante. *Luisa and Devante. Together. Them being a couple? I didn't like it. I got jealous. She... she should be with me, why not me? Why did she pick him?* Joe was at the summit before he even had the chance to realise, and he pulled himself up. Staring at him was a a guard, alarmed that there was an intruder. In one rapid motion, Joe stood up straight and, with a last surge of jealousy, gripped the golden orb tightly. A crack like a whip exploded in the air and the soldier was violently thrown back with such force that the wooden rail at the top of the tower splintered and broke, sending him hurtling down to the ground, where he landed with a loud thud.

Joe rushed to the newly punctured hole he had created and peered down. He saw the body and at once turned away, crouching low on the floor with a lump in his throat. Gulping hard, Joe remembered why he was here and how each second was precious. He stood up to his surprise, saw that Zurman was shuffling along the trail below, and almost within reach of the fallen soldier. He grabbed the man's leg and dragged him unceremoniously to the side, out of view of the many who would busy the street in no time at all. His breathing finally slowing down, Joe gripped the edge of the railing tightly and looked around. Behind him was the Great Wall. Plenty of soldiers going about their patrols, engaging in conversation and looking out to the vast forest beyond where Joe and Zurman had begun their assault. Instinctively, Joe ducked a little to avoid being detected and turned his gaze, searching for the three-tiered roof of the Temple. He spotted it quickly enough, the morning sunrise glinting behind it, making it appear even more grand than it was. Joe continued to survey the landscape and discovered that there was a winding pathway leading up to the shrine, which ended at a giant set of wooden gates. Four men that Joe could see stood guard, though he suspected there were more.

Sitting down, Joe breathed in and collected his thoughts. The orb felt hot in his robes, so he retrieved it and discovered, to his surprise, that it had turned a slightly darker shade. Where before it had been a smooth, golden colour, it was now tinged with a darkness that seemed to spread from an unknown source. Joe put it away and reflected on the jealousy he had suffered at the peak of his climb. He couldn't believe it. He had always been so happy for Luisa and Devante, his two best friends being together, what wasn't to love? *Everything*, he thought with bitterness. Joe let his head gently fall against the wooden tower as he came to terms with the truth: he had feelings for Luisa, genuine feelings and always had. Did it make him a bad person? No, but Joe couldn't shake the sense of guilt that accompanied this revelation. Strangely, Joe could't shake the feeling that he had somehow betrayed Devante, even though he knew nothing of how Joe felt or how he was feeling right now.

"As if things weren't complicated enough, I'm in love with my best friend," Joe said aloud. Shaking his head, partly in amusement and a little in bewilderment. He realised with a jolt that he had to move and get out of there. Zurman was probably waiting for him down below and they needed to evade the morning crowds. Joe scrambled to his feet and looked down. Too late. Doors were open, neighbours were chatting, and people were filling the path. Joe looked with wide eyes at the scene below and at once realised a horrible truth: he was trapped. He frantically searched the platform he was on; there was a crossbow resting against the railing, some bolts, and not much else. A pair of binoculars lay discarded on the floor, along with remnants of a meal the guard must have had last night. *Did he know that was the last thing he would eat?* Joe thought, a fresh wave of guilt rising within him.

Disturbing him from these thoughts were the loud conversations going on below, apparently right beneath him. Joe peeked over the edge and watched a few of the people picking up the splintered wood and examining the ground more closely, discovering to their horror the blood stain of the soldier. Joe watched as a man called over some of his comrades. They pointed to the ground and then, out of nowhere, directed a finger up at the hole Joe had created. Joe fell out of sight and pushed himself back with his feet, dragging himself along the floor. He felt his heart thumping faster and faster, knowing that he was going to be caught within a moment, that it would all be over, and that he would never see Luisa again. The last thought surprised him; even at a time like this, it was Luisa who came to his mind. With fresh awareness, Joe quickly retrieved the orb from his pocket and saw that it was glowing with a golden hue again. *Fear stopped the soldiers in their tracks before* Joe thought. Concentrating hard, Joe imagined a life where he was tortured, maimed and worst of all, never able to see Luisa again. Focussing harder, he tried to picture what would happen if his life ended here, hundreds of years before he was indeed supposed to be born. He didn't want to die, not yet, not when there was so much to be said, so much to be done. Joe closed his eyes tightly and fixated on the one person he was most afraid of losing. Then everything was still.

Opening his eyes slowly and deliberately, Joe strained his ears to listen. There were a few cries coming from the Great Wall. Joe dared to glance behind him and noticed that there were troops who were standing perfectly still, the unaffected guards rushing over to inspect the sudden phenomena. With a burst of urgency, Joe looked down below and saw, to his relief, that everyone was frozen in place. Their eyes searched him, and Joe could feel their surprise, shock, and fear. He pushed those thoughts away as he descended the ladder, reaching the bottom in no time. He felt the stares of the people burning into the back of his head, but again Joe ignored them and darted between the residences where Zurman had dragged the body. Joe skidded around the corner and almost slammed straight into his guide.

"What took you so long?" Zurman asked.

"Sorry, couldn't get out. I used the orb."

"Yeah, I noticed, it's managed to go quite far," Zurman said, pointing ahead of them to the next set of houses that were grouped together beyond the alleyway they were in.

Joe noticed that two women carrying buckets of water

were standing completely still, their bodies frozen in time, just like those in the adjacent street.

"The temple isn't far," Joe stated, distracting himself from the thoughts of how petrified these innocent people must feel. "But I think it's guarded quite heavily. There's an enormous gate and at least four soldiers that I could see, though maybe there are more."

"Doesn't surprise me, how about the path getting there?"

"Fairly simple, winding through these houses up ahead. We should be there in maybe fifteen minutes?" Joe suggested.

"Good, we have time on our side still, but the window of opportunity is closing, and fast. I propose we take a gamble and run through these streets ahead. Hopefully your little magic trick gives us some breathing space," Zurman said with a grin which Joe didn't return. Instead, he simply nodded and set off, taking the lead as Zurman watched their backs. The pair cautiously proceeded through the alleyway ahead and into the clearing beyond. Joe winced as he saw more people trapped in this bubble he had created, unable to move or be free. He whispered the word, "Sorry," as he edged around the frozen humans that occasionally blocked their progress. Zurman stayed quiet behind him, but Joe got the nagging feeling that he was enjoying this. As they moved through the next alleyway, Joe could hear voices again, so he held his hand up for Zurman to stop. Then he sharply inhaled as a squadron of soldiers marched briskly past, their attention fortunately on the Great Wall to Joe and Zurman's left.

"Keep moving," Zurman hissed.

Joe gritted his teeth, his heart beating a little faster and hoping that the coast would be clear when he emerged at the end of the alley. Joe breathed a sigh of relief as he saw a very normal scene before him. Clothes were being washed, conversations had, and there was nothing to suggest that anything out of the ordinary had occurred. He rose up and walked quickly, but not so fast as to arouse suspicion. Zurman followed, keeping his hand firmly on the hilt of his scimitar, just in case they needed to make a quick and messy escape. Joe kept his head low and tried to avoid making eye contact with anyone as he navigated in and out of people going about their daily business. He glanced up and saw that ahead was the winding uphill road that lead to the great gate he had seen from the tower. Poking up just above the enormous gates was the top tier of the temple roof, the rest of it obscured from view by luscious trees that stood taller than the imposing gates which barred entry.

"There it is," Joe whispered behind him. "Any ideas how to get in?"

"I have one, but you'll have to trust me," Zurman answered.

"Oh, great, that's relaxing."

"It'll be fine, just follow my lead." With that, Zurman edged past Joe and walked directly towards the gates, his speed increasing but his limp also becoming more pronounced as the pace quickened.

"What the..." Joe said in a hushed voice as Zurman broke into a jog, and then a run as he closed the distance between himself and the gate.

Joe watched with a mixture of amazement and panic as Zurman charged the nearest guard. The sunlight reflected off of Zurman's blade for the briefest of moments before its curved edge struck the first warrior.

"Oh my God, not again!" Joe protested, now running forward too, without a single thought as to what he could do in this situation. Meanwhile, Zurman skilfully disarmed the next guard and plunged his weapon deep into the soldier's stomach. Joe kept running, and now he heard screams. The people behind him were seeing what was going on.

"Zee!" Joe cried, but it was no use. Zurman kept up his

flurry of destruction and beheaded the next man. Now the civilians were truly horrified and there were shouts of anguish, panic and fear filling the skies. Zurman ignored all of this and simply continued in his killing, the fourth man dying instantly as Zurman threw a small but incredibly sharp blade straight into the rushing man's neck. Joe finally stood next to Zurman with his eyes wide in bewilderment.

"Are you mad? Think of the attention we've attracted!"

"Exactly." Zurman grinned just as the mechanisms of the gate clicked and shifted behind them.

Zurman pulled Joe to one side and crouched. They watched as the immense doors creaked open and more guards spilled out, trying to locate the source of the disturbance.

"Joe, get inside. I'll clear the path here," Zurman instructed before springing up and charging into the four men who had arrived. They all fell down like bowling pins, and Zurman plunged his weapon into flesh before leaping out. The movement caused his leg to give way and Zurman fell down with a cry.

"Go, Joe, don't worry about me! Quick!"

Joe did as he was told and ran past the still struggling soldiers on the floor, the surprise of the attack keeping them grounded for now. Joe didn't look back as he heard steel clash loudly as swords collided. He hoped Zurman would be okay, though there was definitely a part of him that wasn't as worried as it should have been. Instinct told Joe to duck to the right, and he found himself immersed in the lush greenery of the temple grounds. Breathing hard, Joe carefully moved through the bushes, ignoring the scratches and tugs he felt on his skin and clothing. He kept the sanctuary in his view at all times, watching as another set of warriors stepped outside. They were dressed all in black, and Joe was reminded of the assassin from the Golden Pyramid. *Was he one of them?*

The five warriors shut an enormous door behind them with

a thud that reverberated around the garden. They didn't move from the entrance as Joe had suspected, so he advanced on, confident that Zurman could fend off the attackers and keep himself alive. Instead, Joe focussed on how he would gain entry into this imposing fortress. It seemed to be entirely sealed, with only one way in and one way out. Daring to step out from the safety of the thick bushes, Joe moved rapidly and pressed himself against the walls of the temple. He breathed a sigh of relief and shifted around, hoping to discover a rear entrance or storage hole. Joe continued pushing forward, circling the giant temple until he was virtually behind it. Looking back, Joe didn't stop advancing.

He practically walked straight into the pointed tip of Han Ling's outstretched sword.

CHAPTER TWENTY-FIVE

"Frank! Frank!" Luisa called out, staring at the empty space where Lieutenant Frank Williams had been standing just a moment before. Panicking, Luisa put both hands on her head and span around, looking in all directions for any sign of her companion. There was nothing. No trace of him ever having been there, or even that he had disappeared. Luisa became aware of her breaths coming in short, sharp bursts and she stopped herself, leaning against the rough wall for balance.

"Okay, okay," she whispered, finally regaining a measure of control on her breathing. "The stone, get the stone, and this is all over. Where the *hell* is Zurman?" Luisa spoke out loud, frustration at being left alone now taking over her initial shock at seeing Frank disappear.

Luisa walked back to where she and Frank had diverted to escape their pursuer. The space was busier than she remembered. There were people engaging in deep conversations, some of them inspecting strange objects on the ground, which Luisa guessed might be empty bullet casings. Her eyes darted nervously through the crowd, trying to pick out her enemy.

The one advantage she held was that the assassin was dressed all in black and that worked against him in here, in the bright afternoon.

Keeping her head low, Luisa walked quickly and tried to take an educated guess as to how to get back to the harbour, or even the marketplace. Perhaps Zurman was waiting for her already, she thought, hope rising again within her. Suddenly, her stomach dropped, and the brief spark of faith was extinguished as she watched the assassin walking right ahead of her. His blonde hair was unmistakable, yet he had shed his distinctive clothing and was now wearing the same cream-coloured robes as everyone else. His piercing blue eyes scanned the many faces that filled the square and just before seeing Luisa, she ducked down to adjust her sandal.

Breathing quickly, Luisa kept her face shielded as she pretended to fiddle with the strap on her footwear. It was then that she realised the fatal flaw in her plan: she might be obscured from his view, but now she couldn't see *him* either. Not knowing where this man was gave her a fresh wave of anxiety, which she addressed that very instant. Luisa rose from her crouched position and craned her neck to try to peer through the dense crowd. She looked to where the man had been resting a moment before, and her heart skipped a beat when she saw he was no longer in the same position. Keeping herself as inconspicuous as possible, Luisa brushed past several people and walked towards the alleyway. Her logic told her that if he was hunting her down and had come from here, why would he retrace his steps?

Daring to look behind her, Luisa decided that the coast was clear and hurried into the alley, which was just as narrow as the others, though this time it was a shorter route that turned right into a wider street. An uncertain feeling rose within her as she searched around. There were very few people here, just a handful of residents hanging their washing and engaging in friendly conversation. A few birds could be heard chirping away, the merry songs did nothing to quiet the impending feeling of doom Luisa couldn't shake. She resolved to move quickly and quietly, keeping her gaze fixed upon the connecting path ahead, which she prayed would lead her out into the harbour.

Luisa looked both ways before stepping cautiously onto the trail. It was deserted, which did nothing to alleviate the fear in her, but after a few paces she stopped and listened. There it was. The sound was music to her ears. She could hear the gentle lapping of waves and the din of conversation from fishermen and tradesmen, meaning the harbour was just ahead. Luisa let out a laugh, sheer relief washing over her, and she jogged, feeling elated that she was almost at the end of her journey. The alley continued on its short line before turning right, and after a few minutes, Luisa heard the sounds of a bustling port getting louder and louder. She practically ran straight into the blonde man who was standing at the exit of the alleyway.

"No!" Luisa screamed, falling down and scrambling quickly backwards. "Get away!"

But the imposing figure didn't listen, and he walked calmly towards her, Luisa noticed the glint of a knife in his hand as the sun reflected off the blade. His eyes locked with hers and to her surprise, she didn't see anger or hate, but almost a sadness, like this was something that was inevitable and that he took no pleasure from it. Thinking fast, Luisa grabbed a handful of dirt and sand and threw it straight into the man's eyes. He yelled, either from surprise or pain, but it gave Luisa her window of opportunity. She sprang to her feet and rushed past him, feeling his fingers grab for her as she narrowly avoided his grip. She burst out into the open and saw the magnificent sculpture of the Colossus proudly standing tall directly ahead of her. More importantly, she could see the crystal that she needed; an exact replica of the one she had in her possession.

Luisa started running towards the icon. She didn't glance back, but she knew her attacker would be hot on her heels. Luisa thought, *he's going to kill me even if I take the stone. I need to get rid of him*. This alarming realisation caused her to slow a little while her brain tried to calculate an escape route. The delay allowed her attacker to catch up to her, and he was closing in at a rapid pace. Luisa looked around just in time to see him reach into his robes for a weapon. With a jolt of inspiration, Luisa suddenly darted to her right, away from the statue and the harbour. She broke into a full sprint and flew past confused onlookers, who watched as the strange girl ran and ran, being chased by the man with blonde hair. Luisa didn't look back, only ahead, only to the rolling green hills and the sharp rocks that housed a dark secret. She was leading this man directly to the Colossus.

△

Ulrich was surprised by the speed of this young woman; she was keeping a consistent distance between them, and her pace wasn't slowing. Silently, he cursed the fact that he had to leave most of his weapons and armour behind to blend in with the locals. All he had on him was the serrated blade that he never went anywhere without. They were heading straight for an extensive collection of oddly shaped rocks and Ulrich wondered briefly what was going to be hidden within, for that was certainly why he was being led there. He admired the girl's courage and her quick thinking. *A shame*, he thought. In truth, Ulrich took little pleasure in the necessary work he did, but he knew there was simply no other way.

He watched as the girl ran into the jagged rocks and was taken aback at first, as it looked as though she had literally disappeared. Then he saw it, a clever optical illusion that masked the narrow trail that went between the rock formations. Smiling, Ulrich steadily continued along the path and paused. He listened intently; something was stirring up ahead. Gripping his knife tightly, Ulrich crouched low and moved forwards, wondering if the girl was waiting to ambush him. Another clever move, if so. As Ulrich emerged into the clearing, he allowed himself to be surprised. There was no sudden attack, but instead he was in awe of the vast temple that stood before him. It was completely hidden from the ground, but now that he was standing before it, he was amazed he hadn't seen it sooner.

Then Ulrich heard it again. A dull thud, like something heavy being dropped from a great height. Slowly, Ulrich moved around the edge of the vast space he was in, conscious of keeping the exit within a short distance. A quick examination of the landscape had shown that there was no other way in or out, unless the temple itself was an exit. Yet it backed straight into the rocks and looked to be something ceremonial rather than functional. Another thumping sound, this one closer. Ulrich stared at the entrance to the temple and tried to peer inside. Yet he couldn't see anything through the unnatural darkness. One more loud bang, this time the very ground he was standing on shook. Ulrich could sense something was wrong. Every instinct told him to turn back, but he couldn't. This was the mission. It needed finishing. He steeled himself and twirled the knife delicately between his fingers, steadying his nerves for whatever was about to face him. Nothing could prepare him for what was about to emerge from the depths of the temple.

△

Luisa waited with bated breath behind the cluster of rocks immediately to the right of where she and Ulrich had walked through just a moment ago. She had noticed it the first time when she had fled the temple, a space small enough for her to jump into and duck down if necessary. Of course, at the time it was completely useless. The Colossus would have simply picked her up or squashed her. Now, it was lifesaving. Her would-be-attacker was less than two metres ahead of her when it happened. The smooth featureless head of the golden Colossus emerged from the shrine, followed by the rest of its enormous body. Luisa saw the man's body stiffen as he took in this otherworldly sight, and Luisa idly wondered if he had made the connection that the sculpture back down at the harbour was a dedication to a real-life demi-god.

As the Colossus of Rhodes fully appeared from the temple, Luisa was once again transfixed by the enormity of the being. It stood and looked down at the man, perhaps also at Luisa, but she prayed not. She also hoped that her pursuer would be bold and fight, or at least try to flee into the shrine as she had done recently. Either way, she needed time to escape and get to the statue and to finish the mission. Her thoughts drifted again to Zurman. She wondered if he was due to return imminently with whatever weapon he thought was suitable to take down this immense being. An enormous gold fist slammed into the ground, jolting Luisa back to reality. It was aiming for where the blonde-haired man had been standing not a moment before. Luisa crouched low and felt her teeth shake as the shock waves from the impact rippled out from the fresh crater the titan had created.

After the dust cloud cleared, Luisa viewed the assassin running between the legs of the golden being, mimicking almost exactly what she had done. She held her breath as she waited for the right moment to emerge and flee; too soon and she would reveal herself to the man or the behemoth and the entire plan would be exposed. Another sweeping blow from the giant landed with a crash on the ground and Luisa ducked instinctively, though she was in no immediate danger. She quickly poked her head back up and saw with relief that the assassin was heading directly into the temple. With a burst of energy, Luisa jumped out of the hole she was hiding in and ran straight for the path out of there.

△

Ulrich ran as fast as he could, feeling the enormous thing bearing down on him. He had no time to process exactly what he was up against, only that it was incredibly large and clearly not looking to discuss anything. The temple entrance was almost welcoming him in, but just before he ran inside, Ulrich dared to look behind him and try to avoid the next attack. That's when he saw her. Behind the looming, golden giant, Ulrich watched as the girl fled from the hiding place she had been in all along and ran back down the path they had just walked up. He let out a dry scoff, impressed by her tactics and at the same time dismayed that he had been lured so easily into this trap. Something was biting at Ulrich's instinct to get inside and with the giant bringing another fist down to squash him, he didn't need an invitation.

The darkness of the temple was all consuming and after several blinks to adjust to the gloomy atmosphere, there was still no luck in regaining his vision. He knew time was of the essence and that it was running out fast. It would be a matter of moments before the Colossus would enter, so Ulrich kept moving, his hands outstretched to feel for any walls, pillars or anything to guide his way. There wasn't anything. It suddenly dawned on him that the purpose of this shrine was merely to house this extraordinary being, nothing more, nothing less. For the first time in a very long while, Ulrich felt his heart racing as the unfamiliar feeling of panic settled in.

He span around, searching desperately for anything he could use as a vantage point or escape route. His vision was at last returning, but the uplifting development was short lived, for the light source was none other than the Colossus entering its temple. Ulrich watched, feeling the crippling sense of failure as the giant ducked to enter the vast space, fully prepared to decimate the tiny man in front of it. Ulrich closed his eyes and waited, accepting that his life, and thus the mission, was over. He exhaled deeply and accepted his fate, waiting for the crushing final blow of the giant to swiftly end him. Yet it did not come.

Ulrich saw to his disbelief that the Colossus had stopped, seemingly frozen to the spot. Ulrich tried to move, but found his legs were also suspended in animation. Then he realised that his entire body could not do a thing. Fresh panic washed over him. The feeling of having absolutely no control was alarming.

"Who's doing this?" Ulrich shouted into the darkness; no answer came. Then he saw it in front of him. The air itself seemed to blur and bend unnaturally, followed by a white light piercing through the very fabric of reality. Ulrich blinked as the brightness engulfed him and it swept away him from the Temple of the Colossus.

△

Luisa almost tumbled over such was the haste at which she was trying to escape. The rocks slid under her feet and she stretched her hand out to steady herself, only getting a cut from the sharp rocks in return. She didn't care, she couldn't stop. Luisa hurdled out of the covert pathway and rolled onto the grass, using the momentum to continue on, not caring about the flare of pain in her right arm. She had to get to the harbour. She had no idea how long the Colossus would be distracted for, or if the man would realise her plan and chase her down in seconds. All that mattered was that she put as much distance between herself and that temple as she could.

Bursting into the port, Luisa allowed herself a moment to catch her breath. She glanced behind her at the vast openness of the fields and she couldn't see anything, so she decided she had escaped for now. Her eyes were drawn to the mighty statue. It was resplendent in the sun, which was setting as the evening closed in, signalling that time was running out. Taking a deep breath, Luisa walked along the wooden planks of the harbour, careful to avoid eye contact with anyone and simply focussing her mind on how she would retrieve that stone. Without thinking, her slender fingers fumbled over the blue gem in her pocket and she wondered what would happen when she got close to the sculpture. Would there be a signal? She continued walking and was so close now. The effigy of the Colossus was rising higher above her. Eventually she craned her neck to see the top and shielded her eyes from the sun as she stared directly at the gem.

She was at the foot of the sculpture when she heard it. A faint whistling sound was coming from behind her. Luisa turned, and her jaw dropped when she saw one of the large rock pieces from the temple coming straight for her. It landed with the force of a bomb in the sea just beyond where she was standing. Ships were at once capsized, and an enormous wave decimated the harbour. Luisa was caught in the miniature tidal wave, being swept up by the current. She sucked in lungfuls of water and panicked as she struggled to breathe. She had no control as she was pushed and pulled by the flood, which pressed her against a railing which she gripped onto and used to pull herself up. Emerging on dry land, Luisa coughed and spluttered as water emptied, her eyes stinging from the salt and her ears popping from the sudden impact. A few seconds later and another huge rock plummeted from the sky, crashing into houses and burying some of the fleeing civilians.

In less than a minute, the harbour had been wrecked and as a third rock landed squarely in the middle of the area, it was all but destroyed. Luisa groggily got to her feet. The statue was still intact, and the crystal remained where it had always been, proudly held aloft and out of reach of mere mortals. She looked back to the hillside and saw the great golden monster preparing to launch another attack. There was little time remaining, if any at all. She summoned up the last of her strength and headed to the sculpture, leaping across gaps in the pathway as people around her struggled to get out of the water, violent waves pushing them back down. Another rock smashed, this one closer to the edge of the harbour and the fields, so thankfully the damage was minimal. Luisa kept going, her only goal to get to the statue and retrieve the stone.

Luisa jumped onto the plinth and climbed as another rock landed and shattered the remaining parts of the harbour; wood from the boats and walkways splintering into the air, debris raining down on the last few survivors still there. The statue's muscular golden legs were so vast and smooth that Luisa couldn't obtain a purchase on them. She had finally succeeded to clamber onto the foot of the sculpture when another boulder hurtled straight for the Colossus, carving it in half and sending Luisa tumbling into the sea.

As she sank into the wash, Luisa fumbled for her rock in an effort to harness its powers to save her own life. She looked up at the surface as she sank deeper and deeper, when she saw the other gem, now freed from its prison, slowly sinking from above her. Her own stone in her hand, she reached up, desperately trying to touch the other one in a last attempt to survive. Her consciousness fading, she didn't see or feel the objects connect and merge. Just before her world turned black, she was suddenly expelled from the water and on dry land, gasping for air. Blinking, Luisa brought into focus the dimly lit room of the Golden Pyramid. She was back where it all began.

CHAPTER TWENTY-SIX

Joe was tossed roughly onto the cold floor, landing hard at the feet of who he took to be the Emperor. He dared to glance up at the person sitting on the throne and saw dark brown eyes filled with ancient wisdom glaring back at him. The guard who had brought Joe in spoke to the man on the throne in their native tongue. Joe watched as they pointed at him and discussed something; presumably how to kill him. The Emperor held a hand up, and there was silence. Slowly, he rose from his throne and stepped forward towards Joe. The man bent down, his long hair hanging to the floor as he crouched and brought his face inches from Joe and narrowing his eyes.

"You not belong here," he muttered.

Joe gasped, his shock at hearing English being uttered made him unable to answer.

The Emperor's lip curled into a smile.

"What did you say to him?" Han asked his cousin in Chinese.

"I told him that he doesn't belong here," the Emperor responded, standing up and straightening.

"Can you say anything else?"

"I have more words at my disposal," the Emperor remarked. "But for now, I need you to go to the main gate. Our true enemy is there and seeks to reclaim this gift," he gestured to the golden staff next to his throne.

Joe watched the conversation unfold and then saw the object that he knew he and Zurman had been seeking. His pulse quickened as he studied it. There was an opening at one end which looked as though it would perfectly house a small golden ball, just like the one he had in his pocket. With a sudden rush of clarity, Joe tightly squeezed the orb, focussing on the fear he had inside of him. Concentrating hard, Joe kept the thoughts bubbling at the surface, desperately hoping that something would happen. Joe gradually opened his eyes and, to his dismay, saw that nothing changed. It didn't work.

△

Han left the temple and moved into the garden, his personal guard following him as they walked swiftly to the main gate, just in time to see a tall, muscular man behead one of their own. Han stopped in his tracks and felt fear grip him as he recognised the attacker. The bearded man looked up and locked eyes with Han, smiling menacingly.

He spoke in Chinese. "Hello General, it's been a while."

△

"Stand up," the Emperor commanded of Joe, who was once again amazed by his grasp of the English language. He did as he was told and got to his feet, feeling more and more uneasy with every passing second.

"Who are you?" the Emperor demanded.

"J-Joe. I'm Joe."

"What is *Joe*?"

"My name."

"You have army?"

"No, just me," Joe answered quickly, unaware that the Emperor already knew that Zurman was at the gate. Right on cue, the man chuckled, and Joe realised his mistake. "Okay, me and one more," he added.

The Emperor circled Joe, an amused look on his face. "How you come here?" he inquired in broken English.

Joe subconsciously looked down, about to reveal the orb in his robes, but instinct told him otherwise.

"Answer!" the Emperor demanded, making Joe flinch.

"Forest," Joe said hastily.

The Emperor smiled. "Why?"

Joe was silent. He couldn't honestly answer why and didn't know what to say.

"Why!" The Emperor repeated. "This?" he added, gesturing to the golden staff.

Joe studied it and realised it was pointless to lie. "Yes, I think so."

"Think?"

"Yes, I don't know. I'm not here by choice," Joe replied bluntly.

"I don't understand," the Emperor responded, stroking his long beard. "You don't look like warrior."

"I'm not," Joe blurted out.

"Who is your king?"

"King?"

"King, Sultan, who is your master?" the Emperor repeated.

"Nobody, I am alone," Joe answered honestly.

"Who is out there?" The Emperor pointed to the exit of his temple.

"A friend," Joe answered lamely.

The Emperor laughed before answering, "he is not friend."

△

Han's guards rushed Zurman at once, brandishing their weapons and aiming for killing blows instantly. Zurman skilfully ducked and weaved between strikes, blocking where he needed to and moving fast, but back-pedalling due to the overwhelming pressure. Reaching into his robes, he produced a fistful of ash which he threw into the eyes of two of his attackers, giving him a small window of opportunity to put some distance between him and the soldiers. With incredible agility, Zurman back flipped out of the ruckus, but landed on his damaged leg and fell to his knees. Grunting, he stood up and patiently waited for the attackers to charge him, but they didn't. Remaining disciplined, they formed a circle around him, like a pack of wolves about to attack their prey.

General Han stood with his arms folded, watching as his best soldiers had his enemy trapped. He smiled, as he knew what would happen next. He had seen his men perform this manoeuvre countless times. The five soldiers arranged themselves into a semi-circle, with two men standing exactly parallel with the enemy. The three in front would then move as one, with the two at the sides dispatching throwing stars into the legs of their prey, allowing the trio ahead to easily dismember and swiftly kill their opponent. Han watched as his troopers moved into position and waited.

△

"What he tell you?" the Emperor asked Joe.

"Many things," Joe replied, again not deviating from the truth but being deliberately vague.

"He tell you what you looking for?"

"No."

The Emperor chuckled almost knowingly. "But he know, he know."

"How?"

"This weapon, is from gods," the Emperor said, looking at the staff. "It keep me young, when I old, very old."

A puzzled look crossed Joe's face. He didn't quite understand what this had to do with the golden orb in his pocket, but didn't dare question it.

"I was told I could be Emperor forever, if I take this. So I take. I travel, I keep weapon with me, always."

"What does it do?"

"No speak, listen."

Joe promptly shut his mouth and did just that.

"I travel very far, across Europe, looking for man who gave me this. I learn many language, many years away from here," the Emperor paused, sighing perhaps in regret. "He told me I be immortal, but only if I find orb."

Joe's blood ran cold, and the hairs on his neck stood up. *Does he know it's in my pocket?*

"I not find, but I not die. I not grow old, like others. There is great power here, so I share it with my cousin, my General."

Joe hesitated, but he had to know, he needed to ask. "Who gave you the staff?"

The Emperor simply smiled in response.

△

Zurman knew what was coming and was prepared. Time seemed to stretch forever as he watched the guards get into position and get their ambush ready. He knew exactly what was going to happen and acted first. He threw two poison tipped darts out from his hands into the throats of the warriors that were standing at his left and right, jumping as he did to avoid the throwing stars which were millimetres away from hitting him. Zurman turned his attention to the three in front of him and firmly gripped his scimitar and parried the blades as they struck him. Zurman moved fast, ignoring the growing pain in his leg as he slashed and hacked, fending off the attacks but always on the back foot. One soldier landed a glancing blow on Zurman's shoulder, which brought about a yelp of pain.

Zurman took a gamble and reached out to grab the man's throat with his hand. He squeezed, cutting off the air supply and making him drop his weapon. Zurman blocked two simultaneous attacks and, with a grunt, forced the other two backward. The guard who had been choked was on his knees and Zurman was ruthless, killing the soldier with his own blade. Panting, Zurman hurriedly picked up the spare sword that was lying on the ground and armed himself, a weapon in each hand, tipping the odds back in his favour against the last two men standing.

This time, Zurman attacked first, spinning the weapons in controlled arcs that disorientated his enemies. They blocked his onslaught, but Zurman kept coming, fresh adrenaline pumping through his body and fuelling each slash. One warrior tripped and fell backwards, leaving Zurman to quickly disarm the standing guard swiftly and plunge both his swords into the his stomach. Zurman looked down at the last defender, who was crawling away an outstretched hand begging for mercy. Zurman did not hesitate and stabbed the helpless man on the floor. He retrieved his weapon, wiping it clean on the grass, and heard footsteps approaching, followed by a sword being unsheathed. Zurman smiled and then spoke in Chinese, "Now it's just you and I, General Han."

△

The Emperor continued to smile as he saw Joe put together the pieces of the puzzle in his mind. He watched as this stranger, out of his depth, out of his time, was coming to terms with how complex this all really was.

"Who gave you that?" Joe inquired again.

"You know," the Emperor declared.

"Zurman?"

The Emperor nodded in response. Joe scrunched up his face as he thought about this information. His head was spinning. *Why would Zurman give the Emperor the staff?*

"Why?" Joe eventually asked.

"He not say. He came with great treasures, prophecy. He tell us many thing that happened and will happen. He left this as gift and tell us that one day, it need be used to start new world."

"A new world?" Joe repeated aloud, not really to the Emperor.

"Yes, one day, this world end, but life continue, with right people."

"The right people? What does that mean?"

The Emperor smiled, almost sadly. "He tell us, we be part of it, but we know... we know... he lie."

Joe let the words hang in the air as he thought about this recent information. Could he trust the Emperor? Probably not, but he was losing faith in Zurman with each passing second. Joe bit his lip and decided he would take the risk.

"Did Zurman tell you about this?" Joe announced, pulling the golden orb from his pocket.

△

"Why are you here?" Han asked Zurman as he walked towards him, his sword held out threateningly towards his foe.

"It's time for your world to end," Zurman said with a

menacing grin. Han simply shook his head, a mixture of disappointment and sadness.

"We knew you would betray us," Han eventually spoke, still circling Zurman, who simply scoffed at the General's words. "You said we would be part of this new world, that we were chosen."

"You were chosen, just not in the way you thought," Zurman answered, suddenly attacking Han with three fast and deadly strikes, which had the General quickly adjusting his stance, blocking Zurman's attack. A space opened up between both men and they wearily circled each other as before, Han was prepared to launch an attack when Zurman darted forwards again and steel clashed once more as the two frantically traded killing blows, each looking to end the fight quickly but both matched in skill and aggression. Han trapped Zurman's sword on the floor and quickly rammed the butt of his own weapon into Zurman's face. It hit his mouth and blood instantly poured out down his beard and robes.

"What do you mean, chosen?" Han asked, catching his breath as Zurman backed away again.

"You will see," he mumbled, wiping away the blood as he spoke.

"The boy? Who is he?"

"The unwilling pawn," Zurman cooly replied, charging forward again. Han gritted his teeth and met the attack with just as much force as Zurman, and their weapons rang loudly as they clashed. Zurman ducked a horizontal blow from Han and reacted with a diagonal slash of his own. It barely caught the General but it drew blood. Han instinctively grabbed his side, where he felt the glancing strike.

"You're getting slow in your old age," Zurman taunted.

Han responded with a flurry of angry strikes, each one more furious than the last as he pushed Zurman back further and further, the advantage slowly tipping in his favour. He saw the panic in Zurman's eyes as Han kept coming forward, each strike growing in ferocity as the defences of his old foe were crumbling. Just as he felt ready to end the confrontation, a dazzling golden light erupted from the temple and sent shock waves out into the garden, knocking Zurman and Han off their feet, separating them.

△

Joe was flung backwards hard into the wall, The Emperor was sent flying in the opposite direction, crashing over his own throne, which toppled and fell to the floor. Joe blinked the stars out of his eyes and looked in amazement at the sight before him. As soon as he had held out the golden orb, it had been sucked into the staff as though it were an extremely powerful magnet trapping the metallic object. At the point of impact, it had emitted an enormous shock wave and a near blinding light that had knocked everyone in a thousand yard radius off their feet. Joe stood and walked warily past the staff, which floated in the air in an upright position, ready to be taken. He glanced at it but didn't dare touch it and instead went to check on the Emperor.

An audible gasp escaped Joe's mouth when he saw the Emperor. A crumpled ruin of a man was barely stirring on the floor. His once jet-black hair was now as white as snow, and Joe was horrified when the man finally turned to face him. The Emperor's features were completely sunken in, the skin on his face was pulled so tightly over his bones that it scarcely looked like there was any there at all. He was more like a corpse that had somehow been animated. His eyes were unchanged, though they now had a look of utmost panic in them. Reaching out with a bony hand. The Emperor sought to touch Joe and ask for help. In a gruesome moment, Joe watched as the hand snapped clean off at the wrist, causing the Emperor to scream in what was a hoarse and quiet shout. Joe heard another snap as the Emperor tried to get to his feet and he realised that the Emperor's leg must have broken. He landed awkwardly on his palm and chest, and Joe heard more bones splintering.

Joe crouched next to the badly wounded and decrepit old man and eased him on to his back. Blood was spilling out from the Emperor's open mouth, Joe guessed it was from internal organs failing or being punctured by the many shattered bones. The Emperor attempted to speak, but the voice was no more than a whisper. He held aloft his ruined stump of an arm and pointed to the staff.

"Take," was all he could say before his breath gave out. A single tear trickled slowly from the corner of the Emperor's eye and Joe abruptly stood up, feeling a lump forming in his throat. He hesitated at first but gripped the staff tightly and the second he did, was transported out of China.

△

Zurman groggily got to his feet, shaking his head. He looked around for General Han and saw that he on the ground, unmoving ahead of him. Smiling, Zurman walked over slowly and stopped just short of Han's feet, looking down triumphantly on his nearly vanquished foe.

"The years have finally caught up with you," Zurman said with malice, looking down at the half skeleton that was now lying there. Han's eyes darted back and forth; panic etched on his barely recognisable features.

"Ah, General. If you only knew what a great sacrifice you have made today. You have allowed the birth of a new world. The pieces were always in play, yet you didn't know. How could you?"

Han didn't respond, he couldn't. He felt his body failing him at an alarming rate and his breaths came in harsh rasps.

"Yes, better not to talk. Just know that you are part of the most important piece of your history and mine. Worlds will collide and ours will be the one remaining."

Rather than ending Han's misery, Zurman walked on into the temple. General Han looked up at the blue sky, watching as the birds flew overhead and happily chirped. He had failed his Emperor and with that thought, General Han died alone in the grass.

Zurman pushed the doors of the sanctuary open with such a force and that they bashed loudly against the wooden structure. He glanced around, confident that he was alone, and ambled towards the throne, which was on its side. He saw the Emperor lying dead on the floor and chuckled; it was all coming to pass now. Zurman looked for the golden staff and saw it was missing, as was Joe.

"Good," he said into the empty throne room. "There is no escaping now."

With that, Zurman left the temple and fled the Forbidden City, back to his hut in the rolling green fields to prepare the last part of his mission.

CHAPTER TWENTY-SEVEN

Luisa gasped for air as she sat up, choking from the water that had moments ago been filling her lungs. She looked around her in panic, expecting the Colossus to burst through the walls at any second, but there was nothing but an eerie silence surrounding her. She got to her feet, still wearing the clothes from Rhodes, wondering whether the assassin had been killed by the giant. It dawned on her that she didn't have the gem and in a moment of panic; she patted herself down, realising that it was missing.

"Oh no," she said in exasperation, the dread of having gone through such an ordeal all for nothing sinking in. Looking to her left, Luisa saw that there was a doorway and putting her fear aside, she walked towards it, emerging into a wide passage. Torches flickered on the walls and it took her back to when she and Joe had first landed inside the pyramid, which seemed to be a long time ago while still feeling as though it were only yesterday. She guessed it had been a few days, a week at most, but time had lost its meaning recently.

The ground gradually sloped upwards and Luisa could see an opening creep into view. She continued on and eventually emerged onto a balcony, which was one of several within this gigantic hall.

"Woah," she breathed, looking around at the huge pillars that stretched for infinity above her, supporting an unseen roof that must have been incredibly large to cover such a space. She noticed a set of doors which were closed on her right. They had steep steps leading up to them and there was something pulling her towards them unconsciously. Deciding to act upon this instinct, Luisa climbed down the spiral staircase until she found herself in the hall itself.

Her sandals clacked loudly on the marble surface. There was a stillness about the hall that seemed unearthly, as though this place didn't really exist. Then Luisa noticed the tiny golden specks which were suspended in the air. She waved her hand delicately through them and instead of reacting like dust motes as she expected, they seemed to bend and wrap around her arm before returning to their spot. Pulling away, Luisa continued walking alone in this cavernous space, yet feeling she was being watched.

Suddenly, the gates in front of her groaned in resistance as a thunderous noise echoed from somewhere behind the great slabs as they opened. Luisa stopped in her tracks and observed as the rift grew wider, revealing a white light that poured into the dark hall. Then, the doors shuddered once and were still. The gap was wide enough for her to easily walk through, so, cautiously, she approached. As she got closer, she saw that there appeared to be a wall of fog blocking her entrance and her view of what was inside. Luisa stopped and looked up. The doors reached far above her and her mind jumped to various conclusions as to what could be inside. A weapon, another Colossus, a building? Biting her lip, she hesitantly reached out with her hand and brushed the swirling mist.

The second Luisa touched the smoke, something dragged her in. Her world seemed to corkscrew around her, and visions flew past her in a confused mess of flashing images; people, faces and violence until finally it ended. Luisa blinked a few times and then fell backwards in fear. Standing in front of her was a gigantic figure wearing a crown decorated with feathers ready to attack... yet it didn't. Luisa closed her eyes and breathed easily: it was a statue. Craning her neck slightly to inspect it, Luisa recalled a carving she and Joe had seen. She remembered the three spokes of the crown, each containing a jewel. However, this headpiece was missing one. A wave of panic rolled through her as she concluded the lost item must be the gem she had stolen from Rhodes. Walking past the prone sculpture, Luisa noticed the great altar behind the tall figure, as well as the person standing next to it. Approaching with care, Luisa edged forward, not taking her eyes off the man.

"Hello, Luisa," Zurman greeted cooly.

"What is this?" she answered slowly.

"You are at the end of the journey. You have done so well," Zurman replied brightly.

"What happened to you back there? You just left."

"Ah, yes," Zurman said apologetically before continuing. "Things really got out of hand, I had to..."

Zurman's voice was interrupted, and Luisa saw her vision fade to black. There was no altar, no Zurman, just her in a dark room. Then she saw it. White particles at the edge of her vision joined up and formed an outline, the same figure that had met her in the Temple of the Colossus.

"Luisa," a faraway voice spoke.

Luisa panicked and searched around, hoping for an escape, but there was none. Just an empty blackness that surrounded her. She glanced back and the silvery shape was forming a solid entity, a female, and she knew already who it was.

"What's going on!" Luisa cried.

"It's too la..t.e..," came the distorted reply.

"What's too late, what is happening?"

"Yo.. u... time.... need to go... no..w."

Luisa listened to the words and tried to digest the information. She had to go, but where?

"How long do I have?" Luisa asked the spectral figure.

"Be... ware... Zur.... ma..." The voice trailed off and vanished, taking the white outline with it and Luisa was back in the chamber with Zurman, the statue and the altar.

"I had to attend matters in another time," Zurman said, continuing his sentence and clearly not aware that Luisa had just been out of sync with his reality for a moment.

She quickly composed herself, answering with, "I see."

Luisa could still hear the sound echoing inside her head, telling her to beware of Zurman. She was sure that was what she heard, but could she have been mistaken?

"What is this place?" she finally asked.

"This is one of the core chambers of the Golden Pyramid."

"And that thing?" Luisa gestured to the altar behind Zurman.

"This is where we put the crystal, the complete artefact that you have from Rhodes."

"I-I don't have it," Luisa stammered.

"What?!" Zurman rounded on her, his expression suddenly dark, fury twisting his normally handsome features into something grotesque.

"Hey, you abandoned me!" Luisa snapped back, startling Zurman.

Regaining his composure, Zurman descended the short flight of stairs down to Luisa, a broad smile returning on his face. "Luisa, my dear, I am sure that the stone will not be far. You appeared here because the artefact was completed for the first time. It acts as key of sorts, enabling you to be transported back to a specific location at the right moment."

"The Golden Pyramid in two thousand and twenty-one?"

"You got it, so it must be here somewhere. Wait here, I'll look for it." Zurman placed a hand on Luisa's shoulder, squeezing tightly. Previously, this would have been a welcome and friendly gesture. Now Luisa sensed menace in the act. She watched as Zurman casually strolled back down to where she had been and waited until he was out of sight before hurrying over to the altar.

Luisa stared at the barren stone basin. Compared with other items was in the pyramid, it was rather unremarkable. Simple in design, it looked like only a hollow vessel. Luisa walked around it, trying to determine if there was a source of unseen power or anything that might give a clue as to its purpose.

"Lu... is... a."

Luisa span, hearing the distant voice calling her name once more.

"Who's there?"

"Yo..u.. ha..ve... to..stop.... hi.....m."

"Who? How?" Luisa hissed, looking wildly around her for the ghostly figure that she could not see, but felt was with her.

"Th.. e... alt... stop.." The voice trailed off and Luisa looked around with wild eyes, confused and panicked.

Luisa frantically searched her robes again, certain that she must have the gem with her. Her heart skipped a beat when she felt her fingers on the cool and slightly jagged surface of the crystal. She exhaled deeply, but jumped almost a second later.

"Everything okay?" Zurman's calm voice came as he walked around the statue, facing Luisa.

"Yes, yes fine. Just worried and trying to find the rock," Luisa lied.

Zurman walked towards her, his smile fading at the corners and his eyes narrowing. "What are you hiding?" Zurman said, coming ever closer.

Luisa felt a rush of adrenalin through her. She was torn between charging him and running away, or simply allowing him to take the gem from her and do whatever it was he needed to. She couldn't shake the feeling that something was wrong, that Zurman had changed drastically since she had last seen him, but she couldn't quite place it.

"Luisa," he said slowly, getting even closer now and almost within arm's reach. "Do you have the stone?"

She didn't respond and in a moment of inspiration, tried to run past him. Zurman quickly and forcefully stopped her progress, blocking her exit and gripping her neck in an upright headlock.

"Answer me," he stated through gritted teeth.

Luisa gasped, struggling to inhale as Zurman's grip was unrelenting. She tapped his forearm frantically, but he did not loosen his hold on her.

"Give. Me. The stone!" He dropped Luisa, and she spluttered and coughed, clutching her throat. With a vicious look in her eyes, she toyed with lashing out with a kick, but decided against it. Resigned to her fate, she reached into her robes and produced the crystal, which Zurman snatched out of her hands. He began walking briskly to the altar.

Zurman carefully placed the merged blue stones in the basin. At first nothing happened, but then Luisa heard a deep rumbling from behind her. She looked around and screamed as she saw the crowned statue moving stiffly, the figure shifting its enormous weight in what sounded like the first time in eons.

Zurman held her arms, pinning them against her sides and whispered, "Do not worry, he isn't here to harm us, just complete the ritual, watch."

She struggled against his grasp, but gave up. All she could do was examine the giant as it walked slowly and deliberately towards the shrine. Its featureless face declined down to the shining blue crystal. With an effort, the giant slid the crown from his head and deposited it next to the glowing stone. Taking a step back, he gripped the huge altar and twisted anticlockwise. A deep grinding noise reverberated from somewhere far inside the pyramid and further mechanical clunks could be heard as a new whirring sound joined the ensemble. The strange clamour kept going as the uncrowned being turned the altar again. It dawned on Luisa that this was likely an enormous key, turning something on within the pyramid. She shuddered at this realisation, wondering what on earth she had unleashed.

"Let go of me!" Luisa cried, and to her surprise, Zurman did. She tumbled forward, still keeping her eyes on the enormous monster in front of her. "What's happening here?"

"The inevitable. The pieces are all in place and now you can only watch," Zurman said triumphantly, looking on proudly as the giant continued to turn the massive altar.

"Why are you being like this? I thought we were supposed to save the world?"

"You fool!" Zurman laughed coldly. "This isn't for *your* world; this is for *my* world."

Luisa let the words filter through her. At first she was confused, wondering if she had misheard.

"Do you mean for the future, right?"

Zurman turned around, a mocking tone to his speech. "You have no idea, do you? None of you have any idea. All of this," he opened his arms wide and looked around the cavernous chamber, "this was all planned for our return. We built this before you were even swinging from the trees as apes. Everything your species has ever done was because of us, because we made it so, in order to return to our former glory."

Luisa's head was spinning. The words felt unreal. She almost expected Zurman to laugh and say he was joking. But as she watched the altar being turned repeatedly, and she heard the rumblings and noises echoing throughout the pyramid getting more pronounced, she realised that this was far from a joke.

"Who are you?" she asked in a small voice.

"I am your end," Zurman answered, and Luisa realised with horror that the apocalypse she had been fighting to avoid was going to be caused by her.

At last, the looming figure stopped his actions. Gradually, his arms took the blue gem and slotted it neatly into the space in his crown. A burst of energy rippled out, Luisa shut her eyes as dust flew in all directions. Zurman continued to stare triumphantly, watching the crown return to the head of its owner. Luisa gasped as the person convulsed for a second and then paused. Now Luisa could see its face transitioning as the smooth, featureless skin pitted and twisted. Eyes, a nose and a mouth appeared as though fading in to existence. His height remained unchanged, standing several feet above Luisa. A thickly armoured breastplate was now inscribed with detailed scripture, much like the confusing symbols that had been littered throughout the Golden Pyramid. His dark eyes found Luisa and Zurman and studied the pair for a moment. The crowned man however moved and left the room, footsteps echoing loudly in the vast hallway beyond. Luisa became acutely aware of the enormity of the chamber she was in without the presence of the man. She felt Zurman's hand wrap around her arm as he tugged her forward.

"Get off of me!" Luisa protested.

"Come, it's almost time. I think you should see this," Zurman replied.

Luisa resisted, but his grip was strong, and he effortlessly dragged her out into the great hallway. The reanimated man was still walking slowly and methodically ahead of them, stopping when he reached the centre of the room as though waiting for something. Luisa watched, not sure what she was expecting. She got her answer. The immense man stooped down onto one knee and frantically, dug the ground, punching and clawing at the stone floor. Luisa stared at Zurman, who simply looked beyond her at the man, admiring his actions.

At last, the imposing figure stopped. He brushed aside slabs of marble and concrete and unearthed a huge lever. Following this, he hauled the contraption up before decompressing it with some effort. Luisa idly thought that it must have weighed an enormous amount for a person of that size and strength to be struggling. The vast empty hallway was quickly being filled with hazy doorways, seemingly warping into reality. There was a fog around each one that blocked them from being properly seen, as though they lingered between existence and nothingness. More and more kept coming, but none of them fully formed and for a hopeful moment, Luisa thought that something had gone wrong, that whatever Zurman had planned didn't work.

"The king calls his people," Zurman announced. Luisa continued to stare at the enormous man, not talking back to Zurman.

"He was the first, the one who knew what would happen to us. Sacrificing himself in order to construct this incomparable labyrinth you stand in."

Luisa held her gaze, desperately wishing for the mechanism to have failed. Any possibility that whatever the king was doing hadn't worked.

"Do not be alarmed," Zurman said, as though reading her thoughts. "This is just part one of the process. Any minute now, your friend will join us."

"Joe?" Luisa guessed. Even in the circumstances, her excitement at seeing him soon was apparent.

"Yes, he'll be here. And he'll be the one to ensure everything proceeds as it should."

"He'll never help you," Luisa scoffed.

"Young fool," Zurman began. "Much like you, he never had the choice. He didn't even realise what he was truly achieving and never will. You've both served your purpose, but your journey is nearly at an end, whilst ours is just beginning."

Zurman's words were chilling and Luisa simply watched as more and more doors filled the great hall at various levels. The king stood patiently, and they all waited for the fresh horrors that could be unleashed once Joe arrived.

CHAPTER TWENTY-EIGHT

JOE LANDED hard on the cold surface and felt the wind rush out of his lungs. He heard a metallic clang as the golden spear landed noisily nearby.

"What, where am I?" Joe gasped through deep lungfuls of air.

Nobody answered. With shaky arms, Joe pushed himself back to his feet. He glanced around and felt two conflicting emotions. On the one hand, he was glad to be out of China, but here he was, inside the Golden Pyramid once again. He didn't recognise the room he was in, but the smooth stone and confusing runes were unmistakable. He was back where it had all started.

Taking the spear in his grip, Joe noticed the energy of the weapon pulse through him. It startled him and he stared down at the golden spear, wondering what else it could do, for it had obviously transported him here. Turning it over in his palms, the weapon felt light, yet extremely sturdy, precise, and deadly. The golden orb, which Joe had carried for so long, was now embedded at the bottom of the staff. It glowed dimly, pulsating every so often, and Joe noticed the same colours of gold shimmering throughout the length of the spear, making it appear there were something alive inside of it.

Checking his surroundings, Joe saw there was a small opening near the ceiling. It looked like it could have been a vent of some kind, but it was the only way in or out.

"Of all the places..." Joe muttered. He walked closer and saw that he might fit but getting there was a problem. The room itself was probably eight feet tall, and this exit was right at the top. Without a ladder, Joe had no hope of getting there.

"Great, I finally make it back and end up here, a pointless, empty room," Joe spoke. He paced around for a few moments, racking his brain for ideas, when he finally shrugged and pointed the tip of the spear at the hole. Joe was flung back as yellow lightning cracked and sparked into the darkness of the vent.

"What the hell was that!" Joe looked incredulously at the weapon in his hand for answers, electricity still dancing at its point. Readying himself, Joe held it aloft, this time holding it with two hands and bracing himself for the impact. He watched as the energy within the spear built up and shot out, illuminating the room and the narrow passageway above, when the wall cracked and split underneath the vent. Joe could feel a rush of air whip around his face and hair from the exposed splinters he was making in the surface, but remained firm as the lightning continued to dance and inflict further damage.

Finally, the wall gave way completely and crumbled in a loud explosion, sending debris flying in all directions. Joe was knocked off his feet and felt the small stones scatter across his body and clothes, producing tiny cuts where his skin was uncovered. Sitting up, Joe shook himself down, clearing some of the dust from his hair as he did so. He touched his lip and looked at his finger, seeing fresh blood. Ignoring it, Joe stood up and retrieved the spear, shaking his head as he held it.

"You got some party tricks, that's for sure," Joe muttered, walking into the darkness and, once again, into the unknown.

△

Frank heard what sounded like an explosion ring out from within the walls of the pyramid. He had been wandering through tunnels and rooms for hours. Each new chamber looked exactly like the last: empty save for strange pictures on the walls and symbols that made no sense to him. Previously, Frank had heard something deep inside the pyramid stir and create noise, sounding to him like an old factory firing up all of its machines at once to manufacture. Frank didn't dare guess what else could come out of this otherworldly structure. If it could act as a passageway through time, what else could it do?

Exiting yet another vacant room, Frank found himself on a balcony overlooking a network of tunnels and doorways. He blew out a whistle which echoed around the cavernous space and was impressed by the sheer scale of the architecture. At the same time, his stomach growled loudly, and Frank was made acutely aware of how hungry he was.

"Seems like a good place for a pit stop," Frank assessed, digging into his utility belt and retrieving a very squashed protein bar. He grimaced at the sight of it, but knew it was better than nothing, so he unwrapped the snack and took a large bite, savouring the burst of flavour. Leaning on the balcony, Frank surveyed the scene whilst he chewed, thinking that, under different circumstances, he'd love to come back and explore the whole thing. It would likely take months to see everything, he mused, taking another bite.

"What am I doing?" Frank said in bewilderment, stuffing the unfinished bar back into his belt. "That maniac is still out there, and Luisa is somewhere needing my help." Shaking his head, Frank rushed down the sloping staircase onto the level below and passed into another room.

Suddenly, he could hear footsteps. Frank ducked to hug the wall and drew his pistol from the holster in his belt, slowing his breathing. The sound was getting louder. Whoever it was, they were in a hurry and walking fast. Frank tightened his grip on the gun without realising and released the safety, ready to fire if needed. His pulse quickened as the steps grew louder and nearer. Frank braced himself and waited.

△

Joe walked into the empty chamber, looking up and down, hoping for something to catch his eye. But it was unremarkable, so he decided to just move on.

"Hold it," came a voice from behind him.

Joe span around in panic and with that, the spear exploded with a crackle of energy, lifting Joe and the stranger off their feet. Both men landed with a grunt, Joe seeing stars in his vision and struggling to get back to his feet.

"Son of a..." Joe heard from the man in the corner, prompting him to get up quickly. The other man reacted first and held his pistol out, pointing it straight at Joe.

"Don't try anything stupid," the man said with a southern accent.

Joe held his hands up, "please, I don't want any trouble at all."

"Easy son, you don't happen to be an archaeologist, do you?" Frank asked, surmising that this must be the second of his missing persons.

"I, er, well, yeah."

Frank lowered his handgun. "Lieutenant Frank Williams, U.S. Army. Boy, it's been one hell of a journey to find you," Frank finished, walking over to Joe with his hand outstretched.

Joe hesitated, but took his hand and shook it. "Joe Cullins, how did you know?"

"We got a whole operation topside, waiting to come and evac. Now that I've got you, I just need to figure out where Ms. Duarte went..."

"You saw Luisa?" Joe asked, his heart skipping a beat at the mention of her name.

"I sure did. Somewhere very far from here though."

"When? Was she alright? What happened?"

Frank holstered his pistol and stroked the stubble on his chin. "Well, I can't really say *when*, it wasn't our time, as crazy as that sounds."

"Believe me, it doesn't sound crazy," Joe answered. "I've just returned from China, round about the fourteenth century."

Frank's eyes grew wide. "You're kidding me? And how did you get there?"

"That thing." Joe pointed to the discarded weapon on the floor.

"Ah, that thing which nearly blew us both up?"

"Yeah, that," Joe said sheepishly. "I don't really know how it works, see that ball at the end? At first that's all I had, but then in China, the staff was the missing piece and now, well you can see it's a spear which apparently has a short fuse."

"Well, lucky for us, my fuse isn't as short," Frank grinned, and it put Joe slightly at ease. "So I take it there's nothing back that way?" Frank finished, gesturing to the hall where Joe had just entered.

"No, not really. I got stuck in a dead-end room, luckily I was able to get out." Joe elected to leave out just how he escaped, he didn't want Frank thinking he was some kind of lunatic with a dangerous weapon at his disposal. "What's through there?"

"Well, a lot of rooms, a lot of pathways, and a lot of confusion. I've been walking for hours," Frank said, his voice trailing off. "Say, you hungry, kid?"

Joe realised he was indeed famished, and nodded in answer. He looked as Frank retrieved a half-eaten protein bar from one of the pouches on the belt around his waist.

"Sorry, it's all I have, but you can finish it, if you want?"

Joe gladly accepted and stuffed the rest of the snack into his mouth, closing his eyes as he savoured the taste. He hadn't eaten since he and Zurman had left the hut and that was hours, maybe even a full day ago.

Frank watched as Joe made light work of the food and smiled. He seemed like a good kid, caught up in one big mess. He wanted to ask if Joe had seen Ulrich, but decided against it. No need to add anything else into this for now. At the moment, they both needed to find Luisa and then a way out. Oddly enough, Frank was relaxed about the last part. He was sure that General Hoskins would be down here soon enough, if he wasn't already, and that eventually, with all the resources he had at his disposal, everyone would be out of here safe and sound.

"Shall we try some of the passageways?" Joe said, swallowing down the final mouthful of food.

"Well, if you say that way leads to nowhere, I guess we don't have much choice. Stay close and, er, try to warn me if that thing is gonna go off, okay?" Frank looked warily at the golden spear still lying on the ground as Joe went to retrieve it.

△

Luisa watched as the king stopped hoisting the lever and stood aside. All around the hallway were doors, frames and archways, which were blurred by an invisible fog.

"Magnificent, isn't it," Zurman said, surveying the landscape. Hundreds upon hundreds of these gateways filled the room and Luisa saw the need for it being so vast and tall, it was becoming apparent that this grand hallway was built for this very purpose. She didn't respond to Zurman, but her silence was enough of an answer for him.

"It's almost time, your friend is close, I must go to him."

Luisa jolted at the prospect of Joe being near once again. She had missed him and despite herself and the clear peril she found herself in, she couldn't wait to see him.

"You'll wait here for my return and then we shall learn what the Council decides to do with you."

Luisa thought of Elder Alech in the library behind the thrones and wondered if any of those ancient texts would have told her about this moment. She hated the fact that she had rushed out of there so quickly, blinded by Zurman's charisma and charm. She thought about opening her mouth and protesting, but decided it was no use and allowed herself to be led down towards the king, where Zurman left her.

"I'll catch you soon," he said to her in a mocking tone. Again, Luisa didn't respond. She looked up at the king, who peered down at her with his sunken eyes. Glancing around, Luisa couldn't help but be in awe of the sight of these shimmering doorways, most of them suspended in mid-air as if held by invisible strings. They faded in and out of view as reality tried to restrict them from coming into being. Something told Luisa that no matter what the rules of time and space were, nothing was going to stop them from opening. Whatever came through would be the true end of the world she had been trying to prevent.

△

Zurman left the hallway and walked through one of the many doors that led out of the grand arena. He knew Joe was close, but what he didn't know was that Frank was also with him. He quickened his pace and ascended two flights of stairs before emerging on a walkway, which if taken to the right would lead back to the Axis of Time. That's where Joe needed to be, so Zurman took off to the left, hoping to see Joe moving along the floor of the sprawling network of doors and balconies below.

To his surprise, he saw Joe multiple levels below, but he wasn't alone. Frank Williams walked ahead of him, looking left and right and then signalling back to Joe that they were going to head up. Zurman gritted his teeth; this wasn't in the plan. He had gambled by thinking Frank would have been taken out by now, but he had evidently misjudged the man's aptitude for survival. Quickly, Zurman retrieved a small, circular device from his robes, upon which were confusing inscriptions that seemed to overlap each other. On it was a dial, which he frantically turned three times to the right. He peered over the edge of the balcony again. Zurman watched as below, the line that Joe and Frank were on split in two, separating the pair. Frank's alternative route turned to the right and merged with a doorway that was several levels up. Fortunately for Zurman, Frank's attention was solely on Joe, who had remained still. Appearing in front of him was a straight alternative path which would eventually lead him to the Axis of Time.

Zurman held his breath and then exhaled when Joe signalled to Frank that he was going to take the path. Frank waved back with an "okay" and the two quickly moved off. Little did Frank know, thought Zurman, that there was no way out at the other end, but by the time he found out, Joe would have completed his part of the journey.

△

Joe ran, throwing caution to the wind. He had to find Frank again, and fast. He kept moving and could see a clearing and light ahead of him. Joe broke into a sprint and covered the distance in no time, stopping abruptly at the sight before him.

"Woah," he breathed, taking in the magnificence of the Axis of Time.

"Welcome, Joe," he heard a familiar voice call from somewhere above. He looked up, past several balconies and intricate statues, to see Zurman beaming down at him.

"You made it as well?" Joe asked, remembering the seeds of doubt sown by the Emperor in China.

"Yes, yes, it was a hard battle, but we prevailed," Zurman answered, jumping down from the ledges above with cat-like agility, landing next to Joe in an instant.

Joe clutched the spear tightly, his reaction seemingly spotted by Zurman, who spoke again. "Ah, the staff and the orb, they've combined into a powerful weapon, have they not?"

"You knew, didn't you?" Joe asked, and he saw a flicker of surprise pass across Zurman's face.

"Knew what, Joe?"

"You gave them the staff, didn't you? Knowing we would come back and claim it years later. What's really going on here? What are we actually doing?" The spear crackled with energy, which drew an even greater look of shock from Zurman.

"Now, Joe, listen..." In a flash, Zurman thrust a small blade into Joe's side, withdrawing it just as instantaneously.

The agony seared through Joe's body and he fell backwards, clutching at the wound that had been opened. Zurman grabbed the spear and didn't give Joe a second look, instead taking off and heading for the guardian statues on the ground level. Joe looked down at his hand, which was covered in blood, and his vision was going blurry. He could only watch as Zurman got closer to the statue, yet all he could think about was Luisa. He wanted to see her at least one last time.

△

Luisa watched Zurman leave, and as soon as he was out of sight, she made a break for it. The king was incredibly slow to react, a gamble that paid off for Luisa. She guessed that if she moved rapidly enough, he wouldn't be able to chase her, due to being stationary for so long. She darted to her left sharply, hearing the thundering sounds of the giant moving and trying to cut her off. A door was only metres away, but an enormous fist slammed on the ground near her, throwing her off balance. Luisa dared to glance back and saw the ancient king, his eyes blazing with fury. Feeling her heart thump in her chest, Luisa changed her course and ran to her right and up a staircase, deciding that high ground would be the answer. She narrowly avoided another crashing fist, which destroyed the stairs behind her she had been on only moments before. Luisa quickly climbed over the railing and then again rushed to the nearest flight of stairs, taking them two at a time and putting a considerable distance between her and the king. He smashed the wall in protest, having failed in its simple duty. Luisa smirked and tried to recall where Zurman went and follow his path. She knew he was going to meet Joe, and that was the only place she wanted to be right now.

△

Frank turned back almost right away. Something didn't feel right about the sudden shift in the walkway, so he had feigned going this route just long enough not to draw attention to himself. He had watched as Joe ran along the straight exit into a clearing beyond, which Frank dared to believe may be the Axis of Time. Taking a deep breath, Frank jumped down and landed awkwardly on the balcony below. His knees shook with the impact, but he shrugged it off. Instead, he ran, breaking forward and following the same direction of travel as Joe, just a few levels above him.

Luisa burst out of a doorway and ran straight into Frank, both of them startled by one another before laughing and hugging tightly.

"Luisa! Come on, this way, Joe has gone through."

"Okay, there's a big problem that way, so we have to move, now."

"Tell me all about it when we get down there," Frank said, and they both sprinted along the narrow corridor, which was now blocked from the sides and above. They kept their pace and soon emerged into the wide clearing that Frank now knew was the Axis of Time.

"Wow," Luisa said, scanning the many statues, doorways and ledges all around her.

Frank didn't respond. Instead, his eyes were on the prone figure of Joe, laying on the floor clutching at his side. Luisa followed Frank's gaze and screamed when she saw him.

△

Joe blinked slowly and looked up; he thought he heard somebody screaming. *Luisa!* She was climbing carefully but with speed down to reach Joe. Frank was behind her, going just as fast. Luisa skidded to her knees and crouched next to Joe, stroking his hair and holding his face. Tears filled her eyes as she whispered, "Joe," over and over. He managed a weak smile.

"Miss me?" Joe croaked, his voice hoarse. Luisa laughed as tears fell from her eyes. In the background, Frank had prepared a dressing and was coming over.

"Ma'am, if you don't mind," Frank said to Luisa, who moved aside immediately. He applied pressure to Joe's wound and dropped a small vial of liquid over the cut, which made Joe wince in pain.

"Sorry son, alcohol to kill any infection. Hold still, we'll get you fixed right up in no time, you'll see."

Joe watched as Frank applied the gauze but could see Zurman in the distance, placing the golden spear into the hands of the statue standing before a great door.

A flash of blinding light erupted from Zurman's direction. Luisa and Frank turned around to see what was happening and their mouths dropped when they saw the circular doors open wide and reveal an immense mass of energy, whirling and spinning in frantic motions. The statue then moved, much like the king had done, and in seconds, it had taken the spear gifted to it and plunged it into the orb itself. There was a pause of a few milliseconds and then a silent explosion, which was accompanied by a sonic wave that sent a giant shock through them all. A rush of air blew through the enormous chamber, and all three of them covered their eyes.

Nothing happened for a moment. Frank noticed it first, followed by Luisa, and finally Joe. They saw the doorways that filled the Axis of Time shining brightly and form solid entrances. They could hear noises coming from them and knew that any second now, something physical would accompany the sound.

Zurman stood up, having been knocked down by the impact. The statue that had been the ultimate piece of the puzzle had disintegrated, leaving the golden spear on the ground. Zurman took it up for himself and then retrieved a small flip phone from his pocket. He dialled the only number in the contact list and uttered one phrase.

"It's time."

CHAPTER TWENTY-NINE

General Hoskins clicked the phone off and smiled, a genuine, satisfied grin that few had ever seen. He watched as the last remnants of the special forces went into the depths below, the Basin now almost entirely empty. The plan was simple enough. Soon, the best that the U.S. Army had to offer would come face to face with an impossible enemy, one they had no hope of matching. Then, once they were wiped out, there wouldn't be any resistance in a swift yet brutal takeover. First, the United States of America. Then, the rest of the world. It was always written to be this way, Hoskins knew it, and had been prepared for it his entire life. The world was about to change forever, and he would rise from the ashes of this miserable planet and lead his army to usher in a new age.

△

"Frank, what do we do?" Luisa asked, her hands still holding Joe's head.

Lieutenant Frank Williams didn't answer. Instead, his focus

was to his right, the entrance to the Axis of Time that he had discovered what felt like weeks ago. The doors that ran parallel with the ramp were glowing brightly. Runes and symbols danced around their frames, moving like leaves caught up in a gust of wind. He watched as the first figure emerged.

"What... what is that?" Luisa gasped.

Frank wasn't able to respond. He saw an armoured hand come through first, then a thick arm connected to a broad body, all encased in the same dense armour that looked like it could withstand a blast from a tank. A helmet could be seen covering all of the face. Green slits were in place of the eyes and there was an oval grille which acted as a mouthpiece. Finally, the figure was through the portal and on its back was a device that seemed to be a backpack. Luisa jumped when she heard the ignition boosters fire up and the armoured humanoid launched itself high into the air, landing with a loud crunch on the walkway.

Several others followed out of the many doors that lined the vast space between the Axis of Time and the passage leading to it. They all were equipped with the same dark armour and jetpacks. The noise was a cacophony of aggression as the warriors grew in number, all waiting on the path. A few of the soldiers had golden helmets, which Frank assumed marked them out as sergeants. Their jetpacks gave off a blue fire when they soared into the open and when they landed next to their kin, they exchanged a greeting of sorts, placing one hand on their colleague's right shoulder. As the forces kept coming, space was running out, so some were now entering the Axis of Time, gathering in the open courtyard. None of them seemed to pay any attention to Frank, Luisa, or Joe, but they all seemed to be waiting for something.

Luisa heard it first. It sounded like a rumble of thunder before a storm.

"Do you hear that?" Joe croaked, making Luisa smile despite herself. The fact that he was talking was a good thing.

"Come on, we need to get to cover, let's go. Can you walk, Joe?" Frank asked.

"I can try," Joe said, wincing as he climbed to his feet. Luisa put one of Joe's arms over her shoulder, with Frank doing the same on the other side. Luisa and Joe both shared a look. No words were spoken, but they knew what the other meant: *I've missed you.*

"Over here, this will do." Frank ushered the pair into a corner where two walls met under a balcony, so there was some protection from above and their only field of view was straight ahead. Joe was eased to the floor and Frank checked his pistol was loaded, crouching in front of Joe and Luisa.

"How are you feeling?" Luisa asked softly.

"Oh, never better," Joe grinned, closing his eyes and grimacing a little as he sat back against the wall.

"You look great to me," Luisa answered, kneeling so their eyes were level.

"Oh yeah? Makes a change I guess."

"No, you always look good, Joe Cullins."

Joe held out his hand for Luisa, and she squeezed it tightly as they looked at each other for a few moments in complete silence.

The tranquilly was shattered with a booming noise that sounded like a bomb had gone off nearby, echoing all around them. All three of them instinctively covered their heads, but there was no rain of rocks or debris to fall on them. Instead, there had been an enormous hole carved out to their left, coming from inside the Axis of Time. Stepping out first was the giant frame of the king, heading up a battalion of ground troops, who marched in formation around him. Like their airborne counterparts, they had the same black armour, but their eye slits were blue. Now that they were on an even surface with the soldiers, Frank could see just how huge these warriors were. He guessed they were all seven feet tall and on closer inspection. The armour wasn't bulky, but more of an exoskeleton that was shaped around their bodies, meaning the mass came from their own muscular form.

"Oh my... they're massive," Luisa vocalised, exactly what they were all thinking.

"Just keep down, they don't seem to have noticed us yet."

"Have you seen their weapons?" Luisa stated.

Frank had. He saw what looked to be M16 rifles, but their barrels were twice as long and wide. The magazine clips were large and square, far bigger than conventional rounds. Frank tapped the spare ammunition pouches on his belt out of habit, but somehow his bullets didn't feel deadly at all when compared to these behemoths. He glanced down at Joe, whose condition seemed to have stabilised, but without proper medical attention, Frank feared he might not survive much longer.

Luisa read Frank's thoughts. "We need to get him to a hospital."

Frank nodded silently. He agreed, but had no idea how or when they could move him. The troops kept coming, pouring out of the many passageways above and around them incessantly. A jetpack ignited from somewhere to the right of where the group was huddled and the warrior landed only a few feet away. Smoke billowed out from his cooling apparatus and engulfed them, causing Joe to cough loudly. The warrior turned to the corner where they were hidden and stomped over, his head slightly tilted inquisitively. As he got closer, large blades extended out from gauntlets on the warrior's hands. He stopped in front of the three of them, looming as they waited, helpless. Frank toyed with unloading a full clip into the face of the soldier, but decided against it. They were massively outnumbered and outgunned.

Slowly and deliberately, the soldier removed his helmet and showed his face. Fair skinned and shaved completely, including eyebrows, he stared with piercing green eyes.

His mouth worked to form a sentence and in a deep voice, he spoke. "Who are you?"

"That is not of your concern, comrade," Frank answered defiantly.

The soldier glanced at Frank with a blank expression. Frank stood up. He was an entire foot shorter than his opponent, but he didn't flinch.

"Ah, I see you're making friends already."

Everyone turned to look at Zurman, who had arrived just behind the towering soldier.

"You son of a..." Frank began.

"Ah, now, now. We can all be polite and co-operative, can we not?"

"You lied to us," Luisa snarled.

"Did I? I told you we were preventing the apocalypse, and *we are!* Look around, have you ever seen such a force? Who can stop us? Certainly not your pathetic troops," Zurman finished, directing the last scathing remark at Frank, whose stomach dropped when he remembered the soldiers assembled above ground. Good men and women that he knew and worked with. Some had families, most of which Frank had met with his own wife and daughter. Now the outlook looked far bleaker than it had done previously, and Frank felt his heart ache. He wanted to protect his loved ones, but this was a seemingly impossible task.

"What do you want with us?" Frank managed to say, steeling himself and staring at Zurman.

"Well, with these two, some unfinished business remains.

But you? Nothing." With that, Zurman pulled out his pistol and aimed it at Frank. A deafening crack of gunfire followed.

△

"Sir, we are in position outside of the pyramid awaiting instruction, over." Riggs keyed the intercom and waited patiently for General Hoskins to reply.

"Secure the perimeter and wait for those inside to exit. I will be down in a few minutes. Over and out." The message from his General came through loud and clear.

Riggs heard the receiver click off and he attached the device to his belt. Turning to his personal retinue he simply said, "You heard the man, let's get this place locked down."

"Roger!"

Riggs watched as they dispersed and relayed the General's orders to the various squads scattered around the base of the Golden Pyramid. He looked at the large contingent that had amassed for this simple evacuation mission and felt it was slightly over the top. Some of the best soldiers the U.S. Army had were down here. They had summoned divisions from the Navy seals, as well as elite black-ops teams that were usually involved in far more important missions. Riggs shrugged these thoughts away, surmising that as this was clearly an unknown discovery and there was a highly dangerous assassin still at large, this required top priority. There had to be thousands of troops here, with more still coming from above, but what did Riggs know? He had no wish to fill the General's shoes. Decision making on such a grand scale didn't interest him. Riggs just wanted to serve his country and do his family proud, that was it. He idly thought of Frank and hoped that he was alright in there. They had lost contact with him almost forty-eight hours ago and Riggs didn't like it. Frank was always on top of communication and wouldn't just go AWOL. With a last sigh,

Riggs moved into his own position; a makeshift bunker of sandbags and barbed wire providing some degree of cover for him and his squad. He checked his rifle was loaded and waited, as he had been instructed to.

△

His eyes grew wide in a mixture of shock and pain. Blood poured on the ground, flowing freely from the wound. Zurman screamed in agony as he clutched the ruined stump where his arm had been only a few seconds earlier. The warrior who had removed his helmet collapsed in a heap. Luisa and Joe stared in disbelief at the scene in front of them. Luisa gagged and almost vomited whilst Joe closed his eyes and focussed on the pain in his side.

Frank pulled his own weapon up to fire, but Zurman reacted quickly and turned away, just as a second shot rang out and blew a crater into the wall where Zurman's head had been. Frank covered his face as fragments of stone chipped and exploded into him.

"Now! Go now!" Zurman screamed to the assembled troops as he fled into the crowd of soldiers, his eyes darting back and forth on the many levels above to find the source of the shot.

"You! Go up there and find who did this!" Zurman instructed a nearby guard, who nodded in silent acceptance and moved with two compatriots to discover the origin of the shots. Zurman fled into the hallway, still clutching what remained of his arm, the bleeding showing no signs of stopping.

"Do you need assistance?" an old voice croaked from the darkness. Zurman recognised it as belonging to Elder Alech.

"My Lord," Zurman panted.

Alech drew back his sleeves and touched a keypad attached

to his wrist. Seconds later, a soldier on a jetpack scorched through the sky and landed just by the hallway.

"We require an assisted cauterisation and transfusion, sergeant. See to it that it is carried out."

"Yes my lord," with that the commando took off again, rockets blasting him away. Zurman slumped down to the ground and closed his eyes, wheezing.

"You have done well, my old friend. Allow us to take over from here," Elder Alech said, placing a comforting hand on Zurman's head before taking his leave. Behind him, the other members of The Last Table arrived, transported by hovering thrones that glided inches above the floor. They gave Zurman a curt nod as they proceeded through to the mobilised army and joined their ranks.

△

Ulrich moved fast, rapidly disassembling the large caliber sniper rifle and stowing it in his backpack. He retrieved the shotgun that was magnetically clipped to his back and ran, knowing that time was of the essence. Moving with an almost unnatural agility, he leapt down to the level below and paused when he saw the three imposing warriors moving away from the crowd and into one passageway below. Guessing that he would have company soon, Ulrich checked his shotgun was fully loaded and kept advancing. He had to reach the boy and the girl now, before it was too late.

△

"Are you alright?" Frank asked Joe and Luisa. They both nodded in unison.

"What happened?" Luisa asked, still trying to shake from her thoughts the violence she had witnessed.

"We were saved."

"By whom?"

"I have a suspicion, but it makes little sense. It doesn't look like they're very interested in us right now. Keep low, let's try to go inside and to some more shelter. Joe? How you holding up, son?"

Joe groaned in response and managed a weak smile.

"Alright, good enough for me. Let's get you to your feet. There we go, easy does it," Frank grunted with effort as he hoisted Joe up from the floor. "Other side, if you would, sweetheart?" Frank asked Luisa, who immediately moved to help Joe hobble along, the three of them ducking into the nearest empty doorway.

△

Ulrich crouched as an enormous shell whistled past him, the wall behind him exploding from the impact. Ahead were the three soldiers he had seen just a few minutes ago. *They were fast, really fast,* he thought. Running at full speed, Ulrich jumped and fired off a shot. He heard the shells ricochet harmlessly off the armour of the first soldier, who was stomping rapidly towards him. Ulrich landed on the level below and immediately holstered his shotgun to his back, sliding it between the straps of his backpack and fixing it to the magnetic plate. Ulrich pulled out two grenades attached at his hip: one flash and one high explosive. He threw the explosive one first, aiming it at the doorway where the troops were about to emerge. It went off with a loud bang, but Ulrich knew it wouldn't stop them. He kept running and chanced a glance behind him. As expected, his three pursuers emerged through the cloud of smoke seemingly unscathed. Ulrich kept running, looking down below as the vast army of highly advanced soldiers spilled out of the atrium and moved on to the pathway leading back to the Golden Pyramid.

Suddenly, Ulrich lost his footing and the path he was on disappeared. He fell the short distance to the level below and was about to walk through the arched entrance in front of him when it vanished. Puzzled, Ulrich looked around and saw things were evolving all around him. Doors were opening where before there had been a blank wall, yet pathways and other exits were disappearing or moving at the same time.

"The Axis of Time... time is changing," Ulrich whispered to himself, realising just how critical his mission had become and how close he was to failing. He glanced down and saw the girl and the boy being led out of a doorway by the U.S. Army lieutenant and his pulse quickened. *Thank God they're still alive.* A shell ruptured the surface nearby, and Ulrich was reminded suddenly of his assailants. Looking down one last time and inhaling a deep breath, Ulrich tossed his flash grenade behind him as he leapt, clearing several levels and landing on the ground floor while above him. A brilliant white light exploded and temporarily blinded his attackers.

△

Frank nearly collapsed in shock when he saw Ulrich land next to them and almost wipe the three of them out.

"Holy..."

"It's him!" Luisa screamed, feeling utterly helpless as the darkly dressed assassin was right in front of her.

Frank tried to get his pistol, but Ulrich grabbed his wrist to stop him. Frank looked up into the blue eyes of his nemesis and saw that there was fear there.

"There is no time. I have to leave with these two," Ulrich said hurriedly, looking back above him to check that the three soldiers weren't following.

"Like hell you are," Frank retorted.

"Lieutenant Williams," Ulrich began, his eyes darting to the name badge on Frank's chest. "I just saved your life. I need you to trust me at this most critical moment. The fate of our world is at stake and I need these two to come with me, immediately."

Frank could hear the honesty in Ulrich's voice, but he didn't trust him. "You tried to kill them And me!"

"At times, yes, but now it is too late. I sought to stop them causing this, bringing about the end of our planet. I now need to take them with me, back to my time, where we have one last chance to fix this."

"What do you mean, *your time?*" Luisa chimed in.

Ulrich looked her up and down quickly. "You've seen it, haven't you? That man, he took you somewhere, didn't he?"

"Yes, to the future," Luisa replied.

"That isn't the future. That's *their* world. He used you, both of you. They want our world for their own."

"What are you talking about?" Frank asked. He couldn't believe he was standing there having a discussion with Ulrich Kaufmeiner. For months, he'd been only interested in stopping the assassin and now here he was, about to align himself to his cause.

"We don't have time, but I need you to trust me," Ulrich pleaded, looking above him again and seeing the three soldiers standing up and shake their heads. One of them pointed below, and Ulrich's eyes grew wide.

Frank could see the honesty in Ulrich and hear it in his voice. He sucked his teeth and turned his head, looking again at the horde of warriors assembled in the atrium. Exhaling hard through his nose, Frank had come to a decision.

"It's now, or never, Williams. Take these and try to find your men," Ulrich urged, handing Frank the remaining grenades as well as his shotgun. "They stand no chance and you all need to flee. Time is already changing, the Axis itself is forming alternative routes and paths. You two," Ulrich looked to Luisa and Joe, "you must come now."

Luisa studied Frank, who gave a slight nod. She wrestled with her emotions as her instincts told her that for whatever reason, Ulrich was telling the truth. However, she couldn't just forget that he had hunted her and came close to killing her on numerous occasions. Biting her lip, she resigned herself to the fact that for now, Ulrich may be her only hope at staying alive.

"Williams, move now, they're only interested in me. Escape through this path. It will lead you out the back of the pyramid and you can hopefully take some of your troops there and leave this place. Hurry now, you'll make it there just in time to warn them!"

Frank took one last look at Joe and Luisa. In the short time he had known them both, he had grown attached to them. He wanted to stay, but something was screaming at him to go.

"I'll see you both down the road. Be careful and look after yourselves. As for you," Frank stated, now turning to Ulrich. "You better be right, because we will meet again, mark my words."

Ulrich nodded a wordless response and nervously glanced over his shoulder. With a last look, Frank turned and ran along the tunnel that Ulrich had pointed out. He couldn't believe he was taking instructions from this madman, but what other choice did he have?

Ulrich turned to Luisa and Joe. "We'll do proper introductions soon, but this is our one and only chance out of here, so hold still."

Luisa watched as Ulrich took out a circular purple disc from his backpack. The three soldiers landed on the ground floor with a thud and aimed their weapons. Ulrich threw the disc on the ground and grabbed Joe and Luisa's arms. Gunfire rang out as the three attackers took aim at their targets. The shells ripped through the air and were about to tear Joe, Luisa, and Ulrich apart when a crack of lightning erupted from the purple object. In the blink of an eye, they were gone, the large bullets hitting the wall which had been behind the three unlikely allies a second earlier.

CHAPTER THIRTY

FRANK RAN AS FAST as he could, the weight of the shotgun slowing him a little, but he kept going. The torrent of emotions swirling through his mind created a storm of confusion. He had made a decision in the heat of the moment (which he never usually did) and had trusted the one man he had been striving to hunt down for months. *But he saved you.* The thought swam to the front of Frank's consciousness and he gritted his teeth, begrudgingly accepting that he was still breathing thanks to that assassin.

His feet pounded against the familiar stone pathways of the Golden Pyramid. He was putting blind faith in the fact that this wide corridor would lead him to the courtyard where he would undoubtedly find the battalion of the U.S. Army who were expecting a short evacuation operation, not a full-scale war against a far greater enemy. Frank started to sweat and his breathing was becoming laboured, but he kept going. He could see a narrow opening swimming into view, and this boosted Frank's determination. He just hoped he wouldn't be too late.

△

Luisa landed roughly, face down in some tall grass. She groaned as she turned on her back and heard Joe cry out in pain as well. Blinking once, she took in the dull, grey clouds that hung overhead. It was gloomy, to say the least.

"I need a medic!" Luisa heard a British accent call out and at first she wondered who it belonged to, when it all came flooding back. She scrambled to her feet and searched around, surprised at what she saw. They had appeared outside of a tall concrete wall, which looked to have been fortified by mixing together several materials. Two watchtowers had been constructed either side of enormous iron gates, which now creaked open upon hearing Ulrich's cry for help. Luisa had almost forgotten that Ulrich had whisked her and Joe away. It had all happened so fast. One minute, she was sure they were about to be gunned down by those massive troops, and then in the blink of an eye she was here. *Wherever here was.*

"He's been stabbed, lost a lot of blood. Get him to the medical bay now!" Ulrich commanded to the two women who had rushed out with a makeshift stretcher. Ulrich sighed and pushed his blonde hair away from his eyes, removing his backpack and many utility belts that were draped across him, carrying an array of weapons, ammunition and throwing knives. Joe was hoisted up and carried into the garrison, where a small crowd of people had gathered to investigate the disturbance.

"Hey!" Luisa started, walking over to Ulrich.

"Yes?"

"Where are you taking him? What is this?"

"He's going to be looked after, don't worry. And this? One of the last surviving settlements outside of Hoskins' control."

Luisa simply remained still, watching Ulrich as he walked away and greeted some of the community. Commiserations could be heard, pats on the back given, and the overall mood felt bleak.

"Wait!" Luisa hurried to keep up. She felt eyes studying her and whispers among the crowd. She ignored them and caught up to Ulrich, pulling him on the arm and spinning him to face her. Ulrich glared at her in a mixture of disbelief and anger, the look making Luisa question her actions, but she held firm.

"Answers. You tried to kill us, now you bring us here? What for?"

"Follow me, we need to speak to the leader and debrief."

Ulrich turned and led the way, Luisa resigning herself to following along in silence and taking in the new environment she was in. At best it was run down, at worst it was a slum. There were houses that were square concrete blocks, tightly packed together and on top of each other. People were hanging out their washing to dry on lines that zig-zagged overhead, connecting to other abodes running parallel to the street Ulrich and Luisa were walking on. Neighbours gossiped above, and Luisa looked at them without fear, which only seemed to increase the whispers. The street itself was made of tarmac, which surprised Luisa, but it was dotted with potholes and cracks, showing signs of years of wear and tear. It slowly rose at an incline, heading to a castle in the distance. One of the four towers had crumbled, leaving three still standing.

Breaking the silence, Luisa asked, "Where is the medical bay? I heard you say it to those women taking Joe?"

"Up there," Ulrich said, pointing to the castle.

"Oh. Will he be okay?"

"I hope so. Whoever wrapped the bandage did a good job," Ulrich answered.

Luisa smiled. She liked Frank. Her thoughts lingered on him for a moment as she continued her walk without speaking next to her new guide.

△

Frank burst out of the tomb and into the open air once again. Despite the circumstances, it was great to be out of that oppressive structure. Taking a second to catch his breath and take a last sip of the water flask, which was now empty, Frank turned to his left and rounded the corner. To his relief, he saw legions of U.S. Army personnel dotted all over the cavern and the main courtyard.

"Hey!" Frank shouted, waving his arms to grab their attention.

△

"Holy... is that Lieutenant Williams?"

Riggs chuckled. "You're damn right it is, private." Keying his intercom on, Riggs issued out his orders. "Alpha unit, Lieutenant Williams spotted, east side coming about to your three. Do you copy?"

A buzz of static answered Riggs, and then a distorted voice came through.

"Roger that, intercepting now, over."

Riggs sighed. At least Frank was back. He pulled out his binoculars and focussed in on Frank, who was extremely animated in his discussions with the Alpha team sergeant.

"Private, stay here, I'm going over there," Riggs said and left his post.

△

"Son, I am telling you, everyone needs to go topside, now. Riggs, thank God, we need to go, right now!"

"Woah, Frank, what's all this?" Riggs replied, interrupting the conversation he was having with the Alpha team leader.

"There is an army coming for us, right now, from in there," Frank hastily pointed to the front of the pyramid.

"An army? How?"

"There isn't time to explain. Just call tactical retreat now. Get me Hoskins as well, I'll talk to him as we go."

"Okay, slow down. Here, let's speak to the General first."

Riggs thumbed his voice communicator on and tried to hail General Hoskins. "General Hoskins, this is Colonel Riggs. Do you copy, over?"

The steady buzz of static was his only answer.

"General Hoskins, do you copy?" Riggs repeated. Nothing again. "Must be the signal..." Riggs' voice trailed off.

"Major, we have got to move, I implore you!" Frank pleaded with his long-time friend.

"Frank, I can't disobey a direct order from the General. He told us to fortify this area so we wouldn't be caught asleep again by that damn Ulrich. Did you see him in there?"

"Yes, I did, but major, that's not the point," Frank waved a hand dismissively.

"Wait, you saw him? Where is he?"

"He's gone, Riggs! And we need to go as well before it's too la..."

An explosion sounded from the main entrance to the Golden Pyramid. Frank and Riggs whirled around to see smoke billowing from the doorway, obstructing their view. Riggs reacted fast, speaking into his communication device.

"Gimme eyes on that now! All units prepare to fire, but wait for confirmation that this isn't the two missing person..."

Frank grabbed the receiver and spoke into it. "All units, this is Lieutenant Frank Williams. We are under attack. Do not waste any time. Initiate a tactical withdrawal, this is a direct order..."

Riggs snatched the comm back and stared at Frank in disbelief. A tense moment passed between them, but a booming sound rang out from the direction of the monolith and they turned to look once again, just as the familiar shape of a crown emerged from the smoke. The king stomped into the open and surveyed the land. He was now armed with a gigantic sword that was broad and long. Dragging it along the floor, he stopped and pointed it forward, aiming straight for the collection of marines ahead of him.

"Mother of God..." Riggs mouthed.

Frank grabbed Riggs by the coat. "We need to go, right now! Get as many of our men out as we can, there's no time." Frank had barely finished his sentence when the first rows of the enemy streamed out of the monolith, opening fire as they marched out slowly and methodically, fanning out to cover as much ground as they could as quickly as possible. Riggs watched in horror as his men exploded with the force of unthinkably large shells rupturing their bodies. There were screams coming in on the voice channels, confused orders of retreat mangled with dying cries and conflicting commands forcing soldiers to attack.

High above, on the path that led down to the Golden Pyramid, teams of snipers fired their rounds with loud cracks of gunfire. Some were successful, managing to level many of the opposing forces with the impact of their shots. The joy was short lived. Mouths dropped as the warriors who had been hit got to their feet, unharmed, merely knocked back because of the force of the shots. The jetpacks fired up, and they soared high into the air, landing on top of several soldiers, crushing them instantly. In a desperate attempt to survive, the snipers abandoned their guns and drew their knives to fend their attackers off at close range. But the hulking monsters tore them apart with the large blades that extended from their gauntlets. They made quick work of the unfortunate troopers and fired up their jetpacks again, barrelling into more men who were situated up high and continuing the carnage.

Riggs watched in horror as he witnessed the massacre

unfold. More and more of these heavily armoured and deadly warriors kept coming from the pyramid. A number of them were knocked down through the sheer amount of firepower unloaded from stationary machine guns. Eventually Riggs observed that one or two of them had been outright killed, their dark blood staining the sandy coloured stone of the courtyard. But as one fell, ten more would emerge and fill the void. Riggs turned to Frank and nodded, and they ran from the carnage, dragging as many of their comrades with them as they could.

"Fall back, fall back!" Riggs shouted as he watched a crowned figure swipe an enormous blade across the ground and swat a contingent of troops like insects. To his right, the squadrons of Navy Seals had gathered and were firing rockets into the crowd of soldiers streaming out of the pyramid with limited success. They co-ordinated volleys so that there was a constant barrage of fire flowing in. Coupled with the non-stop fire from the mounted machine guns nearby, they were taking out more and more of the enemy. For a fleeting second, Riggs had faith. He had even slowed his run and was watching the battle unfold.

"Riggs, come on!" Frank shouted from above, running with a large group of marines who were fleeing as well. But the Colonel didn't move. He felt as though this could be turned around; that his forces would find their rhythm and with the joint efforts of the best the U.S. Army offered; it would only be a matter of time before they repelled this attack. With a thundering crash, that flame of belief was extinguished. Troops landed from the heavens, smoke trails pouring out of their jetpacks. Within moments they were carving into the Navy Seals, eliminating their fire power. Riggs watched as they blitzed through the ranks of soldiers again and moved on to the mounted machine guns, seeing tiny fires as they dismantled the weaponry and killed the veterans with ease. Finally,

Riggs turned away and ran, leaving behind the total devastation of his units.

Frank and Riggs scrambled to the top of the pathway with a small force of fighters. They ran from the gunfire, the sound of detonations and cries of pain rising from down below. There was nothing more that could be done; their enemy was brutal and overwhelming.

"How did you get down here?" Frank asked as he rushed over the makeshift bridge that had been hastily constructed over the invisible gap on the pathway.

"We used cables and then rappelled down."

"Tell me you left a ladder to get out?"

Riggs shot Frank a warning look, "how dumb do you think I am?"

Frank breathed a sigh of relief, and he could see the temporary rope ladder dangling down from the hole far above. It was hovering just slightly above the ground.

"Is anyone up there?" Frank asked.

"Well, Hoskins and a small squadron, but he ordered everyone down. Didn't wanna let Ulrich slip away again."

Frank nodded in response; his instinct told him that something was amiss with the General. He had never been the most personable of people, but there was an unsettling feeling about the order to send all the best soldiers down to the Great Pyramid to be slaughtered like lambs. Did he know about the invasion? How could he?

An enormous explosion sounded nearby, jolting Frank from his thoughts.

"We gotta go, now!"

"Quite agree, come on," Riggs answered, directing troops to the ladder and urging them to climb at once. In total, there may have been around fifty men and women that had escaped. Down below, the battle raged on, but it wouldn't be long before it was over, and they would be hunted down.

Frank watched anxiously, checking behind him every few seconds, convinced that he would see the dark outline of the enemy appear menacingly over the side of the track. Finally, the last few soldiers were ready to ascend and Riggs pulled Frank along to the ladder.

"Come on, let's get out of here!"

Both men climbed as fast as they could, the ladder swaying as they did, when suddenly they heard the roar of jetpacks close by.

"They're right under us, go go go!" Frank bellowed as the sound of the heavy troops landed one by one on the path they had just left.

"Riggs!" Frank called up. "Tell them to shut the hole, explosives, grenades, whatever, do it now!"

Riggs grunted with effort as he climbed the last few rungs. "But Frank!"

"Just do it!" Frank glanced down and his heart sank as he saw one soldier walk under him and look up. Frank gritted his teeth and yelled. "Now!"

He waited to be buried under debris and sand, but nothing happened. Instead, he felt hands gripping him tightly and hoisting him up, clear of the gap. Frank glanced down and saw the fires light up from the jetpack as the armoured warrior rose to meet the survivors.

"Now! Now!" Frank instructed, and on his mark, grenades were tossed lightly to the edge of the opening, exploding just as the soldier on the jetpack emerged through the gap. He was thrown forward, tumbling through the air as fire peeled off layers of his armour. Behind him, the hole collapsed, pouring sand and rocks into it, but to Frank's dismay, it had been made even wider and potentially easier to climb out of with the right equipment.

"Go, go go!" Riggs shouted while his comrades placed large steel sheeting over the pit, sealing it temporarily.

"Everyone out, find a vehicle and rendezvous back to base, we're getting out of here!" Riggs yelled. All around him there was a frenzy of activity, but nobody seemed to notice the still moving warrior on the ground, who had now stood up. He tried to activate the jetpack, but it was ruined beyond repair, so he hurled it from his back and brandished the long and sharp blades from twin gauntlets.

Frank stared at his enemy and felt his eyes glare right back at him. Frank knew he had no chance at all, but there was no way he would cower. Instead, he ran forward. He would meet his opponent and his end head on, with no fear. Frank closed his eyes for a brief moment as the soldier began to charge, as well. He thought of his wife and daughter and let a tear escape from the corner of his eye. He would miss them dearly. Opening his eyes, Frank pulled out his knife and continued to charge the massive warrior, when a huge truck rammed into the side of Frank's adversary, knocking him a great distance and leaving him in a crumpled heap.

"Get in!" Riggs cried, flinging open the door. Frank didn't need a second invitation. He climbed into the pickup and Riggs floored the accelerator, joining the rest of the convoy that was speeding away from the Basin.

"Did you try Hoskins?" Frank asked Riggs.

"No, he's long gone. He probably had a message come through from the chaos down there and managed to escape."

Frank sat in silence; he didn't believe that, and he doubted Riggs did either. Their truck continued to move along the desert at speed, driving inland towards their base.

Frank saw the sun rising and hoped that the new day would bring answers.

EPILOGUE

Ulrich walked side by side with Luisa as they entered the castle. Much like the village they had just passed, it was run down and in need of repair, but in here there were heavily armed men and women patrolling and moving about. It made Luisa feel uneasy, but once again she found herself with little choice in the matter. People nodded at Ulrich as he passed them. He returned the gesture, but kept his gaze focussed ahead.

"In here," he said to Luisa, opening an elevator door and closing it behind them. They rode it in silence up several levels before an abrupt halt signalled they had reached their destination. Luisa saw that the number "7" had been pressed, but that it went up to nine. They emerged into a wide hallway. A red and gold patterned carpet was laid out on the wooden floor. There were portraits of kings and queens from centuries gone by lining the walls, leading to a doorway that was closed and guarded by two soldiers. They knocked twice on the oak door, and it creaked open as Ulrich and Luisa drew closer. The interior wasn't how Luisa had imagined at all. She had pictured a regal throne room, resplendent with ornate decorations and furniture. Instead, it was a command centre, with a vast screen on the wall directly facing them that showed multiple images on its display. Luisa noticed various news channels; CNN and BBC, to name a few, as well as what looked to be security footage of the castle and the village they had passed through. A woman was watching the large screen with her back turned to the room. In front of Luisa were desks manned by an eclectic mixture of people, huddled behind computers and tapping away on keyboards. It was a hive of activity, with many conversations overlapping each other, but they all stopped as they spotted Ulrich and Luisa.

Hushed whispers circled around the office. Ulrich stood in the walkway between the rows of computers and counters and waited. Luisa looked at some faces of the individuals staring at her. There was a blend of confusion and apprehension among them and Luisa wanted to speak to them all, ask them who they were and what they were doing. Before she could, the woman at the front of the chamber turned around to face Ulrich and Luisa. She spoke with a soft voice in an American accent. Slightly southern, but not overly pronounced.

"Welcome back," she stated, addressing Ulrich. "And you must be Luisa," she added, smiling.

"Yes," Luisa replied.

The woman walked forward, her curly brown hair hung just above her shoulders. Luisa guessed she might be in her late thirties or early forties. She wore a plain top with short sleeves and baggy trousers, which Luisa thought was unusually casual, especially for someone in charge. Her green eyes locked with Luisa's for a brief moment before she turned to Ulrich and kissed him softly on the lips.

"Glad to have you home, honey." She let her hand linger on his face for a second before returning to Luisa. "You must have questions?"

"I do. Where is Joe?"

"He's downstairs, being operated on as we speak."

"Operated?" Luisa repeated, a tone of panic in her voice.

"Nothing to it, sweetie, just a minor op to address the bleeding and stitch him back up. You got him here just in time, he'd lost a lot of blood."

Luisa sighed and felt a lump in her throat. She hated the prospect of Joe being in pain. Regaining her train of thought, she continued, "And where are we?"

"England. York, to be exact. This castle has stood for centuries and we've made it our home."

"Right, what year are we in?"

"Two thousand and fifty-one."

"What? That can't be. I went to the future. It was desolate. Nothing survived the nuclear fallout, I saw it," Luisa replied.

"That wasn't our world, that was theirs. I think we need to get you a hot meal and some rest, then we can explain in full."

Luisa was now aware of how tired and hungry she was, so the offer was enticing, to say the least.

"Okay, thank you. Sorry, what was your name?"

"Grace Williams, I believe you know my father?"

ACKNOWLEDGMENTS

Once more I wish to start by thanking my amazing partner, without whom this book wouldn't even be possible. She has worked tirelessly to edit this novel and ensure it can be the best possible story it can be. I literally couldn't have done this without her. Again. More than that, she is my rock and my inspiration. I couldn't live without her.

Secondly, my two beta readers, Richard and Victoria. Two authors who I highly respect and I am immensely grateful for their input into this story. Thank you for taking the time to read through this book and give me some guidance on a number of points, it was extremely helpful and I am in your debt.

Oliver, who has the greatest creative mind I have ever known. There are a few sections in this book which he had a big input in. Vivid imagination and great storytelling are just some of the tools he has at his disposal, of which he selflessly gave to me for certain scenes. Can't stress how valuable this was and I look forward to many more hours of bouncing ideas off one another.

Ben and Alun, who are a constant source of strength and encouragement. They have been at my side for such a long time and we have been through an enormous amount together as a collective. Nothing I can say here will truly to justice to how much I value and appreciate every moment with the pair of you. P.S. they have a cameo in this story, combined into one character.

Finally, my ever supportive family and friends, who have never ceased to amaze me with their kindness. Writing this story has been bittersweet. Suffering a tremendous personal loss whilst getting this book finished has been challenging to say the least. But every single one of you have stood up and supported me, making sure I was okay and keeping me in your thoughts. There are no words to express my gratitude adequately, so I will simply say thank you from the bottom of my heart.

ABOUT THE AUTHOR

Chris Kenny is an emerging author in multiple genres, with a romance novel titled "The Love Story" being his debut in February 2021. "Original Earth Chronicles" will return with the next instalment in Summer 2021.

Chris balances working a full time job with creating new stories and keeping fit. More importantly than that, Chris ensures his two year old cat is well looked after and loved, often taking naps together on lazy Sundays.

If you want to be the first to know when book two of Original Earth Chronicles is released, please visit his website at https:// chriskennyauthor.com/newsletter, where you can sign up to a monthly newsletter that will provide updates and free content!